PEOPLE YOU SHOULD KNOW

TOP 101 REFORMERS, REVOLUTIONARIES, ACTIVISTS, AND CHANGE AGENTS

EDITED BY NICHOLAS FAULKNER

Britannica
Educational Publishing
IN ASSOCIATION WITH
ROSEN
EDUCATIONAL SERVICES

Published in 2017 by Britannica Educational Publishing (a trademark of Encyclopædia Britannica, Inc.) in association with The Rosen Publishing Group, Inc.
29 East 21st Street, New York, NY 10010

Distributed exclusively by Rosen Publishing.
To see additional Britannica Educational Publishing titles, go to rosenpublishing.com.

First Edition

Britannica Educational Publishing
J.E. Luebering:Executive Director, Core Editorial
Anthony L. Green: Editor, Compton's by Britannica

Rosen Publishing
Nicholas Faulkner: Editor
Nelson Sá: Art Director
Michael Moy: Designer
Cindy Reiman: Photography Manager
Sherri Jackson: Photo Researcher
Introduction and supplementary material by Nicki Peter Petrikowski

Cataloging-in-Publication Data

Names: Faulkner, Nicholas, editor.
Title: Top 101 reformers, revolutionaries, activists, and change agents / edited by Nicholas Faulkner.
Description: First edition. | New York : Britannica Educational Publishing in association with Rosen Educational Services, 2017. | Includes bibliographical references and index.
Identifiers: LCCN 2015050940 | ISBN 9781680485097 (library bound : alk. paper)
Subjects: LCSH: Social reformers--Biography--Juvenile literature. | Political activists--Biography--Juvenile literature. | Revolutionaries--Biography--Juvenile literature. | Social change--History--Juvenile literature.
Classification: LCC HN8 .T67 2017 | DDC 303.48/4092--dc23
LC record available at https://lccn.loc.gov/2015050940

Manufactured in the United States of America

Cover (top left), p. 49 Buda Mendes/Getty Images/Thinkstock; cover (top, center left), p. 58 ullstein bild/Getty Images; cover (top, center right), p. 199 Andrew Burton/Getty Images/Thinkstock; cover (top right), p. 90 Encyclopaedia Britannica, Inc.; cover (bottom left), p. 167 DRN/Getty Images/Thinkstock; cover (bottom, center left), p. 180 Photos.com/Thinkstock; cover (bottom, center right), p. 154 Chris Jackson/Getty Images; cover (bottom right), p. 32 Ralph Orlowski/Getty Images/Thinkstock; p. 7 Sean Gallup/Getty Images/Thinkstock; p. 12 The India Today Group/Getty Images; p. 17 Bill Peters/Denver Post/Getty Images; p. 23 Courtesy The Jimmy Carter Library; pp. 51, 133 Ron Galella/Ron Galella Collection/Getty Images; p. 53 Steve Hansen/The LIFE Images Collection/Getty Images; p. 66 Travis P. Ball/Getty Images Entertainment/Getty Images; p. 70 © Georgios Kollidas/Fotolia; p. 77 Courtesy National Gallery of Art, Washington, D.C., Gift of Thomas Jefferson Coolidge IV in memory of his great grandfather, Thomas Jefferson Coolidge, his grandfather, Thomas Jefferson Coolidge II, and his father, Thomas Jefferson Coolidge III, 1986.71; p. 82 Franco Origlia/Hulton Archive/Getty Images; p. 99 Michael Putland/Hulton Archive/Getty Images; p. 109 Mike Clarke/AFP/Getty Images; p. 113 AP; p. 119 Frederick M. Brown/Getty Images/Thinkstock; p. 127 Courtesy of the Office of U.S. Senator Barack Obama; p. 151 Guillermo Legaria/AFP/Getty Images; p. 160 Spencer Platt/Getty Images/Thinkstock; p. 170 Jean-Claude Francolon/Gamma-Rapho/Getty Images; p. 177 Samir Hussein/WireImage/Getty Images; p. 186 Courtesy National Gallery of Art, Washington, D.C., Gift of Jean McGinley Draper, 1954.9.2; p. 195 Ricardo DeAratanha/Los Angeles Times/Getty Images; p. 197 Mondadori Portfolio/Getty Images; p. 202 Andreas Rentz/Getty Images News/Getty Images ; cover and interior pages border © iStockphoto.com/urbancow

CONTENTS

66

113

127

151

186

199

INTRODUCTION

One of the great strengths of the human race is the ability to change. Over the course of history, people have adapted to vastly different circumstances, and they have changed their environments to better suit their needs. Change does not only occur as a reaction to outside factors, though. Human society is bound to change as well. Sometimes this change begins with just one person, one creative thinker showing that things can be done better than they were done before, or one brave soul standing up against what they believe to be wrong.

For statesmen and politicians, changing the status quo is part of their job, and enacting reforms that improve the life of those they govern is one of the things they are measured by and remembered for, as Abraham Lincoln is for abolishing slavery in the United States.

The pursuit of freedom can lead to revolutions like the ones connected with Thomas Jefferson and Símon Bolívar, but not every revolutionary is as successful; Che Guevara's guerrilla war for a socialist world failed.

Spiritual leaders such as the Dalai Lama, Pope John Paul II, and Pope Francis have shown an influence that goes beyond their religious groups and enters the realm of politics, and Martin Luther's endeavor to reform the medieval Roman Catholic Church resulted in unforeseen political upheaval.

One does not have to be in a position of power to cause change, though. With a single act of defiance against social injustice a person can become a symbol, such as Rosa Parks was for the United States civil rights movement, and sometimes the most unlikely person, such as Joan of Arc, born a simple peasant girl, can change the fate of nations.

Change is often established by force of arms as military leaders such as the Scottish national hero William Wallace or George Washington show, but violence is not always the way. The nonviolent resistance practiced by Mahatma Gandhi and Martin Luther King, Jr., has also proved to be effective, and social work can have a positive effect on many lives, as the examples of Jane Addams and Mother Teresa illustrate. Scientists such as Galileo Galilei and Charles Darwin have influenced how we see the world through their discoveries, opening up new ways of thinking, and innovators have changed the way the world works with their inventions. Without Johannes Gutenberg, for example, this book would possibly not even exist, and neither would the books Upton Sinclair wrote to fight for social justice.

Whether it is brought about by reforms pushed through by powerful politicians or fought for by activists, whether it is established through armed force or nonviolently, change can take many forms, and many deplorable situations have already been changed for the better thanks to the efforts of some of the most remarkable people in history.

JANE ADDAMS

(b. 1860–d. 1935)

An early concern for the living conditions of 19th-century factory workers led American reformer Jane Addams to assume a pioneering role in the field of social work. She brought cultural and day-care programs to the poor, sought justice for immigrants and blacks, championed labor reform, supported women's suffrage, and helped to train other social workers. Addams was cowinner (with Nicholas Murray Butler) of the Nobel Peace Prize in 1931.

Jane Addams was born on September 6, 1860, in Cedarville, Illinois. Her father, John Huy Addams, was a wealthy miller, a state senator, and a friend of Abraham Lincoln. Jane was the youngest of five children. She graduated from Rockford Female Seminary in Illinois in 1881 and was granted a degree the following year when the institution became Rockford College. Following the death of her father in 1881, her own health problems, and an unhappy year at the Woman's Medical College in Philadelphia, Pennsylvania, Jane Addams was an invalid for two years. She subsequently traveled in Europe in 1883–85 and stayed in Baltimore, Maryland, in 1885–87.

In 1887–88 Addams returned to Europe with a Rockford classmate, Ellen Gates Starr. During this trip they visited Toynbee Hall—the world's first social settlement—in London, England. Upon returning to the United States, Addams and Starr decided to create something like Toynbee Hall. They settled in a working-class immigrant district in Chicago, Illinois. There they acquired a large vacant residence built by Charles Hull in 1856, and, calling it Hull House, they moved into it on September 18, 1889. Eventually the settlement included 13 buildings and a playground as well as a camp near Lake Geneva, Wisconsin. Many prominent social workers and reformers—including Julia Lathrop, Florence Kelley, and Grace Abbott—came to live at Hull House, as did others who continued to make their living in business or the arts while helping Addams in social settlement activities.

Among the facilities at Hull House were a day nursery, a gymnasium, a community kitchen, and a boarding club for working girls. Hull House offered college-level courses in various subjects; furnished training in art, music, and crafts such as bookbinding; and sponsored one of the earliest little-theater groups, the Hull House Players. In addition to making available services and cultural opportunities for the largely immigrant population of the neighborhood, Hull House afforded an opportunity for young social workers to acquire training.

Outside of her Hull House work, Addams and other reformers helped to establish the world's first juvenile court, tenement-house regulation, an eight-hour working day for women, factory inspection, and workers' compensation. In addition, Addams strove for justice for immigrants and blacks and advocated research aimed at determining the causes of poverty and crime. In 1910 she became the first woman president of the National Conference of Social Work, and in 1912 she played an active part in the Progressive Party's U.S. presidential campaign for Theodore Roosevelt. At The Hague (Netherlands) in 1915 Addams served as chairman of the International Congress of Women, following which was established the Women's International League for Peace and Freedom. She was also involved in the founding of the American Civil Liberties Union in 1920. In 1931 she was a cowinner of the Nobel Prize for Peace.

Addams wrote many books on her work and experiences. Her best-known writings included *Democracy and Social Ethics* (1902), *Newer Ideals of Peace* (1907), *Twenty Years at Hull-House* (1910), and *The Second Twenty Years at Hull-House* (1930).

For 46 years Addams managed the Hull House settlement. Starr had been forced by ill health to retire about six years before Addams's death on May 21, 1935, in Chicago. In 1961 plans were laid to tear down Hull House to make room for a Chicago campus of the University of Illinois. Despite vehement, worldwide protests against such plans, the properties were sold in 1963. The original building, however, was preserved as a museum.

AI WEIWEI

(b. 1957–d.)

Chinese artist and activist Ai Weiwei produced a multifaceted array of creative work, including sculptural installations, architectural projects, photographs, and videos. While Ai was lauded internationally, the frequently provocative and subversive dimension of his art, as well as his political outspokenness, triggered various forms of repression from Chinese authorities.

Ai was born in 1957 in Beijing, China. Shortly after his birth, communist officials accused his father, the renowned poet Ai Qing, of being a rightist, and the family was exiled to remote locales before being allowed to return to Beijing in 1976, at the end of the Cultural Revolution. In 1978 Ai enrolled at the Beijing Film Academy, though he found more creative and intellectual stimulation as part of a collective of avant-garde artists called Xingxing ("Stars"). He moved to New York City in 1981, where he attended Parsons School of Design (part of what is now the New School) and actively engaged in the city's fertile subculture of artists and bohemians.

Although Ai initially focused on painting, he soon turned to sculpture. There was little market for his work, however, and in 1993, when his father fell ill, he returned to Beijing. Exploring the fraught relationship of an increasingly modernized China to its cultural heritage, Ai began creating works that irrevocably transformed centuries-old Chinese artifacts—for instance, a Han dynasty urn onto which he painted the Coca-Cola logo (1994) and pieces of Ming- and Qing-era furniture broken down and reassembled into various nonfunctional configurations. Between 1994 and 1997 Ai collaborated on three books that promoted avant-garde Chinese art. He later turned toward architecture, and in 2003 he founded the design firm FAKE to realize his projects, which emphasized simplicity through the use of commonplace materials.

In 2005 Ai was invited to write a blog for the Chinese Web portal Sina. Although he initially used the blog as a means of documenting the mundane aspects of his life, he soon found it a suitable forum for his often blunt criticism of the Chinese government. Through the blog, Ai publicly disavowed his role in helping to conceive the design of the National Stadium (popularly dubbed the Bird's Nest) in Beijing, claiming that the 2008 Olympic Games for which the structure had been built were tainted by official corruption and amounted to government propaganda. Furthermore, nearly a year after the 2008

Sichuan earthquake—in which shoddy construction was suspected to have been responsible for the deaths of thousands of children in collapsed public schools—Ai lambasted officials for not having released details on the fatalities and mobilized his growing readership to investigate. The blog was soon shut down, and Ai was placed under surveillance, though he refused to curtail his activities. (He transferred his online presence to Twitter.) Later in 2009 he was assaulted by police in Chengdu, where he was supporting a kindred activist on trial. Among the artworks that resulted from Ai's "citizen investigation" was *Remembering* (2009), an installation in Munich in which 9,000 colored backpacks were arranged on a wall to form a quote, in Chinese, from an earthquake victim's mother.

Ai earned praise in 2010 for his installation, at the Tate Modern in London, of 100 million hand-painted porcelain "sunflower seeds," which were produced by some 1,600 Chinese artisans. Until the exhibit was roped off because of a feared health hazard, Ai had encouraged visitors to walk upon the seeds, considering the fragile sculptures a metaphor for the downtrodden Chinese populace. In April 2011 Ai was detained by Chinese authorities for alleged "economic crimes"—it was later revealed that he was accused of tax evasion—in what was seen as part of a widespread government crackdown on dissent. He was released on bail more than two months later, with Chinese state media reporting that he had confessed to the charges against him. The resulting international media coverage of the incident brought further attention to Ai's art.

MUHAMMAD ALI

(b. 1942–d.)

One of the greatest American heavyweight boxing champions, Muhammad Ali was known as much for his flamboyant self-promotion and controversial political stances as for his boxing ability. His motto was "I am the greatest!" He became the first boxer to win the heavyweight title three times.

Ali was born Cassius Marcellus Clay in Louisville, Kentucky, on January 17, 1942. He began boxing as an amateur at the age of 12. After advancing through the amateur ranks, he captured a gold medal in the 175-pound (79-kilogram) division at the 1960 Olympic Games in Rome, Italy. As a professional fighter, he gained immediate fame when he defeated heavily favored Sonny Liston on February 25, 1964, to win the world heavyweight title. After the Liston bout, Clay announced that he had joined the Nation of Islam, and he soon took the name Muhammad Ali.

Gifted with unusually fast reflexes and excellent coordination, Ali dominated the heavyweight division for the next three years. In 1967 he was convicted of violating the Selective Service Act after refusing, on religious grounds, induction into the U.S. Army during the Vietnam War. He remained free on bail but was stripped of his title and barred from boxing. The U.S. Supreme Court reversed his conviction in 1971.

In New York City on March 8, 1971, he lost a 15-round decision to champion Joe Frazier. In a rematch on January 28, 1974, Ali gained a unanimous decision over Frazier, who by then had lost the heavyweight title to George Foreman. Ali regained the title with an eighth-round knockout of Foreman on October 30, 1974, in Kinshasa, Zaire (now the Democratic Republic of the Congo). Perhaps the high point of Ali's career came in the rubber match with Frazier on October 1, 1975, in the Philippines. Ali emerged victorious in the bout, known as the "Thrilla in Manila," after Frazier's corner called an end to the fight after 14 grueling rounds.

Ali went on to defend his title successfully six more times before losing to Leon Spinks on February 15, 1978. He then won the title for the third time, defeating Spinks on September 15, 1978. Ali retired soon afterward but twice returned to the ring, losing to Larry Holmes in 1980 and to Trevor Berbick in 1981. Ali's career record stands at 56 wins (including 37 knockouts) and 5 losses.

Ali's later years were marked by physical decline. He was thought to have Parkinson disease, which impaired his speech and movement.

He remained very active, however. In 1996 he was chosen to light the Olympic flame at the start of the Games in Atlanta, Georgia, and from 1998 he traveled widely as a United Nations Messenger of Peace. Ali was awarded the Presidential Medal of Freedom on November 9, 2005. That month the Muhammad Ali Center, a cultural gathering place honoring the boxer, opened in Louisville.

KOFI ANNAN

(b. 1938–d.)

The first black African to hold the post of secretary-general of the United Nations (UN) was Kofi Annan. The career diplomat spoke several African languages, English, and French and was well respected in the international community. He won the Nobel Peace Prize in 2001.

Kofi Atta Annan was born in Kumasi, Gold Coast (now Ghana), on April 8, 1938, to Henry and Victoria Annan. His family came from the cape coast on the Atlantic Ocean, but Annan spent most of his childhood in the inland town of Bekwai. His father was the elected governor of the Ashanti province and was a chief of the Fante people. The younger Annan studied at the University of Science and Technology in Kumasi and won a Ford Foundation grant that enabled him to study in the United States at Macalester College in Minnesota. While studying economics there, in 1960, he won the Minnesota state oratorical contest. He received a postgraduate certificate in economics from the Institute for Advanced International Studies in Geneva, Switzerland.

From 1962 to 1971 Annan worked for the UN as an administration and budget officer with the World Health Organization in Geneva. He received a master's degree in management from the Massachusetts Institute of Technology in 1972, where he was an Alfred P. Sloan fellow. From 1974 to 1976 Annan was managing director of the Ghana Tourist Development Company. Those were his only years away from the UN.

Annan's career leading up to the UN's helm progressed from such day-to-day jobs as assistant secretary-general for program planning, budget, and finance, to head of human resources and security coordinator, director of the budget, chief of personnel for the high commissioner for refugees, and administrative officer for the Economic Commission for Africa. When Iraq invaded Kuwait in 1990, Annan was responsible for getting hundreds of thousands of Asian workers out of Kuwait. He was in charge of the UN peacekeeping operations as undersecretary beginning in March 1993. Annan also served as special UN representative to the former Yugoslavia. He was widely praised for his diplomacy in implementing the accord among Bosnian Serbs, Muslims, and Croats. He also led peacekeeping operations in Burundi, Somalia, and Zaire (now the Democratic Republic of the Congo).

Kofi Annan.

After nearly four decades of service to the United Nations, Annan was appointed to lead the organization, marking the first time that a secretary-general was elected from the ranks of the UN staff. He succeeded Boutros Boutros-Ghali in December 1996 as the UN's seventh permanent secretary-general after a contentious nominating period during which the United States was the only member country to position itself against Boutros-Ghali's reelection. Annan quickly gained the support of the Security Council after three other African candidates under consideration withdrew their names from the list of candidates in the hopes of building a consensus for a secretary-general from Africa. Annan was elected by acclamation and immediately set to work on a reform plan to be instituted in 1997.

Annan's vision for the UN included peacekeeping and establishing norms for international law, with an emphasis on the values of equality, tolerance, and human dignity mandated by the UN charter. He brought a deep commitment to a more efficient and leaner UN and an unyielding advocacy for universal human rights. One of his first challenges as secretary-general was to convince the United States to begin paying the $1.4 billion in back dues the country owed. Annan considered the fight against HIV/AIDS to be a personal priority, and he called for the establishment of a global fund to help increase the flow of money for health care in developing countries.

Annan used his influence in several political situations. Among these were his efforts to convince Iraq to comply with Security Council rulings and his role in effecting the transition to civilian rule in Nigeria. In 1999 Annan facilitated an international response to widespread violence in East Timor. Not content to focus solely on the rights of citizens around the world, Annan also tried to improve the position of women who worked in the Secretariat of the UN, and he began to build stronger relationships with nongovernmental organizations. In June 2001 Annan was unanimously reappointed for a second term as secretary-general. Later that year, the Nobel committee bestowed the Nobel Peace Prize jointly to Annan and the UN on what was the 100th anniversary of the venerable award.

In 2005 Annan was at the center of controversy following an

investigation into the oil-for-food program. That program had allowed Iraq—under UN supervision—to sell a set amount of oil in order to purchase food, medicine, and other necessities. A report described major corruption within the program and revealed that Annan's son was part of a Swiss business that had won an oil-for-food contract. Although Annan was cleared of wrongdoing, he was criticized for his failure to properly oversee the program. Annan's second term leading the UN ended in 2006.

In 2007 Annan was named chairperson of the Alliance for a Green Revolution in Africa, an organization helping small-scale farmers. That same year he founded the Kofi Annan Foundation, a nonprofit organization that promotes peace, sustainable development, human rights, and the rule of law.

Annan continued to play a role in international diplomacy. He helped resolve the Kenyan election crisis that began in late 2007, eventually brokering a power-sharing agreement between the government and the opposition in February 2008. In 2012 Annan served as Joint Special Envoy for Syria, which was wracked by civil war, but he was unable to resolve the conflict.

Annan coauthored a number of works. His memoir *Interventions: A Life in War and Peace* (cowritten with Nader Mousavizadeh) was published in 2012.

SUSAN B. ANTHONY

(b. 1820–d. 1906)

For more than half a century Susan B. Anthony fought for women's right to vote. Many people made fun of her. Some insulted her. Nevertheless, she traveled from county to county in New York and other states making speeches and organizing clubs for women's rights. She pleaded her cause with every president from Abraham Lincoln to Theodore Roosevelt.

Susan Brownell Anthony was born on February 15, 1820, in Adams,

Massachusetts. She was active in the temperance movement and an ardent abolitionist. When blacks were given the right to vote by the 15th Amendment, she launched a campaign to extend the same right to women. In 1869 she helped to organize the National Woman Suffrage Association.

In 1890 this group joined the American Woman Suffrage Association to form the National American Woman Suffrage Association. She became the president of the new association in 1892 and held this office until she was 80 years old. In 1872 she voted in the presidential election to test her status as a citizen. For this act she was tried and fined $100, but she refused to pay the fine, declaring that "taxation without representation is tyranny."

At the time when Anthony began her work, women had few legal rights. Today, largely through her efforts and those of her associates, women have opportunities for higher education, the privilege of working at almost any occupation, the right to control their own property and children, the right to hold public office, and the right to vote. She lived to see many of these reforms put into effect. After she died in 1906, both major political parties endorsed women's suffrage. In 1920 the suffrage amendment to the Constitution was ratified. She died on March 13, 1906, in Rochester, New York.

ELLA BAKER

(b. 1903–d. 1986)

Ella Josephine Baker was an American community organizer and political activist who brought her skills and principles to bear in the major civil rights organizations of the mid-20th century.

Baker was reared in Littleton, North Carolina. In 1918 she began attending the high school academy of Shaw University in Raleigh, North Carolina. Baker continued her college education at Shaw, graduating as valedictorian in 1927. She then moved to New York City in search of employment. There she found people suffering from poverty and hardship caused by the Great Depression and was introduced to the radical political activism that became her life's work. In the early 1930s, in one of her first efforts at implementing social improvement, she helped organize the Young Negroes Cooperative League, which was created to form cooperative groups that would pool community resources and thus provide less-expensive goods and services to members.

Baker married T.J. Roberts in the late 1930s and then joined the staff of the National Association for the Advancement of Colored People (NAACP), first as a field secretary and later as national director of the NAACP's various branches. Unhappy with the bureaucratic nature of the NAACP and newly responsible for the care of her young niece, she resigned from her director position in 1946 but worked with the New York branch to integrate local schools and improve the quality of education for black children.

Inspired by the historic bus boycott in Montgomery, Alabama, in 1955, Baker cofounded the organization In Friendship to raise money for the civil rights movement in the South. In 1957 she met with a group of Southern black ministers and helped form the Southern Christian Leadership Conference (SCLC) to coordinate reform efforts throughout the South. Martin Luther King, Jr., served as the SCLC's first president and Baker as its director. She left the SCLC in 1960 to help student leaders of college activist groups organize the Student Nonviolent Coordinating Committee (SNCC). With her guidance and encouragement, SNCC became one of the foremost advocates for human rights in the country. Her influence was reflected in the nickname she acquired: "Fundi," a Swahili word meaning a person who teaches a craft to the next generation.

Baker continued to be a respected and influential leader in the fight for human and civil rights until her death on her 83rd birthday.

BENAZIR BHUTTO

(b. 1953–d. 2007)

The first woman to attain political leadership of a Muslim country in modern times was Benazir Bhutto. In 1988 she was named prime minister of Pakistan to succeed General Mohammad Zia ul-Haq—the

Benazir Bhutto.

man who had seized the office from her father and ordered his execution. She served two terms as prime minister, in 1988–90 and in 1993–96.

Benazir Bhutto was born on June 21, 1953, in Karachi. She studied abroad, earning degrees from Harvard University, in the United States, in 1973 and the University of Oxford, in England, in 1977. Her father, Zulfikar Ali Bhutto, had led Pakistan since 1971, first as president and then as prime minister, and she often accompanied him on his official travels. In July 1977 his government was overthrown in a revolt led by Zia. Her father was imprisoned and then hanged in 1979. She then became the titular head of her father's political party, the Pakistan People's party (PPP).

For the next five years Benazir Bhutto was kept either in prison or under house arrest. Zia sent her into exile in London in 1984. After Zia lifted martial law, she returned home to a triumphant welcome in 1986 and became the foremost figure opposing his rule.

After Zia died under mysterious circumstances in a plane crash in August 1988, free elections were held. Bhutto led the PPP to victory and became prime minister of a coalition government in December 1988. She was unable, however, to do much to combat Pakistan's widespread poverty and increasing crime. In August 1990 the country's president, Ghulam Ishaq Khan, dismissed her government on charges of corruption. Her party was defeated in the next elections, and she became the opposition leader in Pakistan's parliament. In the October 1993 elections, her party won a plurality, and she again became prime minister of a coalition government. Under renewed allegations of corruption and economic mismanagement, however, Bhutto's government was dismissed in 1996 by President Farooq Leghari.

Bhutto went into self-imposed exile in 1999 while still facing corruption charges. Meanwhile, General Pervez Musharraf seized power and became president. In 2007 he finally granted Bhutto amnesty for the corruption charges, and she returned to Pakistan in October of that year. She was assassinated in Rawalpindi on December 27, 2007, as she campaigned for upcoming national elections. Her husband, Asif Ali Zardari, took over as head of the PPP.

Bhutto's autobiography, *Daughter of the East*, was published in 1988.

(It was also published under the title *Daughter of Destiny* in 1989.) Her book *Reconciliation: Islam, Democracy, and the West* was published after her death, in 2008.

SIMÓN BOLÍVAR

(b. 1783–d. 1830)

Six nations—Venezuela, Colombia, Panama, Ecuador, Peru, and Bolivia—venerate Simón Bolívar as their liberator from the rule of Spain. This great statesman, writer, and revolutionary general is known as the George Washington of South America. He inspired men to follow him through trackless wilderness to fight and die for liberty. Bolívar's followers, however, did not support him as loyally in his struggle to set up stable governments.

Simón Bolívar was born in Caracas (now in Venezuela) on July 24, 1783, of a noble Spanish family. Orphaned in boyhood, the youth was educated in Europe. He absorbed the spirit of revolution then widespread in Europe and vowed to free Venezuela.

When Napoleon Bonaparte overran Spain, the restive colonies of Spanish America seized the opportunity to revolt. Venezuela was the first to declare its independence, in 1811. Although that initial revolt failed, for the next 19 years Bolívar continued to lead the fight to free northern South America. His small, poorly equipped forces won amazing victories and met overwhelming defeats. At one time he might be a conquering hero—at another, a fugitive in exile. At the height of his power, between 1825 and 1828, he was president or protector of Gran Colombia (now Venezuela, Colombia, Panama, and Ecuador), Peru, and the newly formed Bolivia.

The spirit of disunion and opposition, however, was strong. Bitter and broken in health, he died at a friend's estate in Colombia on December 17, 1830—seven months after he resigned his offices. Bolívar was a sincere patriot, devoted to the cause of liberty and equality. Years before slavery was officially abolished in Venezuela,

Bolívar liberated his own slaves. He also was a pioneer in urging the formation of a union of American republics.

LOUIS D. BRANDEIS

(b. 1856–d. 1941)

U.S. lawyer Louis Brandeis was an associate justice of the Supreme Court of the United States from 1916 to 1939. Intellectual prowess and an abiding concern for the rights of individuals distinguished his legal career.

Louis Dembitz Brandeis was born in Louisville, Kentucky, on November 13, 1856. His parents, Adolph and Fredericka Dembitz Brandeis, immigrants from Prague (now in the Czech Republic), were married in Madison, Indiana, in 1849. Louis held an outstanding scholastic record in the public schools of Louisville and at the Annen Realschule in Dresden, Germany. Admitted to Harvard Law School without a college degree, he graduated with record-breaking grades while still under the age of 21.

After practicing law for a short time in St. Louis, Missouri, Brandeis grew to be a leader of the Boston bar. Giving his time and talents without pay in matters of public interest, he became known as the attorney for the people. He was responsible for many social and economic reforms and for savings bank insurance, an economic protection plan for workingmen. His book *Other People's Money—And How the Bankers Use It* (1914) helped strengthen the federal antitrust laws.

President Woodrow Wilson nominated Brandeis to the U.S. Supreme Court in 1916. On most important issues he was aligned, often in the minority, with his colleague Oliver Wendell Holmes. Brandeis retired on February 13, 1939. Brandeis University, opened in 1948 in Waltham, Massachusetts, was named for him. Brandeis died in Washington, D.C., on October 5, 1941.

DAVID ROSS BROWER

(b. 1912–d. 2000)

The U.S. environmentalist David Ross Brower spent nearly 70 years in his effort to protect wilderness areas in the United States. He was involved with such groups as the Sierra Club, Friends of the Earth, the League of Conservation Voters, and the Earth Island Institute. His work resulted in the creation of the Kings Canyon, North Cascades, and Redwood national parks and the Point Reyes and Cape Cod national seashores; protection of the Grand Canyon and Dinosaur National Monument from dams; passage of the Wilderness Act in 1964; and innumerable other environmental-protection victories.

Brower was born in Berkeley, California, on July 1, 1912. When he was eight years old, he began taking his recently blinded mother on walks in the Berkeley Hills, and he attributed his interest in the beauty of nature in part to having had to serve as the eyes for someone else. He graduated from high school at age 16 and attended the University of California, Berkeley, for two years, until 1931. In 1933 he joined the Sierra Club. Brower went to work for Yosemite National Park two years later, and in his six years there he ascended its mountain peaks scores of times. He also was able to put his superior climbing skills to good use during his World War II Army service both as instructor and in combat. Upon leaving the Army, he returned to the job he had held before the war, editing for the University of California Press.

In 1952 Brower became executive director of the Sierra Club, a position he held until 1969. During his tenure, the club became a powerful activist organization and saw its membership grow from 7,000 to 77,000, but there were disagreements over the level of activism, and he felt pressured to leave office. He thereupon formed the Friends of the Earth and served as its chairman until disagreements with its board caused him to be dismissed in 1984. Although he was reinstated soon thereafter, he resigned in 1986 and returned to the Sierra Club, whose board he had rejoined in 1982. That same year he

David Ross Brower.

founded the Earth Island Institute in San Francisco to back worldwide conservation projects. Brower remained on the Sierra Club's board until 1998. His autobiography, *For Earth's Sake: The Life and Times of David Brower*, was published in 1990. He died in Berkeley on November 5, 2000.

JOHN BROWN

(b. 1800–d. 1859)

The ideological differences between the North and the South that festered before the American Civil War were reflected in their views of the abolitionist John Brown. To Northerners he was a martyr to the cause of freeing African Americans from slavery. To Southerners he was an insane criminal. To historians he was a man obsessed who chose a lawless course in order to achieve a moral end. Brown regarded himself as an instrument of God.

John Brown was born on May 9, 1800, in Torrington, Connecticut. His father was a tanner, shoemaker, and farmer who had 16 children by three wives. The family moved to Ohio in 1805. Young John was fond of animals and had many different pets, but he learned how to cure hides. He disliked what little schooling he had.

A restless drifter, Brown followed his father's trades, sold wool, and tried surveying. Yet he was barely able to support his growing family as they moved about in Ohio, Pennsylvania, Massachusetts, and New York. At 20 he married Dianthe Lusk. They had seven children. In 1833, a year after she died, he married Mary Anne Day. They had 13 children.

The son of a staunch abolitionist, Brown was convinced that black slavery was a sin against Christianity. In Pennsylvania his home was a station on the Underground Railroad, a secret network to aid fugitive slaves. In New York he settled his family in a black community founded on land donated by an antislavery philanthropist. By the time he was in his 50s, he had finally decided that force was the only way left to banish slavery.

In 1854 several of Brown's sons settled at Osawatomie, in Kansas Territory. Brown joined them in the bloody fights to make Kansas a free state. (One son was killed in a skirmish.) In May 1856 Brown led a small band of men who sought revenge for murders by proslavery mobs and brutally killed five settlers suspected of proslavery beliefs. He became feared as "Old Osawatomie Brown," a ruthless guerrilla leader pitted against the slaveholders. When the Kansas question was settled in favor of freedom, Brown schemed for a slave insurrection in the South itself.

On a rented farm in Maryland he gathered an armed band of 16 whites and five blacks to attack the federal arsenal across the Potomac River at Harpers Ferry (now in West Virginia) on the night of October 16, 1859. He wanted weapons for an "army of emancipation" to liberate other slaves. They took 60 hostages and held out against the local militia but finally surrendered to United States Marines under Colonel Robert E. Lee. Ten of Brown's men, including two of his sons, were killed. Brown was among those wounded and taken prisoner.

Convicted by Virginia of treason, murder, and inciting slaves to rebellion, Brown was hanged on December 2, 1859. At his trial he declared he would "forfeit my life for the furtherance of the ends of justice, and mingle my blood further with the blood of my children and with the blood of millions in this slave country whose rights are disregarded by wicked, cruel, and unjust enactments."

African Americans revered Brown for his long dedication to their welfare. As early as 1847 the great black abolitionist Frederick Douglass described him as a man who was "in sympathy a black man, and as deeply interested in our cause, as though his own soul had been pierced with the iron of slavery."

After the raid on Harpers Ferry, Southerners feared that other Northern radicals would follow Brown's violent example. Many Northerners who had been indifferent to slavery became convinced that abolition was necessary. Historians now believe that Brown's action helped bring on the Civil War. Once the war had begun, Brown was immortalized in a song in which his soul went "marching on."

PEARL S. BUCK

(b. 1892–d. 1973)

The daughter of American missionaries who served in China, Pearl S. Buck was one of the first writers to try to explain the mystery of the Far East to Western readers. For her many books about the wisdom, patience, and suffering of the Chinese peasants, she won the Nobel Prize in 1938.

Buck was born Pearl Sydenstricker on June 26, 1892, in Hillsboro, West Virginia. Her parents returned to their work as missionaries when she was only three months old and soon moved to Zhenjiang, China. She grew up in a house on a hill overlooking the Yangtze River, and her first language was Chinese. Her early stories about what she observed were printed in the weekly children's edition of the Shanghai Mercury.

At 15 Pearl was sent to boarding school in Shanghai, and two years later she entered Randolph-Macon Woman's College in Lynchburg, Virginia. She became class president and won two literary prizes. In 1917 she married John L. Buck, an American agriculturalist in China. They had one daughter, who was intellectually disabled—a story she eventually revealed in *The Child Who Never Grew* (1950).

Buck's first article, "In China, Too," appeared in the *Atlantic Monthly* in 1922. Her first book was *East Wind: West Wind* (1930), followed by the Pulitzer Prize–winning *The Good Earth*. Her most famous work, it was part of the trilogy The House of Earth (1935). Among Buck's more than 85 books were the novels *Dragon Seed* (1942) and *Pavilion of Women* (1946). She wrote some historical novels with an American setting under the pseudonym John Sedges.

Divorced in 1935, she immediately married her publisher, Richard J. Walsh, and stayed in the United States thereafter. She adopted nine children. Buck established an agency for the adoption of Amerasian children and the Pearl S. Buck Foundation, which works for the welfare of Amerasian and other children worldwide. Buck died on March 6, 1973, in Danby, Vermont.

RACHEL CARSON

(b. 1907–d. 1964)

Drawing on her childhood fascination with wildlife and the sea, American biologist Rachel Carson became a scientific writer whose works appeal to a wide range of readers. Her enchanting book *The Sea Around Us*, published in 1951, was a best-seller and the winner of a National Book Award. Her prophetic work *Silent Spring* (1962), about the dangers of pesticides in the food chain, created worldwide awareness of the dangers of pollution.

Rachel Louise Carson was born on May 27, 1907, in Springdale, Pennsylvania. She did her undergraduate work at the Pennsylvania College for Women, where she received her B.A. in 1929. She then went on to earn an M.A. from Johns Hopkins University in 1932. From 1931 to 1936 she taught zoology at the University of Maryland. During this period she also taught in the Johns Hopkins summer school and studied at the Marine Biological Laboratory in Woods Hole, Massachusetts.

Carson accepted a position in 1936 as an aquatic biologist with the United States Bureau of Fisheries (from 1940 called the U.S. Fish and Wildlife Service). She would hold this government post for the next 16 years. From 1949 to 1952 she served as editor in chief of the Fish and Wildlife Service's publications. By that time Carson had become widely known as a science writer. Her first three books were about sea life: *Under the Sea-Wind* (1941), *The Sea Around Us*, and *The Edge of the Sea* (1955) displayed Carson's remarkable talent for combining scientific observation with elegant and lyrical prose descriptions.

After the publication of *The Edge of the Sea*, Carson spent much of the next five years conducting research for *Silent Spring*. The book, which detailed the harmful effects that pesticides such as DDT had on the environment—and particularly on wildlife—became her second best seller and today is regarded as a landmark work in the history of the modern environmental movement. Carson died on April 14, 1964.

JIMMY CARTER

(b. 1924–d.)

In November 1976 Jimmy Carter was elected the 39th president of the United States. His emphasis on morality in government and his concern for social welfare appealed to voters who were disturbed by corruption in government and economic problems.

Carter took office during one of the most severe winters on record. The long period of below-freezing temperatures produced the worst shortage of natural gas in the nation's history. Carter received temporary authority from Congress to allocate natural gas supplies and to regulate prices. He also used the Taft-Hartley Act to end a coal miner's strike.

In April 1977 Carter gave the first of a series of major addresses to the nation on energy, which was to become one of the dominant concerns of his administration. Congress approved several of Carter's energy proposals, including the deregulation of natural gas prices, by 1985, and incentives for such conservation measures as conversion to coal in industry and fuel-saving improvements in the home.

In a second major energy program, announced in April 1979, Carter ordered the gradual decontrol of domestic oil prices, but a court later struck down his order. Congress approved Carter's tax on the so-called windfall profits of oil companies but rejected his request for standby authority for gasoline rationing. A third major set of energy measures included government underwriting of the development of synthetic fuels, which Congress also approved.

The economy became Carter's other domestic concern. Although he emphasized cutbacks in spending, he also approved some measures to stimulate the economy. As the rate of inflation increased, in October 1978 Carter announced the first of several anti-inflation plans, which included voluntary wage and price controls. In November he took emergency measures to protect the declining dollar on world markets.

The cost of living increased more than 13 percent during 1979, and in March 1980 Carter announced new anti-inflation measures. They included credit restraints, which caused a drop in auto and housing sales

Jimmy Carter.

and produced a deep, but short, recession in the United States.

Several other Carter reforms were approved by Congress. They included granting him limited authority to reorganize the federal bureaucracy, changes in Civil Service to reward performance, and deregulation of the trucking, airline, and railroad industries. Carter also won a major reform of the banking system and strengthening of the Social Security trust fund. Congress rejected his proposal for direct election of the president.

In his first official act as president, Carter granted pardons to Vietnam-era draft evaders. The pardons did not extend to deserters or to evaders who had used force or were employees of Selective Service.

While Carter deferred production of the neutron bomb and of the B-1 bomber, he approved full-scale development of the MX missile system. He stressed human rights in foreign affairs, publicly criticizing several countries and specific leaders for their repressive policies. He supported several Soviet dissidents, an action that the Soviet Union denounced as interference in its domestic affairs. Some Latin American governments broke off agreements with the United States over the charges of repression.

The president participated in summit meetings in Europe and Japan. He visited South America, Africa, Asia, and the Middle East, and his wife also traveled on behalf of the administration. After ending travel bans to Kampuchea (now Cambodia), Cuba, North Korea, and Vietnam in 1977, Carter extended full diplomatic recognition to China beginning in 1979.

Carter narrowly won Senate approval of two treaties in which the United States agreed to relinquish control of the Panama Canal and its surrounding zone by the year 2000. Strong opposition delayed ratification of the second Strategic Arms Limitation Talks (SALT II) agreement reached with the Soviet Union.

In 1978 Carter conducted a summit meeting between Israeli Prime Minister Menachem Begin and Egyptian President Anwar el-Sadat that resulted in agreements on principles for a peace treaty. In visits to Egypt and Israel in 1979, Carter negotiated a last-minute acceptance of a formal treaty.

On November 4, 1979, Iranian militants seized the U.S. Embassy in Tehran and took more than 50 Americans hostage. Carter initiated a series of moves to negotiate the release of the hostages. He called off an unsuccessful military rescue in progress in April 1980. (The last hostages were released moments after Carter left office, on January 20, 1981.)

Carter ordered bans on shipments of grain and high-technology goods to the Soviet Union after that country invaded Afghanistan in December 1979. He called for a boycott, which more than 60 countries joined, of the 1980 Olympic Games held in Moscow. Carter won Congressional approval to resume draft registration.

Shortly after his election Carter began to lose the support of many liberal Democrats who were critical of his economic policies. In the 1980 primaries Edward Kennedy defeated Carter in some of the most populous states, including California, New York, Pennsylvania, and Michigan. In July 1980 Carter received the lowest approval rating to that time of any president in the history of modern public-opinion polls. The hostage crisis played a major role in Carter's image of weakness and incompetency.

At the Democratic convention, though Carter was renominated, Kennedy supporters were able to adopt a platform with economic policies that Carter opposed. Carter refused to participate in televised debates that included Republican Congressman John B. Anderson of Illinois, who ran as an independent. Although the polls predicted a close election, Carter's defeat by the Republican nominee, Ronald Reagan, was one of the worst ever suffered by an incumbent president.

In retirement Carter was one of the few modern leaders who did not try to cash in on the presidency. He served as a professor at Emory University in Atlanta and published several books. In 1982 he and his wife founded the Carter Center, in association with Emory, to secure human rights, to resolve conflicts, and to combat disease, hunger, and poverty around the world. His volunteer services ranged from hands-on help in building low-income housing in the United States to continuing international mediation for human rights and peace. He also monitored controversial elections throughout the world. In 2002 Carter visited Cuba to meet with President Fidel Castro; he was the first sitting or former U.S. president to visit that country in nearly 75 years. For his work as a peacemaker and champion of human rights and democracy, both during and after his presidency, Carter was awarded the Nobel Peace Prize in 2002.

CESAR ESTRADA CHAVEZ

(b. 1927–d. 1993)

Hailed by Senator Robert F. Kennedy as "[o]ne of the heroic figures of our time," American labor leader Cesar Chavez was instrumental in changing the working conditions of migrant workers on American farms. An inspirational leader, he organized poor farm laborers into the nation's first successful union of agricultural workers, the National Farm Workers Association, which was the forerunner of the United Farm Workers of America (UFW).

Cesar Estrada Chavez was born on March 31, 1927, near Yuma, Arizona, to Librado and Juana Chavez. The second oldest of six children, Cesar was named for his paternal grandfather who had migrated to the United States from Mexico in the 1880s and had settled on a small ranch in the Gila River valley near Yuma. The Chavez family led a relatively comfortable existence, even in the early years of the Great Depression. But the family soon fell victim to the depression; Librado could not pay the taxes on the land, and the ranch was repossessed in 1937. The family moved to California to look for work. There they became migrant farm workers who traveled from farm to farm to pick fruits and vegetables during the harvests. The life of migrant farm workers proved a precarious existence. Always very poor, they were often cheated by growers and labor contractors and had to live in a succession of migrant worker camps. They also faced racial discrimination wherever they went. Cesar, who sporadically attended more than 30 different schools, left school when he was 15 years old to work full-time in the fields. Two years later, he joined the United States Navy and served in World War II.

After the war Chavez returned to migrant farm work in California. He married Helen Fabela in 1948, and the couple lived temporarily in Delano, California, before moving to San Jose. In 1952, Chavez met Fred Ross, an organizer for a social service group known as the Community Service Organization (CSO). The CSO was a grassroots association concerned with improving the lives of Hispanic Americans. Impressed with Ross and his ideas, Chavez volunteered as a CSO community organizer. Charged with registering voters among the Mexican American population in San Jose, Chavez went door to door, helping some workers with their day-to-day problems, instructing others on becoming United States citizens, and encouraging all to register to vote. He succeeded in registering 4,000 new voters.

In 1954, as a paid employee of CSO, Chavez was sent to organize a new CSO chapter in Oakland, California. Although he was shy, his passion and patience soon garnered impressive results. He then successfully organized new chapters in Bakersfield, Madera, and Hanford. During his work, he became particularly concerned with the plight of migrant farm workers, who were often exploited because of their financial desperation, their lack of group organization, and their lack of fluency in the English language. Chavez became convinced that only a union of farm workers could address the migrant workers' problems. He envisioned a union that, in addition to trying to win contracts and increased wages, would operate a social service program to alleviate many of the farm workers' other problems. In 1958, Chavez became a director of the CSO. During his tenure, he tried to convince CSO leaders to develop a special farm labor union that would work to improve the rights of migrant workers. When the CSO rejected his proposal, he resigned from the organization in 1962.

With the help of Dolores Huerta, a CSO organizer who shared his concern for the plight of migrant farm workers, Chavez founded the National Farm Workers Association (NFWA) in Delano. The founders tirelessly and patiently built the union member by member. By 1964, the union had 1,000 members and was growing fast. In September 1965, the fledgling NFWA joined an AFL-CIO–sponsored union in a strike against major grape growers in Delano. Chavez captured national attention when he became the driving force in what became a five-year California grape pickers strike, and again in 1968 when he led a nationwide boycott of California table grapes. Although the growers often resorted to violent measures to quell the strikes—measures which at times resulted in the deaths of strikers—Chavez insisted that the union adhere to the practice of nonviolence, and the strikers succeeded in forging a national support coalition of unions, church groups, students, minorities, and consumers. Chavez remained in the public eye by fasting and by inviting arrest to dramatize the struggles of farm workers for better pay and safer working conditions. By 1970, with millions of American consumers supporting the grape boycott, most growers signed union contracts that granted higher minimum wage and health insurance benefits for migrant farm workers.

Meanwhile, the NFWA faced a major threat to its survival as an organization. The Teamsters union, having won the support of growers as a conservative alternative to the NFWA, began competing with the NFWA for membership. To counter this measure by strengthening NFWA's membership base, Chavez merged the NFWA with an AFL-CIO farm group in 1966 to form the United Farm Workers Organizing Committee (UFWOC), which became the UFW in 1971. Chavez served as the new organization's president from its inception until his death. The position of the UFW was further strengthened in 1975 when the California Labor Relations Act, the first law to recognize the right of farm workers to organize into unions, was signed by Governor Jerry Brown. Under this law, farm workers had the right to vote for the union that would represent them. The workers voted for the UFW by a large majority, and the Teamsters abandoned the effort to organize farm laborers in 1977.

In the 1970s, Chavez led the UFW in fights against lettuce growers and other agribusinesses. In addition, the UFW experienced an explosive growth in membership and established regional offices throughout the country. But in the early 1980s, the union lost some momentum due to internal dissent and increased political support for the growers. Although union membership dwindled from near 100,000 at its climax to a low of some 20,000 members, Chavez continued his impassioned work for the rights of migrant farm laborers. In the 1980s, he protested against grape growers who used pesticides on their crops, which proved extremely harmful to the workers who harvested the grapes. He called for another boycott of California grapes in 1988. He continued to bring to national attention the plight of farm workers everywhere through media appearances and interviews, hunger strikes, and well-organized boycotts. While in Arizona helping UFW attorneys defend the union against a lawsuit filed by a California-based grower, Chavez died in his sleep on April 23, 1993. Tens of thousands of people attended his funeral. Chavez was posthumously awarded the Presidential Medal of Freedom, the highest civilian honor in the United States, in August 1994.

MICHAEL COLLINS

(b. 1890–d. 1922)

Michael Collins was a leader in Ireland's fight for independence from the British in the early 20th century. He helped form the Irish Republican Army (IRA) and led them in their first uprising against British troops. In 1921 he helped negotiate a treaty that ended the uprising and laid the foundation for Irish independence. The following year he was killed by IRA members who were opposed to the treaty.

Collins was born on October 16, 1890, in Woodfield, in the rural western county of Cork. His teacher at Lisvaird National School and the local blacksmith taught Michael about the 700-year occupation of Ireland by the British and nurtured pro-independence inclinations in him.

When he was 15 Collins moved to London to live with his sister. He worked at various jobs in banks and stock brokerage firms there for the next 11 years. Collins was increasingly interested in Irish republican politics, and he became an admirer of Arthur Griffith, founder of the revolutionary political party Sinn Fein.

At 18, Collins joined the Irish Republican Brotherhood, a secret nationalist group, and in 1916 he enrolled in the Irish Volunteers, an underground military organization. He returned to Dublin in 1916 to take part in an insurrection against the British. The rebellion was quashed in five days, and the British spent the next week systematically executing its leaders. Collins was sent to a prison camp in Wales for seven months.

The experience of the revolt and subsequent imprisonment galvanized Collins's revolutionary spirit. In 1917 he was elected to the executive body of Sinn Fein, quickly proving his dedication to the cause by creating an intelligence network and initiating an arms-smuggling operation. Two years later Sinn Fein announced the formation of the Dáil Éireann, an independent Irish parliament, and Collins was elected minister of finance and director of organization and intelligence. Eamon De Valera, imprisoned in an English jail at the time, was chosen to be president of the provisional government. Together with his friend Harry Boland, Collins executed a daring escape for the new president. At about this time, Collins met Kitty Kiernan, to whom he later became engaged.

The establishment of the Dáil exacerbated an already tense situation, and the war for independence began. Collins was responsible for creating an Irish Republican Army out of the relatively untrained Irish Volunteers. He decided to abandon traditional military tactics in favor of guerrilla warfare, a method that proved to be extremely effective in fighting the British. Collins also created an elite killing squad known as the Twelve Apostles. Within a year they had effectively destroyed the British Secret Service in Ireland.

The British responded with shelling and mass arrests. After a particularly devastating blow by the Twelve Apostles in 1920, British forces fired on a crowd watching a Gaelic football match. Twelve people were killed, and the day became known as Bloody Sunday. Collins's family homestead in Woodfield was also burned.

After three years of bloody fighting, a truce between the English and Irish went into effect on July 11, 1921. De Valera traveled to England to negotiate a treaty, but talks broke down and he returned to Ireland. He later sent Collins and Arthur Griffith, against their will, for a second round of negotiations. After two months, Collins returned to his country with a treaty for an Irish Free State that fell short of complete independence for Ireland, leaving the northern portion of the island under British control. Many speculate that De Valera placed Collins in the bargaining position knowing that the English would not grant full independence. After signing the document on December 6, 1921, Collins told Kitty Kiernan, "I have signed my death warrant."

The Dáil voted to approve the treaty by a vote of 64 to 57, but De Valera was opposed, and a bitter disagreement between pro- and antitreaty forces caused a deep rupture in the ranks of the IRA. Despite Collins's efforts to prevent more bloodshed, the tensions boiled over into a civil war that lasted 10 months.

Collins and Kitty became engaged during this tumultuous time, but Collins did not live to marry or to see his country reunited in peace. During a trip to his home county in August 1922, Collins was shot and killed by antitreaty forces. He was 31 years old. His body was returned to Dublin where tens of thousands of people, including British soldiers, filed past to pay their respects. He was remembered as a hero and a patriot who helped free Ireland from British control.

DALAI LAMA

(b. 1935–d.)

To Tibetan Buddhists, a Dalai Lama is the incarnation of the lord of compassion who takes earthly forms in order to help humankind.

The title is often translated as "Ocean of Wisdom." The Dalai Lama is the head of the religious order called Dge-lugs-pa (or Yellow Hat). Since the order achieved supremacy in Tibet in the mid-17th century, the Dalai Lama has been the spiritual leader of Tibetan Buddhism. Until the mid-20th century, when the 14th Dalai Lama was forced into exile, the Dalai Lama also ruled Tibet politically.

Each Dalai Lama is seen as a rebirth of the first of the line. After the death of a Dalai Lama, monks begin what may be a long search for the child believed to be the new incarnation. They are guided by the state oracle and various other signs. Candidates are examined physically and mentally and are usually asked to identify the personal belongings of the previous Dalai Lama. Once selected, the child is given a comprehensive Buddhist education. An appointed regent rules for the child until he is ready to do so.

HISTORY

The first of the line was Dge-'dun-grub-pa, who lived from 1391 to 1475. His successor, Dge-'dun-rgya-mtsho (1475—d. 1542), established a new monastery at Lhasa, Tibet, which became the seat of the Dge-lugs-pa order. The third of the line, Bsod-nams-rgya-mtsho (1543–88), was the first to be called Dalai Lama during his lifetime. The title was conferred on him as an honor by the Mongol leader Altan Khan.

The fifth Dalai Lama, Ngag-dbang-rgya-mtsho (1617–82), known as the Great Fifth, was a powerful leader. With the help of Mongol troops, he secured the dominance of Dge-lugs-pa over all other sects in Tibet. In 1642 the Dalai Lama was enthroned as Tibet's ruler, both spiritual and earthly.

In the 18th century, Tibet came under the control of the Chinese Qing Dynasty. The succession of Dalai Lamas continued to govern Tibet, however, which remained largely independent for some 200 years. In the early 20th century, China tried to establish direct control of Tibet by force. The 13th Dalai Lama, Thub-bstan-rgya-mtsho (1875—d. 1933), fled to India in 1910. The Tibetans expelled the Chinese troops by 1912, and the Dalai Lama returned, declaring Tibet independent.

The 14th Dalai Lama.

THE 14TH DALAI LAMA

Bstan-'dzin-rgya-mtsho (also spelled Tenzin Gyatso) was born as Lhamo Thondup on July 6, 1935, in the village of Taktser, Qinghai province, China. His parents were peasants of Tibetan birth. He was identified as the 14th Dalai Lama in 1937 and enthroned in 1940. He received an extensive education, and in 1959 he earned a degree equivalent to a doctorate in Buddhist philosophy.

The Dalai Lama assumed his full role as ruler of Tibet on November 17, 1950, at age 15. A month later he fled the advance of Chinese troops, which had entered Tibet in 1949. He returned to Lhasa in 1951 and spent several unsuccessful years attempting to make a peaceful and workable arrangement with China.

In 1959 the Chinese crushed an attempted revolution, killing tens of thousands of Tibetans. The Dalai Lama fled along with about 100 followers. They eventually settled in the Himalayas, in Dharmsala, India. There the Dalai Lama created a government-in-exile and waged a peaceful campaign to end the Chinese military presence. For his efforts, he was awarded the Nobel Peace Prize in 1989. He received the Templeton Prize in 2012.

The Dalai Lama traveled widely, teaching, lecturing, and meeting with many world leaders. Wherever he went, he spoke out against Chinese abuses of Tibetans and the destruction of Tibetan culture. The first Dalai Lama to become a global public figure, he became a spokesman not only for his people but for Tibetan Buddhism. He wrote several books about Buddhism, as well as an autobiography.

After the Dalai Lama reached the age of 70, the question of his successor was repeatedly raised. In the first decade of the 21st century, he declared that the 15th Dalai Lama would be discovered not in Chinese-controlled Tibet but in exile. He later suggested that he might appoint his successor. The Chinese government rejected this idea, declaring that the tradition of selecting a new Dalai Lama by determining the reincarnation of the previous one had to be maintained. In 2011 the Dalai Lama stepped down as the political head of the Tibetan government-in-exile.

CHARLES DARWIN

(b. 1809–d. 1882)

The theory of evolution by natural selection that was developed by Charles Darwin revolutionized the study of living things. In his *Origin of Species* (1859) he provided a scientific explanation of how the diverse species of plants and animals have descended over time from common ancestors. His theory remains central to the foundations of modern biology. Moreover, by demonstrating how natural laws govern the world of living things, Darwin helped usher in a new era in the cultural and intellectual history of humankind.

Charles Robert Darwin was born in Shrewsbury, England, on February 12, 1809. Darwin's father was a successful and wealthy physician; his mother was a daughter of Josiah Wedgwood, the famous British potter. She died when Charles was eight years old, and the boy was reared by three older sisters, who constantly found fault with him.

Darwin was such an indifferent student that his father said, "You care for nothing but shooting, dogs, and rat-catching, and you will be a disgrace to yourself and all your family." He had no interest in the classical languages and ancient history taught in school. Instead, he liked to collect shells, birds' eggs, and coins. He also watched birds and insects and helped his brother make chemical experiments at home.

At the age of 16, Darwin began to study medicine at the University of Edinburgh. There too he found the courses dull, and watching operations made him ill. In 1828 he transferred to Cambridge, intending to become a clergyman. Instead, he devoted most of his time to studying plants and animals and later to geology. He received his bachelor's degree in 1831.

Then came the event that shaped his life—an appointment as unpaid naturalist on the exploring ship *Beagle*. It left England on December 27, 1831, to chart the southern coasts of South America and sail around the world. The voyage, with many side trips on land, lasted until October 1836. During those five years Darwin examined geologic formations, collected fossils, and studied plants and animals. In the jungles, mountains, and islands he visited, he saw evidence of the many geologic changes that have been occurring over the course of eons—for example, the land gradually rising in some places and falling in others. He also considered the great diversity of living things, even in the depths of the ocean where no humans could appreciate their beauty. He thought about how the fossils he collected suggested that some kinds of mammals had died out. And he returned home filled with questions.

Back home, Darwin settled in London and quietly began work on what would become his great theory of evolution, developed largely in 1837–39. Meanwhile, he wrote up the journal of his scientific work on the *Beagle*. He also consulted experts to help him identify the thousands of fossils and specimens he had brought back, and he published the results. In 1839 he was admitted to the prestigious Royal Society.

Darwin married his cousin Emma Wedgwood in 1839, and they eventually had 10 children. He began to avoid society, and in 1842 the couple moved to the isolated village of Downe. This was partly owing to physical illness: a few years earlier, Darwin had begun to experience the heart palpitations and nausea that would plague him for the rest of his life. But he also sought seclusion because he knew that his radical theory would shock and offend Victorian society. Believing in evolution, Darwin said, was "like confessing a murder." And so he continued this work in secret.

In Darwin's time, the nearly universally accepted view was that God had created all species of living things in their current forms and that their attributes were the result of God's design. Nevertheless, Darwin was not the first to suggest that living things might change over time. Since ancient times, people have proposed other ways that plants and animals could have developed. The first broad theory of evolution was proposed in the early 19th century by French naturalist Jean Baptiste Lamarck. He maintained that plants and animals evolved because of an inborn tendency to progress from simple to complex forms. Environment, however, modified this progression and so did use or disuse of parts. He thought that giraffes, for example, developed long necks by straining to reach the leaves of trees, while snakes lost their legs by crawling.

Darwin knew about Lamarck's theory of evolution. His grandfather, Erasmus Darwin, had published several books expounding similar ideas. He felt, however, that early writers on the subject had speculated too much and had not based their theories on a solid foundation of observable phenomena. In developing his theory of evolution, Darwin drew upon observations made in a wide array of scientific disciplines and conducted a great many experiments.

Darwin also happened to read *An Essay on the Principle of Population*, by British economist Thomas Malthus. Malthus had undertaken to prove that human populations tend to increase more rapidly than food and other necessities. The result is a struggle in which some people succeed and become wealthy while others fail or even starve.

Darwin applied this theory to the world of nature. Plants and animals, he knew, reproduce so rapidly that the Earth could not hold them if all their young survived. This meant that there was a constant struggle for space, food, and shelter, as well as against enemies and unfavorable conditions. Certain hawks, for example, struggle, or compete, with each other for the mice they eat, and the poorest hunters go hungry. Mice, in turn, struggle to keep from being caught by hawks. In frigid winters living things struggle against the cold. Some endure it, while others fail to keep themselves warm enough and die. Although Darwin did not coin the phrase "survival of the fittest," his ideas about struggle expressed the same notion.

Struggling and living or dying could not lead to evolution if all members of each living kind or species were exactly alike. Darwin found that members of a single species vary greatly in shape, size, color, strength, and so on. He also believed that most of these variations could be inherited.

Under the constant struggle to exist, organisms with harmful variations are more likely to die before they can reproduce. And, on average, living things with useful variations are more likely to survive and bear young and thus to pass on their helpful variations. When their descendants vary still more, the process is repeated. In other words, the struggle for existence selects organisms with helpful variations but makes others die out. Darwin called this process natural selection.

Over the ages, Darwin believed, changes from natural selection produce a slow succession of new plants, animals, and other organisms. These changes have enabled living things to go into all sorts of environments and become fitted, or adapted, to many different types of life. Darwin called his theory descent by modification, because he proposed that all living things were descended from earlier forms.

Darwin wrote a short sketch of his theory in 1842 and a longer one in 1844. Instead of publishing the second statement, however, he continued his investigations. He also wrote books on coral reefs, volcanic islands, barnacles, and the geology of South America. Not until 1856 did he begin what would be a multivolume work on evolution.

In 1858 he received a manuscript from a young naturalist, Alfred Russel Wallace, who also had developed a theory of evolution by natural selection. With Wallace's approval, short statements by both men were published late in 1858. Darwin went on to write his famous book *On the Origin of Species by Means of Natural Selection*, which appeared in 1859.

The book caused a tremendous stir, and not just in scientific circles. The general public also read, discussed, and vigorously defended or denounced Darwin's theory, which became a popular topic in society salons. Some religious leaders believed that evolution was incompatible with their teachings and so opposed it. Newspapers publicized with great scorn a conclusion that Darwin had been careful to avoid—that humans are descended from apes. Evolutionary imagery spread through many other fields, including literature, economics, and political and social science. During Darwin's lifetime, the scientific community largely accepted his theory of descent, though it was slower to adopt his idea of natural selection.

After completing the *Origin of Species*, Darwin began *The Variation of Animals and Plants Under Domestication*, which showed how rapidly some organisms had evolved under artificial selection, the selective breeding of plants and animals by humans. *The Descent of Man, and Selection in Relation to Sex*, published in 1871, discussed human evolution. Later books dealt with earthworms, orchids, climbing plants, and plants that eat insects.

Darwin became very weak in 1881 and could no longer work. He died on April 19, 1882, in Downe, and was buried in Westminster Abbey among England's greatest citizens.

Darwin himself never claimed to provide proof of evolution or of the origin of species. His claim was that if evolution had occurred, a number of otherwise mysterious facts about plants and animals could be easily explained. After his death, however, direct evidence of evolution was observed, and evolution is now supported by a wealth of evidence from a variety of scientific fields.

Evolution has been rejected by members of some religious groups who prefer their theory of creationism. This attempts to explain some features of plant and animal life through a literal interpretation of the Bible. In the scientific community, however, there is little doubt that the general outline of Darwin's theory of evolution is correct.

EUGENE V. DEBS

(b. 1855–d. 1926)

The only candidate to run for the presidency of the United States from a prison cell, labor organizer Eugene V. Debs had been sentenced to prison for criticizing the government's prosecution of persons charged with violating the 1917 Espionage Act. It was the fifth time he had run for the presidency on the Socialist ticket.

Eugene Victor Debs was born in Terre Haute, Indiana, on November 5, 1855. He left home at 14 to work on the railroad and soon became interested in union activity. In 1875 he helped organize the Brotherhood of Locomotive Firemen. As president of the American Railway Union, he led a successful strike against the Great Northern Railway in 1894. Two months later he was jailed for half a year for his role in a strike against another railway company, the Chicago Pullman Palace Car Company.

Within a few years Debs had become a socialist and a founder of the Socialist Party of America. In 1905 Debs helped found the Industrial Workers of the World, but he soon quit the organization because of its radicalism. He was the Socialist Party's presidential candidate in 1900, 1904, 1908, 1912, and 1920, when he received his highest popular vote—about 915,000. Debs was convicted of sedition, or encouraging opposition to the government, in 1918, and his United States citizenship was taken away. He was released from prison in 1921. He died in Elmhurst, Illinois, on October 20, 1926. His citizenship was restored 50 years after his death.

JOHN DEWEY

(b. 1859–d. 1952)

One of the most notable American philosophers of the 20th century, John Dewey was also a pioneer in educational theory and method. Out of his ideas developed the progressive education movement that was very influential in schools until about 1950. In philosophy he shares with William James and Charles Sanders Peirce the distinction of founding the movement called pragmatism.

Dewey was born in Burlington, Vermont, on October 20, 1859. He attended the University of Vermont and Johns Hopkins University. In 1884 he went to the University of Michigan as an instructor in philosophy and psychology. From 1894 to 1904 he headed a department of philosophy, psychology, and education at the University of Chicago. In 1904 Dewey moved to Columbia University in New York City as professor of philosophy. He remained there for the rest of his teaching career.

Dewey and his wife, the former Alice Chipman, started the Laboratory School at the University of Chicago to test his educational theories. Learning by doing was the heart of his method. The children were given freedom to learn in accordance with their needs and experiences. The faculty was able to study child behavior, a new area of study at the time.

Dewey regarded the school as a community—a part of society. He looked upon education as a process of living, not as preparation for later living. His ideas were incorporated in a number of books, including the influential *The School and Society*, published in 1899, and *Experience and Education* (1938). In philosophy, Dewey's pragmatic theories insisted that the way to test ideas was to check them against their consequences rather than to claim their agreement with supposedly self-evident truth. His philosophy was suited to American life, characterized by its respect for science and technology, its diversity, and its practicality. When faced with a problem, said Dewey, a person must logically examine the options open to him to find the best solution supported by the facts.

This method of inquiry and testing should be applied to moral and social questions, as well as to technological and scientific ones. His theories were set forth in a number of books, including *Reconstruction in Philosophy* (1920), *Experience and Nature* (1925), *Art as Experience* (1934), and *Freedom and Culture* (1939). Dewey retired from teaching in 1930. He died in New York City on June 1, 1952.

FREDERICK DOUGLASS

(b. 1818?–d. 1895)

An escaped slave, Frederick Douglass became one of the foremost black abolitionists and civil rights leaders in the United States. His powerful speeches, newspaper articles, and books awakened whites to the evils of slavery and inspired blacks in their struggle for freedom and equality.

Frederick Douglass was born Frederick Augustus Washington Bailey in Talbot County, Maryland, possibly in February 1818. His father was an unknown white man; his mother, Harriet Bailey, was a slave. He was separated from her and raised by her elderly parents.

When he was seven years old, Frederick was sent to his master, Captain Aaron Anthony, at a nearby plantation. There he first met a brother and two sisters. He later recalled sadly that "slavery had made us strangers."

The following year, Frederick became a servant to Hugh Auld, a relative of Captain Anthony who lived in Baltimore. Frederick persuaded Auld's wife to teach him to read. But Auld believed slaves should not be educated and stopped the lessons. White playmates helped Frederick, and he soon learned to read well. His reading of a book of speeches denouncing slavery and oppression deepened his hatred of slavery.

In 1833 Frederick was sent to work for Auld's brother, Thomas, at a plantation near St. Michael's, Maryland. Frederick's pride angered his new master, who placed him in the hands of a "slave breaker" to "tame" him. One day the two fought, and Frederick emerged victorious. Sometime later he wrote that the fight had been a turning point in his life. "I was nothing before—I was a man now."

In 1835 Frederick was put to work at a farm near Thomas Auld's plantation. In the following year he and other slaves plotted to escape to the North. Their plan was discovered, and they were jailed. Frederick was released and sent back to Baltimore, where he became a ship's caulker. Once, he was attacked by white workers who resented the competition of slave laborers. They went unpunished because the testimony of black witnesses would not be admitted as evidence in a court. For a while in 1838 Hugh Auld allowed Frederick to find his own jobs and to keep part of his wages.

On September 3, 1838, Frederick escaped from slavery. With identification borrowed from a free black seaman, he traveled to New York City. In less than a day he was a free man. Soon after, he sent for Anna Murray, a free black woman from Baltimore. They were married and settled in New Bedford, Massachusetts. He took the name Frederick Douglass.

Douglass read the *Liberator*, an antislavery newspaper published by the white abolitionist William Lloyd Garrison. He eagerly attended antislavery meetings. In 1841 at an antislavery convention, Douglass described his slave life in a moving speech that began his career as an abolitionist.

Douglass became an agent of the Massachusetts Anti-Slavery Society and in this capacity lectured to large assemblies. Soon he became unhappy with merely retelling his memories of slave life. He later said, "It did not entirely satisfy me to narrate wrongs—I felt like denouncing them." In 1841 Douglass campaigned in Rhode Island against a proposed new state constitution that would deny blacks the right to vote. In 1843 he traveled through the East and Midwest to address a series of antislavery assemblies known as the "One Hundred Conventions."

In his travels, Douglass was sometimes attacked by proslavery mobs and often met discrimination. Once, he refused to leave his train seat for a segregated car and had to be forcibly removed.

Many listeners were so impressed by Douglass's appearance and personality that they could not believe he had ever been a slave. He had never revealed his former name or the name of his master. To dispel doubts about his past, he published an autobiography in 1845, *The Narrative of the Life of Frederick Douglass: An American Slave*. Fearful that it might lead to his reenslavement, Douglass fled to Great Britain, where he lectured to arouse support for the antislavery movement in the United States. English Quakers raised money to purchase his freedom, and in 1847 he returned home, now legally free.

That year, Douglass founded a new antislavery newspaper, the *North Star*—later renamed *Frederick Douglass's Paper*—in Rochester, New York. Unlike Garrison, he had come to believe that political action rather than moral persuasion would bring about the abolition of slavery. Douglass also resented Garrison's view that blacks did not have the ability to lead the antislavery movement. By 1853, he had broken with Garrison and become a strong and independent abolitionist.

While in Rochester, Douglass directed the city's branch of the Underground Railroad, which smuggled escaped slaves into Canada. For years he worked to end racial segregation in Rochester's public schools. Douglass hoped that blacks would no longer be employed only as servants and laborers. He proposed that schools be established to train them to become skilled craftsmen.

In 1859 Douglass refused to join the white abolitionist John Brown in his attempt to seize arms for a slave revolt from the federal arsenal at Harpers Ferry, West Virginia. But Douglass did not reject violence as a weapon against slavery. He believed that "it can never be wrong for the imbruted and whip-scarred slaves, or their friends, to hunt, harass, and even strike down the traffickers in human flesh." Douglass was accused of helping Brown and was again forced to flee to England.

In the spring of 1860 he returned to the United States and began campaigning to elect Gerrit Smith, an abolitionist, as president. Later he came out in support of Abraham Lincoln. When the American Civil War began, in 1861, Douglass urged that it be fought to abolish slavery. He applauded President Lincoln's final Emancipation Proclamation of 1863, which freed slaves in the rebellious states, but expressed his disappointment that not all slaves had been freed. Douglass urged the Union Army to use black troops. In 1863 he helped form two black regiments, but the black troops were given lower wages and fewer chances for promotion than white soldiers. Douglass met with Lincoln to request equal treatment for them.

After the Civil War, Douglass held several federal offices. In the

District of Columbia he was appointed to the legislative council in 1871. He became a U.S. marshal there in 1877 and recorder of deeds in 1881. From 1889 to 1891 he served as minister to Haiti.

Douglass fought for passage of the 15th Amendment to the Constitution—ratified in 1870—which gave blacks the right to vote. Later he saw that Southern blacks had returned to virtual slavery under a farming system called sharecropping. He urged the federal government to grant land to blacks.

Douglass earnestly supported women's rights as well. In 1848, at the first women's rights convention in the United States, he had demanded that women be allowed to vote. On the day of his death—February 20, 1895, in Washington, D.C.—Douglass attended a convention for women's suffrage.

Douglass proclaimed his beliefs in justice for the oppressed in the *North Star*: "Right is of no Sex—Truth is of no Color." He wanted blacks to lead the struggle for civil rights. The year he died, he urged a black student to "Agitate! Agitate! Agitate!"

Douglass's first wife died in 1882. They had five children. He married Helen Pitts, a white woman, in 1884. His *Narrative* appeared in expanded editions as *My Bondage and My Freedom* in 1855 and as *Life and Times of Frederick Douglass* in 1881.

W. E. B. Du Bois

(b. 1868–d. 1963)

For more than 50 years W. E. B. Du Bois, an African American editor, historian, and sociologist, was a leader of the civil rights movement in the United States. He helped found the National Association for the Advancement of Colored People (NAACP) and was its outstanding spokesman in the first decades of its existence.

William Edward Burghardt Du Bois was born on February 23, 1868, in Great Barrington, Massachusetts. His parents, Alfred and Mary Burghardt Du Bois, were of African and European ancestry. An excellent student, Du Bois graduated from Fisk University in 1888 and from

Harvard College in 1890. He traveled in Europe and studied at the University of Berlin. In 1895 he received a Ph.D. from Harvard. His dissertation, *The Suppression of the African Slave-Trade to the United States of America, 1638–d. 1870*, was published in 1896 as the first volume of the Harvard Historical Studies.

After teaching Greek and Latin at Wilberforce University from 1894 to 1896, Du Bois studied Philadelphia's slums. In *The Philadelphia Negro*, published in 1899, a pioneering sociological study, he hoped to dispel the ignorance of whites about blacks, which he believed was a cause of racial prejudice. Du Bois taught at Atlanta University from 1897 to 1910 and from 1897 until 1914 directed its annual studies of black life.

In *The Souls of Black Folk* (1903), Du Bois declared that "the problem of the Twentieth Century is the problem of the color-line." He criticized the famous black educator Booker T. Washington for accepting racial discrimination and minimizing the value of college training for blacks. Du Bois felt that blacks needed higher education for leadership. In his essay "The Talented Tenth" he wrote, "The Negro race, like all races, is going to be saved by its exceptional men."

The split between Washington and Du Bois reflected a bitter division of opinion among black leaders. In 1905, at Niagara Falls, Canada, Du Bois joined the more militant leaders to demand equal voting rights and educational opportunities for blacks and an end to racial discrimination. But the Niagara Movement declined within a few years, and he then helped form another group, which in 1909 became the National Association for the Advancement of Colored People (initially called the National Negro Committee). He edited the NAACP's journal, the *Crisis*, in which he often wrote that blacks should develop farms, industries, and businesses separate from the white economy. NAACP officials, who desired integration, criticized this opinion, and he resigned as editor in 1934. He returned to Atlanta University, and in 1940 he launched *Phylon*, a new magazine about blacks' lives.

Du Bois was interested in African blacks and led several Pan-African congresses. He was awarded the Spingarn Medal in 1920 for his efforts to foster black racial solidarity. Although he clashed with Marcus Garvey, the leader of a "back to Africa" movement, and attacked his scheme for an African empire, he lauded Garvey's racial pride.

In his later years Du Bois came to believe that the United States could not solve its racial problems and that the only world power opposed to racial discrimination was the Soviet Union. He was awarded the communist-sponsored International Peace Prize in 1952 and the Soviet Lenin Peace Prize in 1958. Du Bois joined the Communist Party of the United States in 1961 and immigrated to Ghana, where he became a citizen, in 1963. He died there on August 27, 1963. He had been married twice, to Nina Gomer and to Shirley Graham, and had two children.

Du Bois was brilliant, proud, and aloof. He once wrote: "My leadership was a leadership of ideas. I never was, nor ever will be, personally popular." Du Bois wrestled with his conflicting desires for both integration and black nationalism. His Pan-African and communist views removed him from the mainstream of the United States civil rights movement. But he never wavered in his efforts to teach blacks their rights as human beings and pride in their heritage. Among his writings are *Black Reconstruction* (published in 1935) and *Dusk of Dawn* (1940).

MEDGAR WILEY EVERS

(b. 1925–d. 1963)

Although the murder of Medgar Evers deprived the U.S. civil rights movement of a dedicated leader, the event brought national attention to the problems surrounding racial discrimination and segregationist practices in the Southern United States. Evers and his brother Charles were active organizers of local affiliates of the National Association for the Advancement of Colored People (NAACP) in Philadelphia, Mississippi. In 1954, Medgar Evers became the first Mississippi field secretary of the NAACP.

Medgar Wiley Evers was born on July 2, 1925, in Decatur, Mississippi. The third of four children born to James and Jessie Evers, Medgar was raised in a devoutly religious family. As a child and young adult, he lived daily with the discrimination and humiliation brought forth by the Jim

Crow laws that enforced racial segregation throughout the Southern states.

After the Japanese attack on Pearl Harbor in 1941, Evers enlisted in the U.S. Army and served in Europe during World War II. Following his discharge from the military after the war, Evers enrolled at Alcorn Agricultural and Mechanical College (now Alcorn State University) in Lorman, Mississippi, graduating in 1952 with a degree in business administration. While at school he participated in numerous clubs and held several student offices. His outstanding academic and service record at Alcorn led to his inclusion in *Who's Who Among Students in American Colleges*.

Following graduation, Evers and his wife moved to Mound Bayou, Mississippi, where he worked as an insurance agent while organizing local chapters of the NAACP in the Mississippi Delta. He also encouraged local boycotts by African Americans of businesses and services that engaged in discrimination and segregation. In 1954 he attempted to enroll in law school at the University of Mississippi but was refused admission. His continued efforts to enforce integration of Mississippi schools garnered attention from the head offices of the NAACP, and that same year he was named as the organization's first field secretary in Mississippi.

Following his appointment as field secretary for the NAACP, Evers moved his family to Jackson. He continued to encourage and participate in antisegregation actions, including several local boycotts that gained national attention. In Jackson, Evers also began to investigate violent crimes perpetrated against African Americans. In 1962, Evers's efforts to help James Meredith gain admission to the University of Mississippi brought much needed federal support after Meredith's entrance to the institution was barred by the governor and blocked by rioting. Although Meredith's eventual admission to the school was a triumph for the civil rights movement in general, it also drew further attention to Evers. Although his outspokenness and dedicated activism earned him the admiration of many, it also led to increased animosity from local segregationists.

On June 12, 1963, Evers was shot in the back as he returned home from his office late at night. He died within an hour of the ambush. Evers was buried in Arlington National Cemetery; later that year, he was posthumously awarded a Spingarn Medal. Byron de La Beckwith, a local white segregationist, was charged with Evers's murder but was set free in 1964 after two trials resulted in hung juries. The case was reopened in the mid-1990s, however, and in 1994 Beckwith was convicted of the crime he had committed 31 years before. Although Beckwith's attorneys tried to appeal the conviction, it was upheld by the Mississippi Supreme Court in 1997. Beckwith remained in prison, where he died in 2001.

HENRY FORD

(b. 1863–d. 1947)

In 1896 a horseless carriage chugged along the streets of Detroit, with crowds gathering whenever it appeared. Terrified horses ran at its approach. The police tried to curb this nuisance by forcing its driver, Henry Ford, to get a license. That car was the first of many millions produced by the automotive pioneer.

Henry Ford was born near Dearborn, Michigan, on July 30, 1863. His mother died when he was 12. He helped on the family farm in summer and in winter attended a one-room school. Watches and clocks fascinated the boy. He went around the countryside doing repair work without pay, merely for the chance to tinker with machinery.

At 16 Ford walked to Detroit and apprenticed himself to a mechanic for \$2.50 a week. His board was \$3.50, so he worked four hours every night for a watchmaker for \$2 a week. Later he worked in an engine shop and set up steam engines used on farms. In 1884 he took charge of a farm his father gave him. He married and seemed settled down, but after two years he went back to Detroit and worked as night engineer for the Detroit Edison Company.

Ford built his first car in a little shed behind his home. It had a two-cylinder engine over the rear axle that developed four horsepower, a single seat fitted in a boxlike body, an electric bell for a horn, and a steering lever instead of a wheel. In 1899 Ford helped organize the Detroit Automobile Company, which built cars to order. Ford wanted to build in quantity at a price within the reach of many. His partners objected, and Ford withdrew.

In 1903 he organized the Ford Motor Company with only $28,000 raised in cash. This money came from 11 other stockholders. One investor put just $2,500 into Ford's venture (only $1,000 of it in cash). He drew more than $5 million in dividends, and he received more than $30 million when he sold all of his holdings to Ford in 1919.

Early automobile manufacturers merely bought automobile parts and assembled the cars. Ford's objective was to make every part that went into his cars. He acquired iron and coal mines, forests, mills, and factories to produce and shape his steel and alloys, his fuel, wood, glass, and leather. He built railroad and steamship lines and an airplane freight service in order to transport his products.

Mass production was Ford's main idea, and he replaced workers with machines wherever possible. Each worker was given only one task, which he did repeatedly until it became automatic. Conveyors brought the job to the worker instead of having the worker waste time going to the job. To cut shipping costs, parts were shipped from the main plants in the Detroit area and assembled into cars at branch plants.

Ford also won fame as a philanthropist and pacifist. He established an eight-hour day, a minimum wage of $5 daily (later raised to $6), and a five-day week. He built a hospital in Detroit with fixed rates for service and physicians and nurses on salary. He created the Edison Institute, which included Greenfield Village and the Edison Institute Museum and trade schools. The village featured reproductions of Independence Hall, Thomas Edison's early laboratory, and other famous old buildings. Greenfield Village and the museum, now known as the Henry Ford Museum, are still open to the public as part of the complex called The Henry Ford. During World War I Ford headed a party of pacifists to Norway in a failed attempt to end the war, but during both World War I and World War II his company was a major producer of war materials.

In 1945 Ford yielded the presidency of the company to his 28-year-old grandson, Henry Ford II. Ford died on April 7, 1947, at the age of 83. Most of his personal estate, valued at about $205 million, was left to the Ford Foundation, one of the world's largest public trusts.

FRANCIS I

(b. 1936–d.)

Following the resignation of Benedict XVI on February 28, 2013, Francis I became the 266th bishop of Rome and the head of the Roman Catholic church. He was the first pope from South America and the first from the Jesuit order.

Jorge Mario Bergoglio was born on December 17, 1936, in Buenos Aires, Argentina, the son of Italian immigrants to that country. He studied chemistry at the University of Buenos Aires but then switched to philosophy and theology. He was ordained a priest in 1969 and subsequently served as the superior of the Jesuit province of Argentina (1973–79). In 1992 he was appointed an auxiliary bishop of Buenos Aires. He became archbishop of Buenos Aires in 1998.

Francis I.

In February 2013 Pope Benedict XVI resigned, citing old age and health concerns. A conclave was convened in early March so that Benedict's replacement could be elected and installed before the impending Easter holiday.

Bergoglio was elected on the fifth ballot and chose the name Francis.

Francis took charge of a church at a crossroads. In the early 21st century Roman Catholics constituted more than one-sixth of the world's population, many of them in Latin America and Africa. Yet scandals, particularly the clergy sexual-abuse scandals that first arose in the 1980s and '90s, had undermined the church's stature, particularly in the United States and Europe. In his earliest public addresses and in his first public mass, Francis called for spiritual renewal within the church and increased attention to the plight of the poor, and he sternly condemned the forces that diverted the church from its ministry and set it at risk of becoming a "pitiful NGO." He also reached out to his political opponents, Yet he incensed some traditionalists by appearing on that occasion in a simple tunic rather than in the more traditional papal garments. He further drew traditionalists' ire when he washed the feet of two young women, including aMuslim, in a juvenile detention center during the traditional Maundy Thursday reenactment of Jesus's washing of the feet of the Twelve Apostles. (Church tradition held that women could not participate in the ceremony because the Apostles were men.) He also took the unprecedented step later in 2013 of appointing a council of eight cardinals to advise him on church policy.

BETTY FRIEDAN

(b. 1921–d. 2006)

U.S. author and feminist Betty Friedan was best known for her book *The Feminine Mystique* (1963), which challenged the traditional roles of women. In 1966 she cofounded the National Organization for Women (NOW), a civil rights group dedicated to achieving equality of opportunity for women.

Bettye Naomi Goldstein was born on February 4, 1921, in Peoria, Illinois. In 1942 she graduated from Smith College with a degree in psychology. She spent a year on graduate work at the University of California at Berkeley and then moved to New York City. After working

Betty Friedan.

at various jobs until 1947, she married Carl Friedan (divorced 1969). For the next 10 years she lived as a housewife and mother in the suburbs of New York while doing freelance work for a number of magazines. In 1957 Friedan circulated a survey among her Smith classmates and discovered that many of them were, like her, dissatisfied with their lives. To further her research, she began an extensive study on the topic, including more detailed questionnaires, interviews, and discussions with psychologists and other experts on behavior. She eventually published her findings in her 1963 landmark book, *The Feminine Mystique*.

The Feminine Mystique was an immediate and controversial best seller and was translated into a number of foreign languages. Its title came from a term Friedan used to describe a feeling of personal worthlessness that resulted when a woman accepted a designated role that required her to be intellectually, economically, and emotionally reliant on her husband. Friedan's main thesis was that women were subjected to a widespread system of delusions and false values under which they were encouraged to find fulfillment, even identity, vicariously through the husbands and children to whom they were expected to cheerfully devote their lives. This restricted role of wife-mother led almost inevitably to a sense of unreality or lack of general spiritual well-being in the absence of genuine, creative, self-defining work.

As president of NOW from 1966 to 1970, Friedan directed campaigns for greater representation of women in government, for child-care centers for working mothers, and for legalized abortion and other reforms. At one time NOW was one of the largest and possibly the most effective organization in the women's movement. After relinquishing the presidency, Friedan helped to organize the Women's Strike for Equality—held on August 26, 1970, the 50th anniversary of woman suffrage—and was a leader in the campaign for ratification of the proposed Equal Rights Amendment to the U.S. Constitution. She was a founding member of the National Women's Political Caucus (1971), and she became director of the First Women's Bank and Trust Company in 1973.

Friedan authored a few books throughout her career, including *It Changed My Life: Writings on the Women's Movement* (1976); *The Second Stage* (1981), an assessment of the status of the women's movement; and *The*

Fountain of Age (1993), an exploration into the psychology of old age. She published her memoir, *Life So Far*, in 2000. Friedan died on February 4, 2006, in Washington, D.C.

JOHN KENNETH GALBRAITH

(b. 1908–d. 2006)

When the noted American economist John Kenneth Galbraith published his book *The Affluent Society* in 1958, he gave a name to the remarkable prosperity the United States had been enjoying since the end of World War II. He also criticized economic policies that did not pay enough attention to public services.

John Kenneth Galbraith.

Galbraith was born in Canada, in Iona Station, Ontario, on October 15, 1908. After graduating from the University of Toronto in 1931, he went on to earn a doctorate at the University of California at Berkeley in 1934. He taught successively at Harvard and Princeton universities for the next several years. During the war he worked in the federal government's Office of Price Administration, and in the years 1943 to 1948 he was an editor of *Fortune* magazine. He taught at Harvard from 1949 until 1961, when President John F. Kennedy appointed him ambassador to India. He returned to Harvard in 1963.

In addition to his teaching, Galbraith was continuously involved in public affairs. In 1945 he served as director of the United States Strategic Bombing Survey, studying the effects of bombing on Japan and Germany. He aided in the postwar reconstruction of both countries as well. As a proponent of liberal politics, Galbraith was involved in the presidential campaigns of Adlai Stevenson, John F. Kennedy, Eugene McCarthy, and George McGovern. Among his other publications are *American Capitalism* (1951), *New Industrial State* (1967), *Ambassador's Journall* (1969), and *The Age of Uncertainty* (1977). Galbraith died on April 29, 2006, in Cambridge, Massachusetts.

GALILEO

(b. 1564–d. 1642)

Modern physics owes its beginning to Galileo, who was the first astronomer to use a telescope. By discovering four satellites of the planet Jupiter, he gave visual evidence that supported the Copernican theory. Galileo thus helped disprove much of the medieval thinking in science.

Galileo Galilei, who is generally known only by his first name, was born in Pisa, Italy, on February 15, 1564. His family belonged to the nobility but was not rich. His father sent him to study medicine at the local university. Galileo, however, soon turned to a career in science.

In 1583 Galileo discovered the law of the pendulum by watching a chandelier swing in the cathedral at Pisa. He timed it with his pulse and found that, whether it swung in a wide or a narrow arc, it always took the same time to complete an oscillation. He thus gave society the first reliable means of keeping time.

A lecture on geometry kindled his interest in mathematics, and he got his father's consent to change his studies. Lack of money forced him to leave school in 1585, and he became a lecturer at the Academy of Florence.

The next year he attracted attention with discoveries in hydrostatics. His work in dynamics won him an appointment as lecturer on mathematics at the University of Pisa in 1589.

He soon made enemies with his arguments against what he considered mistakes in the science of the day. According to a popular story, he dropped weights from the Leaning Tower of Pisa to prove his views concerning falling bodies. His writings, however, do not mention such an experiment. In any case, resentment against his views drove him out of Pisa in 1591.

In 1592 the University of Padua offered Galileo a professorship in mathematics. About 1609, after word from Holland of Hans Lippershey's newly invented telescope reached him, he built his own version of the instrument. He developed magnifying power until on January 7, 1610, he saw four satellites of Jupiter. He also saw the mountains and craters on the Moon and found the Milky Way to be a dense collection of stars.

Galileo moved to Florence in September 1610 and was a philosopher and mathematician there for many years. In 1609 Johannes Kepler published his laws of planetary motion based upon the Copernican theory. Galileo supported this view strongly. In 1616 he received a formal warning that the theory was contrary to the teachings of the Roman Catholic Church. Nevertheless, he again supported the Copernican view in a dialogue, *The Great Systems of the Universe*.

During his last eight years Galileo lived near Florence under house arrest for having "held and taught" Copernican doctrine. He became blind in 1637 but continued to work until his death on January 8, 1642. Nearly 342 years later, Galileo was pardoned by Pope John Paul II, and the church finally accepted his teachings.

Galileo's contributions to mechanics include the law of falling bodies, the fact that the path of a projectile is a parabola, the demonstration of the laws of equilibrium, and the principle of flotation. He devised a simple thermometer and inspired a pupil, Evangelista Torricelli, to invent the barometer. Galileo's great contribution to scientific thinking was the principle of inertia. Before his time everyone followed Aristotle's theory that when an object moved, something had to act continuously to keep it moving. Galileo countered this with the theory that if a body is moving freely, something must happen to stop it or to make it change direction.

INDIRA GANDHI

(b. 1917–d. 1984)

An aggressive fighter in the struggle for Indian independence, Indira Gandhi was the first woman prime minister of India. She was the only child of Jawaharlal Nehru, who became India's first prime minister.

Indira Nehru was born on November 19, 1917, in Allahabad, India. While she was growing up, her family was active in the nonviolent resistance movement led by Mahatma Gandhi against Great Britain's colonial rule of India. At the age of 12 she joined the movement by organizing thousands of Indian children to run errands and do odd jobs to aid the adults who were working for independence.

Indira's education was intermittent. She attended school in India and Switzerland for short periods. More often she studied at home. In 1934 she studied art and dancing at the university at Santiniketan. Later she attended Oxford University in England.

In March 1942 Indira Nehru married Feroze Gandhi, a friend from her student days in England. A few months later they were arrested after she spoke at a public meeting in defiance of a British ban. She was imprisoned for 13 months. After India achieved independence in 1947, Gandhi toured refugee camps to aid victims of a Hindu-Muslim religious war. She accompanied her father on his official visits all over the world and campaigned for him during elections.

Beginning in 1959, Indira Gandhi served for a year as president of the Indian National Congress, the majority political party. She became the minister of information and broadcasting in the cabinet of Prime Minister Lal Bahadur Shastri, who succeeded Nehru after his death in May 1964.

When Shastri died in January 1966, Gandhi was elected prime minister by the Congress party. She was returned to office in the general elections of 1967 and 1971. Her government faced crop failures and food riots, poverty, student unrest, and resistance from the many different language groups to the adoption of Hindi as the nation's official language. In 1971 Gandhi led India in a successful war against

Pakistan to separate East and West Pakistan and establish the nation of Bangladesh.

In 1975 Gandhi was convicted on two counts of corruption in the 1971 campaign. While appealing the decision, she declared a state of emergency, imprisoned her political opponents, and assumed emergency powers. Governing by decree, she imposed total press censorship and implemented a policy of large-scale sterilization as a form of birth control. When long-postponed national elections were held in 1977, Gandhi and her party were soundly defeated.

Reelected to Parliament in 1978, Gandhi was soon expelled and jailed briefly. While misconduct charges were still pending, she campaigned as an activist who would curb inflation and crime. A landslide victory returned her to office in 1980. Faced with the problem of Sikh extremists in the Punjab using violence to assert their demands for an autonomous state, Gandhi ordered the Indian army on June 6, 1984, to storm the Golden Temple at Amritsar, the Sikhs' holiest shrine, which had been converted into an armory. Hundreds of Sikhs died in the attack. Gandhi was assassinated by her own Sikh bodyguards as she walked to her office on October 31. Her only surviving son, Rajiv, succeeded her as prime minister. He served until 1989 and was campaigning for reelection when he too was assassinated, on May 21, 1991.

MAHATMA GANDHI

(b. 1869–d. 1948)

Throughout history most national heroes have been warriors, but Gandhi ended British rule over his native India without striking a single blow. A frail man, he devoted his life to peace and brotherhood in order to achieve social and political progress. Yet less than six months after his nonviolent resistance to British rule won independence for India, he was assassinated by a religious fanatic.

Gandhi was one of the gentlest of men, a devout and almost mystical Hindu, but he had an iron core of determination. Nothing could change his convictions. This combination of traits made him the leader of India's

Mahatma Gandhi.

nationalist movement. Some observers called him a master politician. Others believed him a saint. To millions of Hindus he was their beloved Mahatma, meaning "great soul."

Mohandas Karamchand Gandhi was born on October 2, 1869, in Porbandar, near Bombay. His family belonged to the Hindu merchant caste Vaisya. His father had been prime minister of several small native states. Gandhi was married when he was only 13 years old.

When he was 19 he defied custom by going abroad to study. He studied law at University College in London. Fellow students snubbed him because he was an Indian. In his lonely hours he studied philosophy. In his reading he discovered the principle of nonviolence as enunciated in Henry David Thoreau's "Civil Disobedience," and he was persuaded by John Ruskin's plea to give up industrialism for farm life and traditional handicrafts—ideals similar to many Hindu religious ideas.

In 1891 Gandhi returned to India. Unsuccessful in Bombay, he went to South Africa in 1893. At Natal he was the first so-called "colored" lawyer admitted to the supreme court. He then built a large practice.

His interest soon turned to the problem of fellow Indians who had come to South Africa as laborers. He had seen how they were treated as inferiors in India, in England, and then in South Africa. In 1894 he founded the Natal Indian Congress to agitate for Indian rights. Yet he remained loyal to the British Empire. In 1899, during the Boer War, he raised an ambulance corps and served the South African government. In 1906 he gave aid against the Zulu revolt.

Later in 1906, however, Gandhi began his peaceful revolution. He declared he would go to jail or even die before obeying an anti-Asian law. Thousands of Indians joined him in this civil disobedience campaign. He was imprisoned twice. Yet in World War I he again organized an ambulance corps for the British before returning home to India in 1914.

Gandhi's writings and devout life won him a mass of Indian followers. They followed him almost blindly in his campaign for *swaraj*, or "home rule." He worked to reconcile all classes and religious sects, especially Hindus and Muslims. In 1919 he became a leader in the newly formed Indian National Congress political party. In 1920 he launched a noncooperation campaign against Britain, urging Indians to spin their own cotton and to boycott British goods, courts, and government. This led to his imprisonment from 1922 to 1924. In 1930, in protest of a salt tax, Gandhi led thousands of Indians on a 200-mile (320-kilometer) march to the sea to collect their own salt. Again he was jailed.

In 1934 he retired as head of the party but remained its actual leader. Gradually he became convinced that India would receive no real freedom as long as it remained in the British Empire. Early in World War II he demanded immediate independence as India's price for aiding Britain in the war. He was imprisoned for the third time, from 1942 to 1944.

Gandhi's victory came in 1947 when India won independence. The subcontinent split into two countries (India and Pakistan) and brought Hindu-Muslim riots. Again Gandhi turned to nonviolence, fasting until Delhi rioters pledged peace to him. On January 30, 1948, while on his way to prayer in Delhi, Gandhi was killed by a Hindu who had been maddened by the Mahatma's efforts to reconcile Hindus and Muslims. An epic motion picture based on his life won several Academy Awards in 1983.

In January 1997, nearly 50 years after his assassination, the ashes of Mahatma Gandhi were spread in the Ganges river during a ceremony honoring his memory in Allahabad, India. Tushar Gandhi, the Mahatma's great-grandson, performed the act of dispersing the remains as thousands of onlookers chanted slogans in remembrance of the man who had succeeded, however briefly, in unifying a nation historically divided along religious and ethnic lines.

LEYMAH GBOWEE

(b. 1972–d.)

Leymah Roberta Gbowee is a Liberian peace activist known for rallying women to pressure leaders into ending Liberia's civil war. She was one of three recipients, along with Ellen Johnson Sirleaf and Tawakkul Karmān, of the 2011 Nobel Peace Prize, for their nonviolent efforts to further the safety and rights of women and their participation in peace-building processes.

Gbowee graduated from high school at age 17, with plans to continue her education. Her plans were interrupted, however, when Liberia became engulfed in civil war that began in 1989. She and her family were forced to flee from their home in the Liberian capital of Monrovia and eventually escaped to a refugee camp in Ghana. She later returned to Liberia and trained as a trauma counselor, working with former child soldiers who fought in Liberia's civil war.

Gbowee joined the Women in Peacebuilding Network (WIPNET) and quickly became a leader within the organization. Moved to action by the pain and suffering that she witnessed, Gbowee mobilized women of various ethnic and religious backgrounds to protest against Liberia's ongoing conflict. The WIPNET-led group, which eventually became known as the Liberian Mass Action for Peace, demonstrated against the war by fasting, praying, and picketing at markets and in front of government buildings. Dressed in white and present in great numbers, day after day, the women were difficult to ignore. Gbowee was eventually granted a meeting with Liberia's president, Charles Taylor, and pressed for peace. In 2003 Taylor and Liberia's opposing factions attended peace talks in Ghana that were organized by international parties in an attempt to bring an end to the Liberian conflict. Gbowee followed the Liberian leaders to Ghana, where she led a group of hundreds of women in surrounding the meeting place. They refused to let Taylor and the other leaders leave until an agreement was reached.

After the war Gbowee continued to advocate for peace and the empowerment of women. She served as a commissioner on Liberia's Truth and Reconciliation Commission (2004–05). In 2006 she was one of the founders of the Women Peace and Security Network–Africa (WISPEN-Africa), an organization active in several western African countries that encouraged the involvement of women in peace, security, and governance issues. She was named executive director of WISPEN-Africa the next year. Also in 2007 she received a master's degree in Conflict Transformation from Eastern Mennonite University in Harrisonburg, Virginia.

In addition to the 2011 Nobel Peace Prize, Gbowee received numerous other awards, including the Blue Ribbon for Peace (2007), awarded by the Women's Leadership Board of the John F. Kennedy School of Government at Harvard University, and the John F. Kennedy Profile in Courage Award (2009). She was featured in the 2008 documentary *Pray the Devil Back to Hell*, which profiled the attempts of several Liberian women to force an end to Liberia's civil war. In 2011 Gbowee published her memoir, *Mighty Be Our Powers: How Sisterhood, Prayer, and Sex Changed a Nation at War*, with Carol Mithers.

CHARLOTTE PERKINS GILMAN

(b. 1860–d. 1935)

U.S. feminist, lecturer, writer, and publisher Charlotte Perkins Gilman was a leading theorist of the women's movement in the United States. She fought for economic independence for women and believed in redefining domestic and child-care chores as social responsibilities.

Charlotte Anna Perkins was born on July 3, 1860, in Hartford, Connecticut. She grew up poor and had a limited education, although she did attend the Rhode Island School of Design for a time. In May 1884 she married artist Charles W. Stetson. The domestic routine of marriage, however, did not suit her, and after the birth of her daughter about a year later she suffered from melancholia, which resulted in a complete nervous collapse. In 1888 she moved with her young daughter to Pasadena, and six years later she divorced her husband. Soon afterward he remarried, and she sent her daughter to live with the couple.

After Perkins moved to California, she began writing poems and stories for various periodicals. One of her most popular stories was "The Yellow Wall-Paper." It was published in the *New England Magazine* in January 1892. The story gave a realistic portrayal of the mental breakdown of a physically pampered but emotionally deprived young wife. In 1893 Perkins published *In This Our World*, a volume of verse. During the next year she coedited the *Impress*, the periodical of the Pacific Coast Woman's Press Association. She also became a noted lecturer during the 1890s on such social topics as labor, ethics, and woman's place. In 1896 Perkins was a delegate to the International Socialist and Labor Congress in London, where she met some leading socialists, including George Bernard Shaw and Sidney and Beatrice Webb.

In 1898 Perkins published a manifesto called *Women and Economics* that drew much notice and was eventually translated into seven languages. Though radical for the time, her book advocated economic independence for women and exposed many of the contemporary ideas surrounding womanhood and motherhood as romanticized customs. She thought that domestic and child-care responsibilities were social issues to be undertaken by those suited and trained for them. In 1900 Perkins married a cousin, George H. Gilman. She kept writing, authoring in 1904 *Human Work*, which continued the arguments of *Women and Economics*. In *The Man-Made World* (1911) she delineated the virtues and vices of men and women and attributed the ills of the world to the dominance of men. Other books include *The Crux* (1911), *Moving the Mountain* (1911), *His Religion and Hers* (1923), and *The Living of Charlotte Perkins Gilman: An Autobiography* (1935).

Gilman edited and published the *Forerunner*, a monthly magazine of feminist articles, views, and fiction, from 1909 to 1916. She also contributed to other periodicals. In 1915 she cofounded the Woman's Peace Party with Jane Addams, but otherwise she did not become involved in organized movements. After unsuccessfully being treated for cancer, Gilman committed suicide on August 17, 1935, in Pasadena, California.

MIKHAIL GORBACHEV

(b. 1931–d.)

The last president of the Soviet Union was Mikhail Gorbachev. He served as the country's president in 1990–91 and as general secretary of the Communist Party of the Soviet Union from 1985 to 1991. Gorbachev introduced reform programs to make the Soviet Union's political system more democratic and to restructure the economy. His goal was to improve the Soviet Union, but his efforts led to the breakup of that country in 1991 as well to the downfall of communism in eastern Europe.

Mikhail Sergeyevich Gorbachev was born on March 2, 1931, in Privolye, in the Stavropol territory of southwestern Russia, in the Soviet Union. He began studying law at Moscow State University in 1952. In that year he also joined the Communist Party. After his graduation in 1955, Gorbachev joined the Komsomol, the Young Communist League, and rose steadily in party organizations in Stavropol and the surrounding region.

In 1971 Gorbachev was elected to the Central Committee of the party, and he was appointed a party secretary of agriculture in 1978. He was made a full member of the Politburo, the governing body of the Soviet Union, in 1980. He was its youngest member. Gorbachev was named to succeed Konstantin Chernenko as the Communist Party's general secretary in March 1985. In 1988 Gorbachev became Soviet president and chief of state. At the age of 54, he became the youngest man to head the government of the Soviet Union since Joseph Stalin had come to power in the 1920s. Gorbachev was also the first general secretary of the

Communist Party not to have served in the armed forces during World War II.

Shortly after taking office in 1985, Gorbachev initiated a series of policies aimed at a complete restructuring of Soviet society. The terms *glasnost* ("openness") and *perestroika* ("restructuring") came into common use as he tried to undo 70 years of economic stagnation and political repression. Through a restructuring of the constitution and open elections he also brought a measure of democracy to Soviet politics. It became evident within a few years that Gorbachev's goal was to combine reform with retention of a modified communist system. As a democratic movement grew, however, opponents insisted that communism had proved totally unworkable. They demanded the adoption of a free-market economy, a step Gorbachev was unwilling to take.

While progress in domestic renewal was often slow and uncertain, Gorbachev gained some stunning triumphs in foreign policy. He withdrew all Soviet troops from Afghanistan by early 1989. He also began troop reductions in eastern Europe. After summits in 1985, 1986, and 1987, he and U.S. President Ronald Reagan signed the Intermediate-Range Nuclear Forces (INF) Treaty on December 8, 1987, in Washington, D.C. This treaty called for both the Soviet Union and the United States to destroy certain missiles that could carry nuclear warheads. The two leaders met twice in 1988, in Moscow and again in New York City, where Gorbachev addressed the United Nations. Gorbachev and U.S. President George Bush held summits in 1989 and 1990.

Gorbachev's bold foreign policy actions, added to his encouragement of democracy in the Soviet Union, had a completely unintended consequence: the collapse of communism in eastern Europe in 1989–90. Gorbachev was subsequently named the 1990 winner of the Nobel Peace Prize. The first communist head of state to be so honored, he was recognized for promoting the political changes in eastern Europe and for ending the Cold War.

Despite his popularity outside the Soviet Union, Gorbachev faced serious problems at home by 1990 because of a worsening economy. He was proving himself a reluctant reformer and was challenged by a democratic movement headed by Boris Yeltsin, president of the Russian

Republic. At the same time, old-line communists opposed reform. On August 19, 1991, they staged a coup to remove Gorbachev from power. Yeltsin, however, rallied the people, and the coup failed within 72 hours. Events then moved rapidly. Yeltsin had become the leading power in the country. The Communist Party was banned. The Baltic States received their independence in September. By December the Soviet Union had come apart. Eleven of the remaining former republics formed the Commonwealth of Independent States. Gorbachev, with no nation to rule, resigned his office on December 25 and went into retirement.

In 1996 Gorbachev ran for president of Russia but won less than 1 percent of the vote. He nevertheless remained active in public life, as a speaker and as a member of various global and Russian think tanks. In 2006 Gorbachev and Russian billionaire and former lawmaker Aleksandr Lebedev bought nearly half of the newspaper *Novaya Gazeta*, known for its willingness to challenge government policies.

ALBERT GORE, JR.

(b. 1948–d.)

A leading moderate voice in the United States Democratic party, Al Gore served as a congressman and senator before becoming vice president in the administration of President Bill Clinton. Gore earned a reputation as a dedicated crusader for a variety of high-profile issues, especially protecting the environment.

Albert Gore, Jr., was born in Washington, D.C., on March 31, 1948. His father was a Democratic congressman and senator from Tennessee. A bright and hard-working student, Gore graduated with honors from Harvard University in 1969. He then enlisted in the United States Army, serving as a military reporter until 1971. Upon his return, Gore studied philosophy and law at Vanderbilt University while working as a reporter for the *Tennessean*, a newspaper based in Nashville, Tennessee.

In 1976 Gore was elected to the House of Representatives, where he served until winning a seat in the Senate in 1984. His entry into

Al Gore.

presidential politics came in 1988, when he unsuccessfully sought the Democratic nomination. In 1992 Bill Clinton, the Democratic presidential candidate, selected Gore to be his running mate. Gore became vice president when Clinton defeated the incumbent Republican George Bush. Working closely with President Clinton, Gore played a primary role in forging policy in such areas as arms control, technology, health, and the environment. Gore and Clinton were reelected in 1996 to a second term.

Gore announced his candidacy for the presidency in 1999. After easily winning the Democratic nomination, he faced George W. Bush, the Republican governor of Texas, in the 2000 election. Gore's campaign focused on the economy, health care, and education. Gore initially fell far behind in public-opinion polls, but he narrowed the gap after selecting highly regarded Senator Joe Lieberman from Connecticut as his running mate.

The extraordinarily close election proved to be one of historical proportions. Gore won the popular vote by more than 500,000 votes, but the count in the electoral college was so tight that a winner could not be declared until the results from one pivotal state, Florida, were finalized. After a mandatory machine recount in Florida had Bush leading by fewer than 1,000 votes, Gore sought manual recounts in several heavily Democratic counties with widespread reports of irregularities in the vote count. For more than a month the election remained unresolved as Florida state courts and federal courts weighed arguments by the Bush and Gore campaigns. The legal battle eventually reached the United States Supreme Court, which made the controversial decision to stop the recounts. With his legal options exhausted, Gore conceded the election on December 13. The final tally in the electoral college was 271 for Bush and 266 for Gore.

Gore subsequently devoted much of his time to environmental issues. His writings include *Earth in the Balance* (1992) and *An Inconvenient Truth* (2006). The latter was a companion book to the Academy Award–winning documentary of the same name about climate change. In 2007 Gore was awarded, with the United Nations' Intergovernmental Panel on Climate Change, the Nobel Peace Prize for his efforts to raise awareness about global warming.

CHE GUEVARA

(b. 1928–d. 1967)

The leftist revolutionary Ernesto "Che" Guevara was passionately devoted to world revolution through guerrilla warfare. He believed that the only way to end the great poverty of the masses in the developing world was armed revolution to establish socialist governments. He played a major military role in the Cuban Revolution of the late 1950s, and in the early years of Fidel Castro's Marxist government, Guevara made significant contributions to Cuba's new economic order. He later led guerrilla fighters in Africa and South America and wrote about the theories and tactics involved in guerrilla warfare. Guevara became an icon of leftist radicalism and anti-imperialism. He was executed by the Bolivian army, with the assistance of the U.S. Central Intelligence Agency.

Ernesto Guevara de la Serna was born in Rosario, Argentina, on June 14, 1928. In school he excelled as a scholar and as an athlete. Early in life he began absorbing socialist thought from his readings. In order to avoid serving in the army under Argentina's dictator Juan Perón, he left the country soon after earning his medical degree at the University of Buenos Aires in 1953. He traveled throughout Latin America and saw firsthand the economic problems and poverty of the region. He was in Guatemala in 1954 when a coup supported by the U.S. Central Intelligence Agency overthrew the elected government, which had been trying to bring about social and economic reform. Guevara became convinced that the United States would always oppose leftist governments and that revolution was the only answer. He left afterward for Mexico, where he met Fidel Castro and his brother Raúl. For the next several years he was involved in the revolution that succeeded in 1959 in overthrowing the Cuban dictator Fulgencio Batista.

Guevara became a Cuban citizen and for the next five years held a number of important posts in Fidel Castro's new government. By the end of 1964, Guevara's radicalism came increasingly into conflict with the more moderate position of the Cuban government. He left Cuba in the hopes of fomenting popular uprisings in Africa. After a failed attempt to lead a Marxist insurrection in the Congo, Guevara returned to Cuba, where he remained until his continued insistence on exporting revolution to other countries brought him again into conflict with Castro and Cuba's Soviet backers.

Late in 1966, he traveled to Bolivia, believing that a peasant-based revolution would both topple the Bolivian government and prove to be the first of a series of such agrarian revolutions throughout South America. For 11 months Guevara led an unsuccessful guerrilla war in the mountains of Bolivia. On October 8, 1967, the Bolivian army wounded and captured Guevara, along with the last remnants of his guerrilla supporters. Bolivian officials ordered that Guevara be executed.

After Guevara was shot, his body was flown to the town of Vallegrande. En route to Vallegrande, soldiers severed his hands from his body to keep as proof that they had killed the legendary revolutionary. After one day, his body mysteriously disappeared. The Bolivian government later admitted to having removed the body of Guevara, as well as those of his followers, in order to prevent the graves from becoming a shrine to the fallen revolutionaries. Nevertheless, Guevara became a hero, martyr, and legend to revolutionaries everywhere, and his book *Guerrilla Warfare*, published in 1961, was celebrated as the textbook for the tactics of revolution.

The whereabouts of Guevara's body remained unknown until 1997, when it was discovered in a mass grave near Vallegrande. His remains were flown back to Cuba and buried in an official memorial.

JOHANNES GUTENBERG

(b. 1395?–d. 1468)

German craftsman Johannes Gutenberg is believed to have developed the first printing press. He did not actually invent printing, nor did he print the first book. He was also not the first in the world to use movable type, blocks with individual raised letters or other characters that can be arranged and rearranged to print words. However, his

Johannes Gutenberg.

press made printing practical, and his method of using movable metal type endured almost unchanged for five centuries.

Gutenberg's printing process was one of the world's greatest inventions. Before Gutenberg, printing was used mainly to reproduce pictures, playing cards, designs on cloth, and similar items. The designs were cut in wood, stone, or metal and transferred to parchment or vellum.

Sometimes a few words of explanation were cut into the printing block, but that was generally the limit of text printing. Some books were produced by this method of block printing, but most were copied by hand, one by one, by monks or professional copyists. This was a laborious process, so there were few books and only the rich could afford them. Gutenberg's development of the printing press with movable type made it possible to produce a large number of books or other texts quickly. This major development led to a great increase in literacy and the spread of knowledge and new ideas throughout society.

Johannes (or Johann) Gensfleisch zur Laden zum Gutenberg was born in Mainz, Germany, in the late 14th century. His father belonged to the upper classes and held a prestigious managerial position in the mint, where designs were stamped on gold coins. This may have given the boy the idea of printing from metal. After his father's death, Gutenberg moved to Strassburg (now Strasbourg, France), probably between 1428 and 1430. He was skilled as a metalworker, and he also became a gem cutter and taught crafts to several pupils. In 1438 he became a partner in a block printing firm.

In secret, Gutenberg began to experiment with wood and metal type. He probably did not know that the Chinese had printed from movable type about ad 1040 but had later discarded the method. Gutenberg invented movable type for the Western world. He used sand molds to cast his type, and he adapted the presses used in wine making, papermaking, and bookbinding to create a printing press. He used an oil-based printing ink. By late 1448 he had returned to Mainz to set up his own press.

In 1450 Gutenberg went into partnership with the wealthy Mainz financier Johann Fust. In his new shop Gutenberg set type for a Türkenkalender (Turkish Calendar), which was printed in 1454, and for his masterpiece, the famous Gutenberg Bible. The Bible was completed before or in 1455, when he quarreled with his partner. Fust won a lawsuit against him, and Gutenberg lost control of his printing establishment. Most experts agree that the magnificent Psalter, printed in 1457 by Fust and Peter Schöffer (his son-in-law), resulted from the intricate work left by Gutenberg.

After the lawsuit, little is known of Gutenberg. Traditionally, it was thought that he was ruined financially. Scholars now believe that Gutenberg may have operated another printing shop through the 1450s and maybe into the 1460s. He was probably not living in extreme poverty in his last years. In 1465 the archbishop of Mainz awarded him a pension, giving him a set quantity of grain, wine, and clothing each year and exempting him from certain taxes. Gutenberg probably died in Mainz on February 3, 1468.

The copies of the Gutenberg Bible that remain—about 50 in all—are among the world's most valuable books. The text is also called the 42-line Bible because most of its pages have columns that are 42 lines long. It was printed in three volumes. The Library of Congress and the national libraries of Britain and France have complete and perfect sets.

ABBIE HOFFMAN

(b. 1936–d. 1989)

Abbie Hoffman, who received psychology degrees from both Brandeis University (1959) and the University of California, Berkeley (1960), was active in the American civil rights movement before turning his energies to protesting the Vietnam War and the American economic and political system. His acts of protest blurred the line between political action and guerrilla theater, and they used absurdist humor to great effect. In August 1967 Hoffman and a dozen confederates disrupted operations at the New York Stock Exchange by showering the trading floor with dollar bills. In October of that year he led a crowd of more than 50,000 antiwar protesters in an attempt to levitate the Pentagon and exorcise the evil spirits that he claimed resided within.

Hoffman's ethic was codified with the formal organization of the Youth International Party (Yippies) in January 1968. Later that year Hoffman secured his place as a countercultural icon when he joined thousands of protesters outside the Democratic Party's national convention in Chicago. Before the demonstrations degenerated into a street battle between police and protesters, Hoffman and Yippie cofounder Jerry Rubin unveiled Pigasus, a boar hog that would serve as the Yippies' presidential candidate in 1968. These exploits, among others, led to Hoffman's being named a defendant in the so-called Chicago Seven trial (1969), in which he was convicted of crossing state lines with intent to riot at the Democratic convention; the conviction was later overturned.

After he was arrested on charges of selling cocaine (1973), Hoffman went underground, underwent plastic surgery, assumed the alias Barry Freed, and worked as an environmental activist in New York state. He resurfaced in 1980 and served a year in prison before resuming his environmental efforts. He was the author of such books as *Revolution for the Hell of It* (1968), *Steal This Book* (1971), and an autobiography, *Soon to Be a Major Motion Picture* (1980). Hoffman's life—in particular, his underground period and his efforts to draw attention to the Federal Bureau of Investigation's Cointelpro operations—were dramatized in the film *Steal This Movie* (2000).

JESSE JACKSON

(b. 1941–d.)

The first African American to ever seek nomination for the U.S. presidency, civil rights leader Jesse Jackson established himself as a dominant political force throughout the 1980s. A highly articulate and dynamic public speaker, he is known for his impassioned advocacy for empowerment, peace, and social justice. He founded such organizations as Operation PUSH (People United to Save Humanity) and the National Rainbow Coalition and is widely recognized as an international ambassador of peace.

Jesse Louis Jackson was born in Greenville, South Carolina, on October 8, 1941, and was raised by his mother and stepfather. An excellent student and athlete, he was awarded a football scholarship to the University of Illinois. He later transferred to North Carolina Agricultural and Technical College, where he became active in the civil rights movement. After graduating in 1964 with a bachelor's degree in sociology, Jackson went on to pursue postgraduate work at the Chicago Theological Seminary. The following year, however, he put his studies on hold in order to join the Southern Christian Leadership Conference (SCLC) under Martin Luther King, Jr., in his battle to advance the civil rights movement. Shortly thereafter, King appointed Jackson as director of the SCLC's Operation Breadbasket in Chicago, an organization dedicated to helping African Americans find jobs and other services. While serving with the organization, Jackson was ordained a Baptist minister in 1968. In 1971 Jackson founded Operation PUSH in Chicago, a self-help organization that continued the work of Operation Breadbasket by encouraging African Americans and disadvantaged people to become economically empowered and by helping to open up more opportunities for them in employment, business, and education. Throughout his career, Jackson demonstrated his dedication to young people, campaigning widely for education and against drug abuse and gangs, with his famous slogan, "I am somebody." In the late 1970s, he founded PUSH-Excel, a motivational program targeted at helping inner-city and underprivileged children and teenagers to succeed in school.

A powerful negotiator, Jackson also became involved in foreign affairs, working for peace and justice internationally. In 1979 he traveled to South Africa to speak out against apartheid—an oppressive system in which the African majority was denied the same rights and privileges as the non-African minority. In 1984 he gained the freedom of U.S. Navy pilot Lieutenant Robert Goodman, whose plane was shot down over Lebanon. Later that year he traveled to Cuba, where he achieved freedom for 48 Cuban and Cuban American prisoners. In 1990 Jackson met with Saddam Hussein in Iraq and persuaded him to release U.S. hostages that were captured during Iraq's invasion of Kuwait. He returned to Cuba in 1994 to meet with Fidel Castro and was sent on a peace mission to Nigeria later that year by President Bill Clinton. In 1997 Jackson was appointed as Special Envoy of the President and Secretary of State for the Promotion of Democracy in Africa by President Clinton and Secretary of State Madeleine

Albright. Jackson also traveled to Belgrade, Yugoslavia, in 1999, where he convinced President Slobodan Milošević to release three U.S. prisoners of war who were captured during the war in Kosovo.

Jackson's prominence as an international figure had a powerful influence on the African American community. This influence was instrumental to his voter-registration drive, which helped to elect the first African American mayor of Chicago, Harold Washington, in April 1983. Jackson displayed his skill as a politician even further in 1984 when he broke new ground by campaigning for the Democratic presidential nomination. With an even stronger political base, he campaigned for the nomination again in 1988 when, out of seven contenders, he finished a strong second. Shortly after the 1984 election, Jackson launched the National Rainbow Coalition, based in Washington, D.C. He used this organization as a vehicle to lobby for political empowerment, changes in public policy, increased voting rights, more social programs for the poor and disabled, alleviation of taxes for the poor, and equal rights for African Americans, minorities, women, homosexuals, and other oppressed people.

In 1989 Jackson moved his official residence from Chicago to Washington, D.C., where it was believed he would run for mayor. Instead, he was elected in 1990 to the office of statehood senator, a lobbying position created by the Washington, D.C., city council in support of a bill that would grant statehood to the district. In 1996 Jackson returned to Chicago and Operation PUSH and the National Rainbow Coalition merged into one organization—the Rainbow/PUSH Coalition—which carried on the work of both organizations.

For his dedication to the civil rights movement and his promotion of world peace and social justice, Jackson received several honors. In 1991 the United States Postal Service placed Jackson's likeness on a cancellation stamp, making him only the second living person in U.S. history to be so honored. Jackson received the Martin Luther King, Jr., Nonviolent Peace Prize in 1993 and was awarded the Presidential Medal of Freedom in 2000 by President Clinton. He also received more than 40 honorary doctorate degrees and earned a master of divinity degree from the Chicago Theological Seminary in 2000.

THOMAS JEFFERSON

(b. 1743–d. 1826)

The author of the Declaration of Independence in 1776, Thomas Jefferson was later the third president of the United States, serving from 1801 to 1809. During his presidency the territory of the United States doubled with the Louisiana Purchase. To investigate the vastness of this newly acquired land in the West, he dispatched two of the most famous explorers in U.S. history, Meriwether Lewis and William Clark, to blaze a trail through the Rocky Mountains to the Pacific Ocean. In the first overseas war in U.S. history, Jefferson sent military forces to the Mediterranean Sea to crush Tripoli's piracy threats.

In 1769 Jefferson was elected to the House of Burgesses, Virginia's representative assembly, in Williamsburg. He employed his comprehensive knowledge of law to support the colonial opposition to British legislation and taxation. He emphasized that Great Britain had no legal authority to govern and delegate authority in the colonies.

Jefferson's first published essay, "A Summary View of the Rights of British America" (1774), insisted upon independence from Great Britain as the only solution to liberate the oppressed colonies. When his essay was published, most of the Virginia legislature was not prepared to accept such a radical position against Great Britain. However, over the next year hostilities between the colonists and British authorities reached a boiling point, and the American Revolution began in Massachusetts at the Battles of Lexington and Concord in 1775.

In that same year the Virginia legislature appointed Jefferson as a delegate to the Second Continental Congress in Philadelphia. The Continental Congress recognized his idea for the colonies to secede from British rule as the best course of action.

On June 11, 1776, Jefferson was selected to a committee, which included John Adams and Benjamin Franklin, to outline a formal document justifying the reasons for declaring independence from Great Britain. The committee members admired Jefferson's talent for

Thomas Jefferson.

influential writing and chose him to prepare the first draft. His words expressed what a majority of colonial citizens desired when he wrote: "We hold these truths to be self-evident, that all men are created equal, that they are endowed by their Creator with certain unalienable Rights, that among these are Life, Liberty, and the pursuit of Happiness."

The Continental Congress adopted the Declaration of Independence on July 4, 1776, which officially announced the separation of the 13 colonies from Great Britain. Jefferson and other delegates signed it, but he was not credited as the principal author until 1790. Between 1776 and 1777 the Continental Congress wrote the Articles of Confederation, which was ratified in 1781 as the first constitution of the United States.

JOAN OF ARC

(b. 1412?–1431)

One of the most romantic figures in European war history was Joan of Arc, a peasant girl who saved the kingdom of France from English domination. She has also been called the Maid of Orléans and the Maid of France. When she was only 17 years old, Joan inspired a French army to break the English siege of the French city of Orléans and to win other important victories.

Joan of Arc (in French Jeanne d'Arc) was born in the village of Domrémy, in the Meuse River valley, probably in 1412. She was the daughter of a wealthy tenant farmer. From her mother she learned how to spin, sew, and cook and also to love and serve God. She spent much of her time praying in church.

For almost 100 years France and much of Europe had been fighting in what became known as the Hundred Years' War. The English occupied much of northern France and the Duke of Burgundy was their ally. Because the impoverished French king, Charles VII, had not yet been crowned, he was still called the Dauphin. Reims, where the coronation ceremonies for French kings had been held for 1,000 years, was in enemy hands. The valley where Joan lived was constantly overrun by armies and guerrilla bands.

Joan was only about 13 when she first saw a heavenly vision. She later claimed that St. Michael had told her to be a good girl, to obey her mother, and to go to church often. For some time, however, she told no one of the visions. When St. Catherine and St. Margaret commanded her to journey to the Dauphin in order to inspire his armies to clear the way to Reims for the coronation, she told her parents and others. Her father refused to let her go.

Joan's visions continued to command her. Her friends, who believed that she was truly inspired, secured boy's clothing and a horse for her. Several rode with her on the long trip to the Dauphin's court at Chinon. Perhaps as a test, the Dauphin made one of his courtiers pretend to be the king. Joan, however, went directly to the true king and greeted him. The Dauphin and his councillors were not entirely convinced of her mission, however. Months of doubt and indecision followed while she was questioned.

Slowly an army was gathered. The Dauphin equipped Joan with armor, attendants, and horses. A special banner was made for Joan to carry into battle. On one side were the words "Jesus Maria" and a figure of God, seated on clouds and holding a glove. The other side had a figure of the Virgin and a shield, with two angels supporting the arms of France.

When the army at last moved toward Orléans, Joan was not its commander, but her presence inspired the soldiers with confidence. At Orléans, after Joan disapproved of the plans made for entering the besieged city, her own plan was adopted. From the city she led a series of sallies that so harassed and discouraged the English that they withdrew. In one of the skirmishes Joan was wounded.

On May 8, 1429, the victory was celebrated by the first festival of Orléans. The army entered Reims on July 16. The next day the Dauphin was crowned king as Joan stood by with her banner.

A decision was made to attack Paris, but the new monarch's hesitation and indecision prevented Joan's soldiers from concerted attack. Nevertheless, Compiègne and other nearby towns were taken. A French attack on a Paris salient was driven back and Joan was again wounded. Charles VII disbanded his army for the winter and retired southward. Through the cold months Joan chafed at royal delay.

In the spring she returned to Compiègne, now besieged by forces of the Duke of Burgundy. On May 23, 1430, Joan, on a sortie into the Burgundian lines, was separated from her soldiers and captured.

As a prisoner at Beaurevoir, she attempted to escape, but was injured in the leap from the donjon tower. Later she was sold to the English, who vowed that she would be executed. They removed her to Rouen, where she was held in chains.

Although the English wanted Joan's death, they desired her to be sentenced by an ecclesiastical court. The Burgundian-controlled University of Paris provided the charges of heresy and witchcraft. It also provided some of the members of the court. Other members came from areas under English occupation. Chief of the court was the bishop of Beauvais.

Joan was handed over to this bishop on January 3, 1431. The sittings began on February 21 and continued intermittently for months. Joan's appeal to be sent before the pope for judgment was denied. On May 23 she was condemned to be burned unless she recanted. She had been held for many months in chains, threatened with torture, and harassed by thousands of questions. In spite of all this, she had maintained her shy innocence, often confounding her oppressors with simple, unaffected answers to tricky questions. St. Catherine and St. Margaret, she said, still counseled her.

Faced with death in the flames, she recanted, but many historians think she did not understand what was meant in the statement of recantation. As a result of her submission, her punishment was commuted from death to life imprisonment. This leniency enraged the English, however, and it was not long before she was accused of relapsing from her submission. On May 30, 1431, when she was only 19 years old, Joan was turned over to civil authority and burned to death at the stake.

Charles VII had made no effort to save Joan. Some 25 years later he did aid her family to appeal the case to the pope, and in 1456 a papal court annulled the judgment of 1431. On May 16, 1920, Joan of Arc was canonized a saint by the Roman Catholic church.

SAINT JOHN PAUL II

(b. 1920–d. 2005)

The first Polish pope was John Paul II, who was the 264th bishop of Rome. His 26-year reign as head of the Roman Catholic Church—from 1978 until his death in 2005—was one of the longest in church history. John Paul II made extraordinary efforts to reach out to people around the world, to both Roman Catholics and those of other faiths. Traveling a far greater distance than did all the popes before him combined, he took 104 trips abroad. The crowds that came to hear him speak were sometimes among the largest ever assembled, and he reached still more people through televised broadcasts. He maintained an impressive touring schedule even after becoming visibly ill with Parkinson disease and severe arthritis in the 1990s.

John Paul II was also an ardent advocate for universal human rights and world peace. His experiences as a young man during World War II had profoundly demonstrated to him the importance of combatting violence, religious intolerance, and political oppression. He strove to improve the church's relationship with Judaism and Islam, becoming the first pope to enter a synagogue and the first to enter a mosque. A powerful opponent of communism, his nonviolent activism was credited with helping lead to the peaceful dismantling of the Soviet Union. At the same time, he was a sharp critic of unbridled capitalism and Western-style materialism.

On theological issues, John Paul II was very conservative, more so than his three immediate predecessors. He did not, for instance, change the requirement that the clergy must remain celibate or bans on the ordination of women, homosexual activity, divorce, and artificial contraception. He also vigorously opposed abortion and euthanasia, which he characterized as a "culture of death." Bishops and teachers of theology who disagreed with church doctrine were disciplined, and some were relieved of their posts. Among the problems the church encountered during John Paul II's reign were a drop in the number of priests and nuns

Saint John Paul II.

and a decline in church attendance.

He was born Karol Józef Wojtyła on May 18, 1920, to working-class parents in Wadowice, Poland. His mother died when he was eight, and his older brother died a few years later. His father, a pious and disciplined man who was a lieutenant in the Polish army, became the dominant influence in his life. Wojtyła was an outgoing but serious boy, an excellent student, and an avid athlete who enjoyed playing soccer (association football) and skiing.

After graduating from high school as class valedictorian, Wojtyła entered Jagiellonian University in Kraków in 1938 to study literature and philology. After Germany invaded Poland in 1939, however, the Nazis closed the university. Wojtyła continued to study in secret. To avoid being deported to a concentration camp, he worked in a quarry and then in a chemical factory considered to be critical to the war effort; he later was the first pope in modern times to have worked as a laborer. He also was active in an underground theater group that produced plays in Polish, which was forbidden under Nazi rule.

During the war Wojtyła witnessed immeasurable cruelty and suffering, including the deportation and slaughter of the Jews of Kraków as well as of Polish priests and many of his professors. Amid these horrors, he was deeply influenced by the work of Jan Tyranowski, a tailor who ran a youth ministry for a local church. He introduced Wojtyła to the writings of the Carmelite Spanish mystics, and his example working with young people inspired hope that the church could change the troubled world. Wojtyła's father, his sole remaining close relative, died in 1941. He soon decided to become a priest and began studying in an illegal seminary. In August 1944, Nazi troops swept through Kraków, seizing all able-bodied men. For the rest of the war Wojtyła hid in the archbishop's palace, disguised as a cleric. After World War II ended, he studied at a seminary in Kraków.

Wojtyła was ordained in 1946. After receiving a Ph.D. degree in philosophy from Pontifical Angelicum University in Rome in 1948, he returned to Poland to become a parish priest and a student chaplain. He continued the study of ethics, earned a second doctorate, and taught ethics and theology at the Catholic University of Lublin. In 1958 he became the youngest Polish bishop when he was appointed auxiliary bishop of Kraków.

In the early 1960s Wojtyła participated in the Second Vatican Council. He so impressed the church leadership that he was named archbishop at the end of 1963. He became a cardinal in 1967. As a spokesman for the large Roman Catholic population of Poland, he defended the church and the right to freedom of worship within a communist system that suppressed religious activity. Unable to use the government-controlled media, he began traveling throughout the country to talk to the people, and he became skilled at addressing large crowds.

Upon his election as pope on October 16, 1978, he was only 58 years old. He was the first non-Italian pope in 455 years. John Paul II adopted both the name and the less formal style of his predecessor, John Paul I. To avoid a conflict with a soccer (association football) match, for example, he scheduled his coronation for noon. In matters of theology and most official policy, however, John Paul II supported traditional church doctrines. An exception was the customary Vatican policy of neutrality, which he abandoned as he campaigned for religious freedom and national independence, supporting, for example, Poland's Solidarity movement. His visits to Brazil, the Philippines, Haiti, Paraguay, Chile, and even non-Catholic South Korea were credited with weakening authoritarian rule in those countries.

In January 1979 John Paul II attended a conference of Latin American bishops in Mexico. He became the first pope to visit a communist country when he traveled to his native Poland in June of that year. He was also the first pope to visit a United States president in the White House. In October he addressed the United Nations General Assembly while on his six-city tour of the United States. Dubbed the "pilgrim pope," he visited 44 nations in the first 10 years of his reign. Fluent in eight languages, he was often able to address crowds in their native tongue.

The pope was shot and seriously wounded during an assassination attempt by Mehmet Ali Agca, a Turkish gunman, in St. Peter's Square on May 13, 1981. On May 12, 1982, when the pope went to Portugal's Shrine of Our Lady of Fátima to give thanks for his recovery from the gun wounds, another attack on his life was attempted. A rebel Spanish priest, carrying a bayonet, was subdued by security guards. John Paul II forgave Agca in person in 1983. In 2000 the church announced that the 1981 attempt on the pope's life had been foretold in the third prophecy revealed to three children at Fátima in the early 20th century.

In December 1989 Mikhail Gorbachev became the first Soviet leader to visit the pope. During the visit Gorbachev pledged that all Soviet citizens (including Muslims and Jews) would be guaranteed greater religious freedom and invited the pope to visit the Soviet Union. The Roman Catholic church and the Soviet Union reestablished diplomatic relations in 1990 after a break of 67 years.

At the invitation of Cuban President Fidel Castro, the pope visited Cuba in 1998. He preached against both the communist government's long suppression of religion and the U.S. embargo against Cuba, which he described as "unjust and ethically unacceptable." The Cuban government released about 300 prisoners after his visit.

John Paul II was a champion for world peace throughout his pontificate. He firmly opposed, for example, violence in Northern Ireland, the Persian Gulf War, the NATO bombing of Yugoslavia in 1999, and the U.S.-led invasion of Iraq in 2003.

Throughout his reign, John Paul II also emphasized the need for the Roman Catholic church to reconcile with other religions and to apologize for past wrongdoings, including brutalities committed against indigenous peoples, women, ethnic and racial minorities, people of other faiths, and suspected heretics. In a statement of 1998, he officially apologized for the church's failure to speak out against the Nazi persecution of the Jews. In 2000 he made a historic visit to Jerusalem, meeting with Israeli Prime Minister Ehud Barak at the Yad Vashem Holocaust memorial and with Muslim leaders at the Al-Aqsa Mosque. John Paul II also worked to heal the long breach between the Vatican and Italy, and in 2002 he became the first pope to address the Italian parliament.

An admirer of the scientific search for truth, the pope issued statements supporting the theory that the human body developed through the gradual process of evolution. He also acknowledged that the church had been wrong to denounce Galileo in the 17th century for teaching that the Earth revolves around the sun.

John Paul II canonized more than 480 people, more than doubling the number of Roman Catholic saints. Among them were the church's first Amerindian, Roma (Gypsy), and Chinese saints. He also broadened the membership of the Sacred College of Cardinals, appointing many new cardinals from developing countries. By the time of his death, John Paul II had installed nearly all the cardinals who were eligible to choose his successor.

During his reign, John Paul II revised several major church texts. On January 25, 1983, he approved the first revision of the Roman Catholic church's canon law since it had been codified in 1917. The new code, however, did not change any of the more controversial prohibitions of the church. Although the rule on the celibacy of the clergy was not changed, some married priests were accepted into the church, mainly as transfers from other denominations. John Paul II also introduced the Reform of the Roman Curia and the new Code of Canons for the Eastern Catholic Churches. In 1992 he introduced the first revision to the Roman Catholic catechism in more than four centuries. On October 16, 2002, the 24th anniversary of his election as pope, he added an additional set of meditations, or "mysteries," to the rosary, a method of reciting prayers that had not been changed in hundreds of years.

In 2002 the Roman Catholic church faced widespread allegations, predominantly in the United States, that priests had sexually abused minors and that church leaders had long attempted to cover up the scandal. In April of that year, John Paul II summoned the U.S. cardinals to the Vatican to address the issue, and they later negotiated a new national policy for handling accusations of sexual misconduct.

In addition to issuing encyclicals and other official writings, John Paul II published volumes of poetry and books about faith and ethics, including *Love and Responsibility* (1960), a work on sexual morality. In *The Acting Person* (1969), he discussed his philosophy that a person's actions, and not his thoughts or statements, define what that person stands for. His other books include *Crossing the Threshold of Hope* (1994), *Gift and Mystery: On the 50th Anniversary of My Priestly Ordination* (1997), and *Memory and Identity* (2005).

Despite worsening health in his later years, John Paul II continued to travel and to maintain, as much as possible, the dynamic style of his pontificate, until he became seriously ill in early 2005. He died in Vatican City on April 2, 2005. In January 2011 the Vatican recognized the recovery of a French nun from Parkinson disease as a miracle performed by John Paul II; he was beatified on May 1, 2011, and canonized with Pope John XXIII on April 27, 2014.

TAWAKKUL KARMĀN

(b. 1979–d.)

Tawakkul Karmān is a Yemeni women's rights activist who received the Nobel Peace Prize in 2011 for her role in leading a pro-democracy protest movement. She shared the prize with Ellen Johnson Sirleaf and Leymah Gbowee, who were also recognized for leading nonviolent campaigns for women's rights and democratic freedoms.

Karmān was born into a politically active family in Taʿizz. When she was young, her family moved to Sanaa, where her father, ʿAbd al-Salām Karmān, a lawyer, served as minister of legal affairs before resigning in 1994 over the government's war against secessionists in southern Yemen. She graduated from the University of Science and Technology in Sanaa with a degree in commerce in 1999 and later earned a master's degree in political science. After completing her education, Karmān began a career in journalism, writing articles, producing documentary films, and disseminating news alerts via text messages. When she encountered restrictions and threats from the Yemeni government, Karmān and several of her colleagues founded Women Journalists Without Chains in 2005 to advocate for women's rights, civil rights, and freedom of expression. In 2007 Karmān began staging weekly sit-ins in Sanaa to demand a variety of democratic reforms. She continued the practice for several years and was arrested multiple times for her activism. Although Karmān was a senior member of the Iṣlāḥ (Reform) party, Yemen's main Islamist opposition party, she occasionally clashed with the party's religious conservatives. In 2010, for example, she criticized members of her own party for opposing legislation to raise the legal marriage age for women to 17.

On January 23, 2011, as a protest movement known as the Arab Spring swept through the Middle East and North Africa, shaking some of the region's longest-standing governments, Karmān was arrested after leading a small protest in Sanaa against the government of ʿAlī ʿAbd Allāh Ṣāliḥ, the president of Yemen. Her arrest sparked larger protests, which soon developed into mass demonstrations against the

Ṣāliḥ regime. Karmān, released the following day, soon became a leader of the movement, helping to set up the protest encampment on the grounds of Sanaa University, where thousands of protesters staged a sit-in that lasted for months. For her role in leading protests, Karmān was awarded the Nobel Peace Prize in October 2011. At age 32, Karmān was one of the youngest-ever recipients of the prize.

FLORENCE KELLEY

(b. 1859–d. 1932)

Florence Molthrop Kelley was a social reformer who contributed to the development of state and federal labor and social welfare legislation in the United States.

Kelley graduated from Cornell University in 1882. After a year spent conducting evening classes for working women in Philadelphia, she traveled to Europe, where she attended the University of Zürich. There she came under the influence of European socialism; her translation of Friedrich Engels's *The Condition of the Working Class in England* in 1844 was published in New York in 1887. She returned to the United States in 1886 with her husband, Lazare Wischnewetzky, whom she had married in 1884. In 1889 she published a pamphlet, *Our Toiling Children*.

In 1891 she and her husband separated; they were subsequently divorced, and she moved to Chicago and resumed her maiden name. Kelley became a resident at Jane Addams's Hull House settlement and quickly took her place among the most active and effective workers there. In 1892 she conducted parallel investigations into slum conditions in Chicago and into sweatshops in the tenements. Her reports, together with her contributions to *Hull-House Maps and Papers* (1895), presented a vivid picture of miserable working and living conditions. The Illinois law of 1893 that limited working hours for women, regulated tenement sweatshops, and prohibited child labor was in large part the result of her findings, and in consequence she was appointed to the post of chief factory inspector for Illinois. To further the prosecution of violators, Kelley enrolled in the law school of Northwestern University; she graduated in

1894 and was subsequently admitted to the bar.

In 1899 Kelley moved to New York City to become general secretary of the new National Consumers League, which had grown out of Josephine Shaw Lowell's Consumers' League of New York. She retained the post until her death. She took up residence at Lillian Wald's Henry Street Settlement and set about the work of promoting federal legislation on hours and wages and child labor, as well as other reforms. She organized some 60 local and state Consumers' Leagues and traveled and spoke indefatigably for the cause. Among her publications are *Some Ethical Gains Through Legislation* (1905) and *Modern Industry* (1913); she edited Edmond Kelly's *Twentieth Century Socialism* (1910). With Wald she led in organizing the New York Child Labor Committee in 1902, and in 1904 she was a founder of the National Child Labor Committee. Her efforts contributed greatly to the creation of the U.S. Children's Bureau in 1912.

Kelley was a founder of the National Association for the Advancement of Colored People in 1909, and for several years she served as vice president of the National American Woman Suffrage Association.

JOHN F. KENNEDY

(b. 1917–d. 1963)

In November 1960, at the age of 43, John F. Kennedy became the youngest man ever elected president of the United States. Theodore Roosevelt had become president at 42 when President William McKinley was assassinated, but he was not elected at that age. On November 22, 1963, Kennedy was shot to death in Dallas, Texas, the fourth United States president to die by an assassin's bullet.

Kennedy was the nation's first Roman Catholic president. He was inaugurated in January 1961, succeeding Republican President Dwight D. Eisenhower. He defeated the Republican candidate, Vice President Richard M. Nixon, by little more than 100,000 votes. It was one of the closest elections in the nation's history. Although Kennedy and his vice presidential running mate, Lyndon B. Johnson, got less than half of

Portrait of John F. Kennedy.

the more than 68 million votes cast, they won the Electoral College vote. Kennedy thus became the 14th minority president.

He was the youngest man and the first Roman Catholic ever elected to the presidency of the United States. His administration lasted 1,037 days. From the onset he was concerned with foreign affairs. In his memorable inaugural address, he called upon Americans "to bear the burden of a long twilight struggle...against the common enemies of man: tyranny, poverty, disease, and war itself." He declared:

> *In the long history of the world, only a few generations have been granted the role of defending freedom in its hour of maximum danger. I do not shrink from this responsibility—I welcome it....The energy, the faith, the devotion which we bring to this endeavor will light our country and all who serve it—and the glow from that fire can truly light the world. And so, my fellow Americans: ask not what your country can do for you—ask what you can do for your country.*

The administration's first brush with foreign affairs was a disaster. In the last year of the Eisenhower presidency, the Central Intelligence Agency (CIA) had equipped and trained a brigade of anticommunist Cuban exiles for an invasion of their homeland. The Joint Chiefs of Staff unanimously advised the new president that this force, once ashore, would spark a general uprising against the Cuban leader, Fidel Castro. But the Bay of Pigs invasion was a fiasco; every man on the beachhead was either killed or captured. Kennedy assumed "sole responsibility" for the setback. Privately he told his father that he would never again accept a Joint Chiefs recommendation without first challenging it.

The Soviet premier, Nikita Khrushchev, thought he had taken the young president's measure when the two leaders met in Vienna in June 1961. Khrushchev ordered a wall built between East and West Berlin and threatened to sign a separate peace treaty with East Germany. The president activated National Guard and reserve units, and Khrushchev backed down on his separate peace threat. Kennedy then made a dramatic visit to West Berlin, where he told a cheering crowd, "Today, in the world of freedom, the proudest boast is 'Ich bin ein [I am a] Berliner.'" In October 1962 a buildup of Soviet short- and intermediate-range nuclear missiles was discovered in Cuba. Kennedy demanded that the missiles be dismantled; he ordered a "quarantine" of Cuba—in effect, a blockade that would stop Soviet ships from reaching that island. For 13 days nuclear war seemed near; then the Soviet premier announced that the offensive weapons would be withdrawn. Ten months later Kennedy scored his greatest foreign triumph when Khrushchev and Prime Minister Harold Macmillan of Great Britain joined him in signing the Nuclear Test-Ban Treaty. Yet Kennedy's commitment to combat the spread of communism led him to escalate American involvement in the conflict in Vietnam, where he sent not just supplies and financial assistance, as President Eisenhower had, but 15,000 military advisers as well.

Because of his slender victory in 1960, Kennedy approached Congress warily, and with good reason; Congress was largely indifferent to his legislative program. It approved his Alliance for Progress (Alianza) in Latin America and his Peace Corps, which won the enthusiastic endorsement of thousands of college students. But his two most cherished projects, massive income tax cuts and a sweeping civil rights measure, were not passed until after his death. In May 1961 Kennedy committed the United States to land a man on the Moon by the end of the decade, and, while he would not live to see this achievement either, his advocacy of the space program contributed to the successful launch of the first American manned spaceflights.

He was an immensely popular president, at home and abroad. At times he seemed to be everywhere at once, encouraging better physical fitness, improving the morale of government workers, bringing brilliant advisers to the White House, and beautifying Washington, D.C. His wife joined him as an advocate for American culture. Their two young children, Caroline Bouvier and John F., Jr., were familiar throughout the country. The charm and optimism of the Kennedy family seemed contagious, sparking the idealism of a generation for whom the Kennedy White House became, in journalist Theodore White's famous analogy, Camelot—the magical court of Arthurian legend, which was celebrated in a popular Broadway musical of the early 1960s.

Joseph Kennedy, meanwhile, had been incapacitated in Hyannis Port by a stroke, but the other Kennedys were in and out of Washington. Robert Kennedy, as John's attorney general, was the second most powerful man in the country. He advised the president on all matters of foreign and domestic policy, national security, and political affairs.

In 1962 Ted Kennedy was elected to the president's former Senate seat in Massachusetts. Their sister Eunice's husband, Sargent Shriver, became director of the Peace Corps. Their sister Jean's husband, Stephen Smith, was preparing to manage the Democratic Party's 1964 presidential campaign. Another sister, Patricia, had married Peter Lawford, an English-born actor who served the family as an unofficial envoy to the entertainment world. All Americans knew who Rose, Jackie, Bobby, and Teddy were, and most could identify Bobby's wife as Ethel and Teddy's wife as Joan. But if the first family had become American royalty, its image of perfection would be tainted years later by allegations of marital infidelity by the president (most notably, an affair with motion-picture icon Marilyn Monroe) and of his association with members of organized crime.

JOHN MAYNARD KEYNES

(b. 1883–d. 1946)

An economist, journalist, and financier, Englishman John Keynes is best known for his revolutionary economic theory on the causes of prolonged unemployment. His enduring fame rests on a theory that recovery from a recession can best be achieved by a government-sponsored policy of full employment.

John Maynard Keynes was born in Cambridge, England, on June 5, 1883. He was educated at Eton and Cambridge, where he studied under Alfred Marshall, the leading Cambridge economist. Here Keynes's interest in politics and economics grew. After leaving Cambridge he became a civil servant and worked for the government's India Office. His experience there formed the basis of his first major work, which is still the definitive examination of pre-World War I Indian finance. He returned to Cambridge as a lecturer in economics, but the onset of World War I brought him back to English government employment. His valuable experience as an economic adviser at the Versailles Peace Conference led him to write his scathing book *The Economic Consequences of the Peace*, published in 1919, in which he argued against excessive reparations requirements of Germany after the war.

Keynes then followed a financial career in London, where he was regarded as a conventional economist until the depression of the 1930s. In *The General Theory of Employment, Interest and Money* (1936), Keynes departed from his classical theories. He put forth his ideas about government responsibility and commitment to maintaining high employment. He claimed that because consumers were limited in their spending by the size of their incomes, they were not the source of business cycle shifts. The dynamic participants were business investors and governments.

During World War II most Western democracies affirmed their commitment to this philosophy. Keynes played a central role in British war financing and in 1944 was chief British representative at the Bretton Woods Conference that established the International Monetary Fund and the World Bank. His last major public service was his brilliant negotiation in 1945 of a multibillion-dollar loan granted by the United States to Britain. On April 21, 1946, exhausted and overstrained by wartime exertion, Keynes died in Firle, Sussex, England.

BILLIE JEAN KING

(b. 1943–d.)

The first woman professional athlete to be paid more than $100,000 in a single year was Billie Jean King, in 1971. Perhaps the greatest woman doubles player in tennis history, she was also an activist for women's rights. She helped to organize the Women's Tennis Association and to establish a women's pro tour in the early 1970s.

Billie Jean Moffitt was born in Long Beach, California, on November 22, 1943. She began playing tennis at an early age. In 1965 she married Larry King, and in the 1970s the couple pioneered team tennis.

King holds the record for British titles with a total of 20 championships. She won the women's doubles at Wimbledon in 1961–62 and 1965 before achieving her first major singles triumph there in 1966. She also won the Wimbledon singles in 1967–68, 1972–73, and 1975; women's doubles in 1967–68, 1970–73, and 1979; and mixed doubles in 1967, 1971, and 1973–74.

King won the U.S. women's singles in 1967, 1971–72, and 1974; women's doubles in 1964, 1967, 1974, 1978, and 1980; and mixed doubles in 1967, 1971, 1973, and 1976. She was the only woman to win U.S. singles titles on four surfaces—grass, indoor, clay, and hard court.

In a match billed as the Battle of the Sexes at the Houston Astrodome on September 20, 1973, King defeated Bobby Riggs. Riggs, who had many years before been a Wimbledon and U.S. champion, had criticized the quality of women's tennis. The match set two records: the audience of more than 30,000 was the largest to witness a tennis event, and the $100,000 purse was the largest won by a player.

King retired from competitive tennis in 1984. In the mid-1990s she served as coach for several Olympic and Federation Cup teams. King published two autobiographies, as well as other books on tennis. In 2009 she was awarded the U.S. Presidential Medal of Freedom.

MARTIN LUTHER KING, JR.

(b. 1929–d. 1968)

Inspired by the belief that love and peaceful protest could eliminate social injustice, Martin Luther King, Jr., became one of the outstanding black leaders in the United States. He aroused whites and blacks alike to protest racial discrimination, poverty, and war. A champion of nonviolent resistance to oppression, he was awarded the Nobel Peace Prize in 1964.

Martin Luther King, Jr., was born in Atlanta, Georgia, on January 15, 1929. His father, Martin, Sr., was the pastor of the Ebenezer Baptist Church, a black congregation. His mother, Alberta Williams King, was a schoolteacher. Martin had an older sister, Christine, and a younger brother, Alfred Daniel.

Martin encountered racism at an early age. When he was six, his friendship with two white playmates was cut short by their parents.

When he was 11 a white woman struck him and called him a racial slur.

A bright student, he was admitted to Morehouse College at 15, without completing high school. He decided to become a minister and at 18 was ordained in his father's church. After graduating from Morehouse in 1948, he entered Crozer Theological Seminary in Chester, Pennsylvania. He was the valedictorian of his class in 1951 and won a graduate fellowship. At Boston University he received a Ph.D. in theology in 1955.

In Boston King met Coretta Scott. They were married in 1953 and had two sons, Martin Luther III and Dexter Scott, and two daughters, Yolanda Denise and Bernice Albertine.

King had been impressed by the teachings of Henry David Thoreau and Mahatma Gandhi on nonviolent resistance. King wrote, "I came to feel that this was the only morally and practically sound method open to oppressed people in their struggle for freedom." He became pastor of the Dexter Avenue Baptist Church in Montgomery, Alabama, in 1954.

In December 1955 King was chosen to head the Montgomery Improvement Association, formed by the black community to lead a boycott of the segregated city buses. During the boycott King's home was bombed, but he persuaded his followers to remain nonviolent despite threats to their lives and property. Late in 1956 the United States Supreme Court forced desegregation of the buses. King believed that the boycott proved that "there is a new Negro in the South, with a new sense of dignity and destiny." In 1957 King became the youngest recipient of the Spingarn Medal, an award presented annually to an outstanding black person by the National Association for the Advancement of Colored People.

In 1958 King became president of a group later known as the Southern Christian Leadership Conference (SCLC), formed to carry on civil rights activities in the South. King inspired blacks throughout the South to hold peaceful sit-ins and freedom rides to protest segregation.

A visit to India in 1959 gave King a long-awaited opportunity to study Gandhi's techniques of nonviolent protest. In 1960 King became copastor of his father's church in Atlanta. The next year he led a "nonviolent army" to protest discrimination in Albany, Georgia. King was jailed in 1963 during a successful campaign to achieve the desegregation of many public facilities in Birmingham, Alabama. In a moving appeal, known as the "Letter from Birmingham Jail," he replied to several white clergymen who felt that his efforts were ill timed. King argued that Asian and African nations were fast achieving political independence while "we still creep at a horse-and-buggy pace toward gaining a cup of coffee at a lunch counter."

In 1964 King became the youngest recipient of the Nobel Peace Prize. He regarded it not only as a personal honor but also as an international tribute to the nonviolent civil rights movement. In 1965 King led a drive to register black voters in Selma, Alabama. The drive met with violent resistance. In protest of this treatment, thousands of demonstrators conducted a five-day march from Selma to the capitol in Montgomery.

King was disappointed that the progress of civil rights in the South had not been matched by improvements in the lives of Northern blacks. In response to the riots in poverty-stricken black urban neighborhoods in 1965, he was determined to focus the nation's attention on the living conditions of blacks in Northern cities. In 1966 he established a headquarters in a Chicago, Illinois, slum apartment. From this base he organized protests against the city's discrimination in housing and employment.

King combined his civil rights campaigns with a strong stand against the Vietnam War. He believed that the money and effort spent on war could be used to combat poverty and discrimination. He felt that he would be a hypocrite if he protested racial violence without also condemning the violence of war. Militant black leaders began to attack his appeals for nonviolence. They accused him of being influenced too much by whites. Government officials criticized his stand on Vietnam. Some black leaders felt that King's statements against war diverted public attention from civil rights.

King inspired and planned the Poor People's Campaign, a march on Washington, D.C., in 1968 to dramatize the relationship of poverty to urban violence. But he did not live to take part in it. Early in 1968 he traveled to Memphis, Tennessee, to support a strike of poorly paid sanitation workers. There, on April 4, he was assassinated by a sniper, James Earl Ray. King's death shocked the nation and precipitated rioting by blacks in many cities. He was buried in Atlanta under a monument inscribed with the final words of his famous "I Have a Dream" address.

Taken from an old slave song, the inscription read: "Free at Last,/ Free at Last,/ Thank God Almighty,/ I'm Free at Last."

King's brief career greatly advanced the cause of civil rights in the United States. His efforts spurred the passage of the Civil Rights Act of 1964 and the Voting Rights Act of 1965. His energetic personality and persuasive oratory helped unite many blacks in a search for peaceful solutions to racial oppression. Although King's views were challenged by blacks who had lost faith in nonviolence, his belief in the power of nonviolent protest remained strong. His writings include *Stride Toward Freedom: the Montgomery Story* (1958); *Strength to Love* (1963); *Why We Can't Wait* (1964); *and Where Do We Go from Here: Chaos or Community?* (1967).

In 1977 King was posthumously awarded the Presidential Medal of Freedom for his battle against prejudice. In 1986 the United States Congress established a national holiday in King's honor to be observed on the third Monday in January.

JOHN LENNON

(b. 1940–d. 1980)

During his career with the Beatles, and later as a solo performer, John Lennon wrote and sang some of the most enduring songs of the 20th century. His impact on music and culture in the 1960s was immeasurable and continued well beyond his murder at age 40 by a crazed fan.

John Winston Lennon was born into a troubled household on October 9, 1940, in Liverpool, England. When the child was three, his father left home; soon thereafter, Lennon's mother Julia found herself unable to care for the boy, and he was sent to live with an aunt in the Liverpool suburb of Woolton. Although he continued to see his mother frequently, the separation had a strong impact on the sensitive boy. In 1957, Lennon's mother was killed when an automobile struck her while she stood outside his aunt's home. The teenager witnessed the accident, which was to haunt him for the rest of his life.

Bright but increasingly bored at school, Lennon grew into a rebellious teenager, cutting class frequently and spending his time drawing and writing stories. His gift for drawing, which later led him to enroll in art school, was accompanied by a strong interest in music, particularly recordings by American rock and roll artists such as Gene Vincent. Lennon received his first guitar from his aunt while in his early teens and taught himself to play. At 15 he formed his first band, a skiffle group called the Quarrymen that later included fellow teenagers Paul McCartney and

John Lennon.

George Harrison. Over the next few years, the band evolved, adding members and changing names. Lennon and McCartney began to write songs together. In 1962 the band—having added drummer Ringo Starr to their lineup—recorded their first single, a Lennon-McCartney composition called "Love Me Do." The record was an immediate hit in England, and within a year the band's recordings were receiving airplay on U.S. radio stations.

In 1964 the band traveled to the United States to appear on *The Ed Sullivan Show*, generating among their fans the hysteria that came to be called Beatlemania. Lennon's quick mind and sarcastic wit was a highlight of the band's first film, *A Hard Day's Night* (1964), and soon earned him the nickname of The Smart Beatle. A book of his drawings and stories, *In His Own Write* (1964), was published to critical acclaim. Over the next two years, the band's mass appeal continued unabated, prompting Lennon to remark to a reporter in 1966 that the band was more popular than Jesus Christ. The controversial statement generated a backlash that led to their records being banned in some towns. Lennon later apologized for the statement.

Drained by the demands of live performances, the Beatles stopped touring in 1966, choosing to focus on studio work, though Lennon took time off from recording to appear in the film *How I Won the War* (1967).

Lennon was the only married member of the group at the onset of Beatlemania in 1964; in 1962 he had married Cynthia Powell, with whom he had a son, Julian. By 1968 Lennon had divorced Powell, having begun an association with Japanese artist Yoko Ono, whom he had first met in an art gallery in 1966. Ono's avant-garde films and art installations fascinated Lennon, and soon they were collaborating on experimental recordings such as *Unfinished Music No. 1: Two Virgins* (1968), which featured a cover photograph of Lennon and Ono in the nude. At Lennon's insistence, Ono began attending all of the Beatles' rehearsals and recording sessions, an intrusion that drove a wedge into Lennon's relationship with his bandmates, particularly McCartney.

Lennon and Ono married in 1969 and continued to generate publicity by staging events that intrigued, amused, and annoyed Beatle fans. Increasingly vocal in their opposition to the Vietnam War, the couple used their honeymoon in Amsterdam, The Netherlands, as a protest statement, spending the week in bed and inviting reporters to discuss the probability of world peace. In 1970, the Beatles announced that they had broken up, and while fans blamed Ono for the band's demise, Lennon steadfastly insisted that the group had simply run its course.

In 1971, Lennon and Ono moved to New York City and continued to collaborate on musical projects. Lennon's public statements regarding politics and war came under suspicion from the Nixon Administration, who saw his popularity with youth as a security threat. The government began deportation proceedings, using a drug arrest from years past as the legal basis for denying him residency. Lennon eventually won the case and was allowed to remain in the United States. He continued his recording career with several albums, notably *Mind Games* (1973), *Walls and Bridges* (1974), and *Rock 'n' Roll* (1975), though his greatest solo success was the title song from his second album, *Imagine* (1971). At the end of the 20th century the song was voted in some polls as the one of the greatest pop songs of all time.

In 1973 Lennon and Ono separated for 18 months, during which time Lennon moved to Los Angeles, California. In 1974 Lennon made what would be his last public performance, as a surprise guest at an Elton John concert in New York City. Having reconciled with Ono by 1975, Lennon retired to their home in the Dakota apartments in New York, staying out of the spotlight to focus on raising their son Sean, who was born on Lennon's 35th birthday.

In late 1980 Lennon and Ono returned to the music world with a joint effort, *Double Fantasy*. The collection of songs was greeted with critical praise and commercial success, and Lennon's comeback seemed assured. On December 8, 1980, Lennon and Ono were returning home from a recording session when he was shot in front of his home by a deranged fan. Although Lennon was rushed immediately to a nearby hospital, within an hour he was dead. The fan was later convicted of murder.

Ono continued to manage the estate of John Lennon, and in 1984 she released *Milk and Honey*, an album of songs recorded during the sessions for *Double Fantasy*. In 1994 Ono gave home recordings of two of Lennon's works-in-progress to the surviving Beatles, who were assembling a three-volume anthology of unreleased works. McCartney, Harrison, and Starr added instrumentation and vocals to the tracks and in 1995 released the first new Beatles songs in 25 years. Lennon was inducted posthumously into the Rock and Roll Hall of Fame twice—with the Beatles in 1988 and as a solo artist in 1994.

JOHN L. LEWIS

(b. 1880–d. 1969)

From 1920 to 1960 John L. Lewis was president of the United Mine Workers of America (UMWA). He also worked for unionization of the steel, automobile, and other mass-production industries and organized the Congress of Industrial Organizations (CIO), a labor organization. Demanding and unyielding, he aroused passions with his thunderous oratory and kept industry in turmoil throughout his long and dynamic career.

John Llewellyn Lewis was born in Lucas, Iowa, on February 12, 1880. His father, a coal miner from Wales, was active in the Knights of Labor. Lewis quit school at 12, and at 17 he became a coal miner. He educated himself with the help of a schoolteacher, marrying her in 1907. He also directed a debating club and took part in amateur theatricals.

At 26 years old, Lewis was a delegate to a UMWA convention. In 1920 he was elected president of the organization. The membership was then about 700,000, the largest union in the American Federation of Labor (AFL).

Under Lewis's leadership, eight unions in the AFL promoted organizing drives on an industry-wide basis. When the AFL convention of 1935 rejected the plan, Lewis formed a Committee for Industrial Organization, which later became the Congress of Industrial Organizations. The group was regarded as a rival organization and in 1936 was expelled by the AFL. Lewis served as president of the new CIO until 1940. He then pulled the UMWA out of the CIO with much criticism, but he retained the miners' support. When Lewis retired in 1960, there were only 200,000 UMWA members, but their wages were high, and they were excellently insured. Lewis died in Washington, D.C., on June 11, 1969.

ABRAHAM LINCOLN

(b. 1809–d. 1865)

The 16th president of the United States, Abraham Lincoln, ranks among the greatest of all American statesmen. Many historians also place him among the greatest men of all time. Lincoln came to the presidency at a time of great crisis, with the country at the brink of a civil war that threatened to split North from South. Combining his roles as statesman and commander in chief, Lincoln led the federal armies to victory and held the Union together. Along the way he brought about the end of slavery in the United States.

Lincoln has become a myth as well as a man. Apart from his historical role as savior of the Union and the Great Emancipator of the slaves, he has been celebrated for his remarkable life story and his fundamental humanity. Born in a log cabin on the frontier, Lincoln made his own way in life to rise to the country's highest office. He did so while remaining a firm idealist who would not be swayed from the right course of action, a man of kindly and brave patience, and a believer in what he called the "family of man."

Lincoln's legacy is complex, however. In his own time, many Southerners believed him to be the destroyer of their liberty and their way of life. Today, some conservative historians continue to criticize Lincoln for using the power of the national government to trample states' rights. In Lincoln's view, though, the Union had to be preserved at all costs. It was worth saving not only for its own sake but also because it embodied an ideal, the ideal of self-government. His passion as a spokesman for democracy is a key element of Lincoln's unique and enduring appeal—both for his fellow countrymen and also for people throughout the world.

Lincoln was deeply devoted to the cause of personal freedom. Yet, as president, he was at first reluctant to adopt an abolitionist policy. There were several reasons for his hesitancy. He had been elected on a platform pledging no interference with slavery. He was concerned about the possible difficulties of incorporating nearly four million African Americans, once they had been freed, into the country's social and political life.

Above all, Lincoln felt that he must hold the border slave states in the Union. He feared that an abolitionist program might push them toward the Confederacy. In August 1862 he wrote: "My paramount object in this struggle is to save the Union, and it is not either to save or to destroy slavery. If I could save the Union without freeing any slave, I would do it; and if I could save it by freeing all the slaves I would do it; and if I could save it by freeing some and leaving others alone, I would also do that."

Yet Lincoln knew that the slavery question must be settled if the United States, founded on the principles of liberty and equal rights for all, were to survive as a country. He realized that the Union must be preserved, as a free nation, if democratic government was to succeed in the world.

As antislavery sentiment rose, Lincoln worked out a plan to emancipate, or free, the slaves. According to his proposal, the slaves were to be freed by the states. The emancipation process was to be gradual. The slaveholders were to be compensated, with the federal government sharing the cost. The newly freed blacks were to be colonized outside the United States. Congress approved the plan, but the border slave states rejected it. In addition, few African American leaders wanted to see their people sent abroad.

Lincoln did not abandon hope for the eventual success of his gradual plan. Still, he took quite a different step by drawing up another proposal. His Cabinet approved issuing the new proclamation after the next Union victory. The summer of 1862 passed with no victory. Then, on September 17, Union forces stopped the advancing Confederate armies at Antietam, Maryland.

On September 22, 1862, Lincoln put forth his preliminary proclamation. It promised freedom for slaves in any Confederate state that did not return to the Union that year. When the South ignored him, he issued the final Emancipation Proclamation on January 1, 1863. It was a landmark moment. It transformed the war from a struggle to preserve the Union into a crusade for human freedom.

Lincoln justified the Emancipation Proclamation as an exercise of the president's war powers. Yet even he doubted whether it fell within his authority under the Constitution. After the war, the slaves freed by the proclamation could have possibly been enslaved again had nothing else been done to confirm their freedom. But something else was done. In 1865 Lincoln urged Congress to approve the 13th Amendment to the Constitution, which outlawed slavery in the United States.

In July 1863 the Union armies turned back the Confederate forces at Gettysburg, Pennsylvania. The Battle of Gettysburg was the only battle on Northern soil.

On November 19, 1863, the battlefield was dedicated as a national cemetery. The chief speaker was Edward Everett, a noted orator. As an afterthought, Lincoln was invited "to make a few appropriate remarks." He worked and reworked his speech, seeking to make it as perfect as possible.

The crowd listened for two hours to Everett's extravagant oratory. Lincoln then rose slowly, put on his glasses, glanced at a slip of paper, and then spoke gravely in his clear, high-pitched voice. He began by invoking the Declaration of Independence: "Four score and seven [87] years ago our fathers brought forth on this continent a new nation, conceived in Liberty, and dedicated to the proposition that all men are created equal."In a little less than three minutes he finished his Gettysburg Address, ending with the words "from these honored dead we take increased devotion to that cause for which they gave the last full measure of devotion—that we here highly resolve that these dead shall not have died in vain—that this nation, under God, shall have a new birth of freedom—and that government of the people, by the people, for the people, shall not perish from the Earth."

Lincoln thus framed the Civil War as a struggle to preserve the ideals of the Declaration of Independence—equality and freedom for all—under which the country had been created. The war was being fought, he asserted, not just to ensure a Union victory over the Confederacy, but to bring about a "new birth of freedom" by ending slavery in the United States. Democracy, memorably described in this address as "government of the people, by the people, for the people," was a recurring idea in most of Lincoln's major speeches.

Lincoln thought that his Gettysburg Address was a failure, as did most of the newspapers. However, it soon came to be recognized as one of the noblest speeches ever made. Everett wrote to him: "I should be glad if I could flatter myself that I came as near the central idea of the occasion in two hours as you did in two minutes."

To win the war, Lincoln had to have politicians and the public behind him. Therefore he gave much of his time and attention to politics, trying to attract the support of as many people as possible. Fortunately for the Union cause, Lincoln was a president with rare political skill. He had the knack of appealing to fellow politicians and talking to them in their own language. He had a talent for smoothing over personal differences and holding the loyalty of politicians who disagreed with one another.

Opposition to Lincoln and war remained strong among Democrats in the North. A few "peace Democrats" even collaborated with the enemy. In dealing with people suspected of treason, Lincoln at times authorized his generals to make arbitrary arrests. He let his generals suspend several newspapers, though only for short periods. He believed that he had to allow the temporary sacrifice of some liberties guaranteed by the Constitution in order to maintain the Union and thus preserve the Constitution as a whole.

Considering the dangers of the time, Lincoln was quite liberal in his treatment of political opponents and the press. He was by no means the dictator critics often accused him of being. Nevertheless, his suspension of some civil liberties disturbed Democrats, Republicans, and even members of his own Cabinet.

Within the Republican Party, Lincoln faced divisions and personal rivalries that caused him as much trouble as did the Democrats. He and most other party members agreed fairly well upon their main economic aims. With his approval, the Republicans put into law the essential parts of the program he had advocated from his early Whig days. These included a protective tariff, a national banking system, and federal aid for internal improvements, in particular for the construction of a railroad to the Pacific coast. The Republicans disagreed among themselves, however, on many matters regarding the conduct and purposes of the war.

The big issue was the "reconstruction" of the South. As Southern states were retaken by the federal armies, the president and Congress put forth plans for bringing them back into the Union. Late in 1863 Lincoln proposed his "ten percent plan." It stated that a state government could be reestablished when 10 percent of the state's voters had taken an oath of loyalty to the United States. Some Republicans, called Radicals, rejected Lincoln's proposal. They thought he was being too easy on the rebel states. The Radical Republicans passed a stricter bill, which the president vetoed.

The Republicans nominated Lincoln for reelection in 1864. As in 1860, Lincoln was the chief strategist of his own campaign. He took a hand in the management of the Republican Speakers' Bureau and advised state committees on campaign tactics. He also did his best to enable as many soldiers and sailors as possible to vote.

By the time of the election in November 1864, however, Lincoln was nearly exhausted by the burden of the war and grief at the death of his son Willie in the White House. Wherever he turned he read or heard criticism of himself and his generals. He prepared a memorandum for his Cabinet, forecasting his defeat in the coming election. The people, however, at last rallied and reelected him, with Andrew Johnson as vice president.

When Lincoln gave his second inaugural address on March 4, 1865, the end of the war was in sight. He looked forward to welcoming the Southern states back into the Union and to making their readjustment as easy as possible. He expressed that thought in these words: "With malice toward none, with charity for all, with firmness in the right as God gives us to see the right, let us strive on to finish the work we are in; to bind up the nation's wounds, to care for him who shall have borne the battle and for his widow and orphan, to do all which may achieve and cherish a just and lasting peace among ourselves and with all nations."

Little more than a month later, on April 9, 1865, General Robert E. Lee surrendered his Confederate Army to General Ulysses S. Grant. On April 11 the Stars and Stripes of the United States were raised over Fort Sumter, where the war had begun.

To celebrate the end of the war, Lincoln took Mary and two guests to Ford's Theatre on the night of April 14. During the third act of the play, *Our American Cousin*, John Wilkes Booth, a young actor who was proslavery and a Confederate sympathizer, crept into the presidential box and shot Lincoln in the head. Booth then leapt onto the stage, and, brandishing a dagger, he escaped. He was shot and killed on April 26 in a Virginia tobacco barn when soldiers and detectives surrounded and set fire to it.

Soldiers carried the unconscious president across the street to the nearest residence, a boardinghouse. On April 15, 1865 he died without regaining consciousness at 7:22 in the morning.

Many thought of Lincoln as an American martyr. The assassination occurred on Good Friday, the day on which Christians commemorate the crucifixion of Jesus. On the following Sunday, known as "Black Easter," hundreds of speakers read sermons about Lincoln's death. One declared, "Jesus Christ died for the world; Abraham Lincoln died for his country." The growth of the president's reputation after his death was thus influenced by the timing and circumstances of his murder, which won for him a kind of sainthood.

The first assassination of a U.S. president shocked the country, and it was especially saddening coming so soon after the bitterly divisive Civil War. Lincoln's death was met with a tremendous outpouring of public grief, as the country mourned both its president and its numerous fallen soldiers. It is thought that some 25 million people—a majority of the country's population—attended memorial services for Lincoln held in Washington and unofficially throughout the country on April 19. On April 21 a funeral train began carrying the president's body from Washington back home to Springfield, Illinois, stopping in 10 cities along the way for public memorial services and viewings of the body. Huge crowds gathered to pay their respects to Lincoln, with people sometimes waiting in line several hours to view the body. The train arrived in Springfield on May 3, and the following day Lincoln was buried there in Oak Ridge Cemetery. The Lincoln Memorial in Washington, was dedicated to him in 1922. The Abraham Lincoln Presidential Library and Museum opened in Springfield in 2004–05.

LIU XIAOBO

(b. 1955–d.)

Chinese literary critic, scholar, and human rights activist Liu Xiaobo called for democratic reforms and the end of one-party rule in

China. In 2010 he became the first Chinese recipient of the Nobel Peace Prize.

Liu graduated from Jilin University in 1982, and he continued his studies at Beijing Normal University, earning a Ph.D. in 1988. By then Liu had already established himself as a prolific and erudite critic, rising to prominence in 1986 with a stinging examination of modern Chinese literature. He undertook a lecture tour of Norway and the United States in 1988–89, returning to Beijing as the pro-democracy movement in that city began to gather strength.

In the days leading up to the Tiananmen Square incident of 1989, Liu served as an adviser to the student protesters, and he joined protest leaders in a weeklong hunger strike. After the Chinese military forcibly cleared the square on the night of June 3–4, Liu went into hiding. He was arrested on June 6, and he spent 21 months in prison for his role in the protests. Upon his release, Liu continued his criticism of the Chinese Communist Party, and he was arrested in 1996 for advocating the release of those still imprisoned as a result of the Tiananmen Square protests. He spent the next three years in a labor camp.

Protesters march for the release of Liu Xiaobo.

In 2008 Liu helped draft Charter 08, a 19-point program that called for greater political freedoms in China and concluded with the signatures of more than 300 academics and intellectuals. Liu was arrested hours before the document's release onto the Internet, and, at a trial the following year, he was sentenced to 11 years in prison for subversion. He was awarded the Nobel Peace Prize in 2010, but neither Liu nor any member of his family was permitted to attend the ceremony in December of that year. In his absence, Norwegian actress Liv Ullmann read a statement that Liu had made to a Chinese court the previous year. It read, in part, "I have no enemies and no hatred. Hatred can rot away at a person's intelligence and conscience. Enemy mentality will poison the spirit of a nation, incite cruel mortal struggles, destroy a society's tolerance and humanity, and hinder a nation's progress toward freedom and democracy."

MARTIN LUTHER

(b. 1483–d. 1546)

The Protestant Reformation in Germany was inaugurated by Martin Luther in 1517. It was his intent to reform the medieval Roman Catholic church, but the firm resistance of the church to Luther's challenge led instead to permanent divisions in the structure of Western Christianity.

Luther was born in Eisleben in the province of Saxony on November 10, 1483, to Hans and Margaret Ziegler Luther. Shortly thereafter the family moved to Mansfeld, where Hans worked as a miner. The young Luther studied at Magdeburg and Eisenach before attending the University of Erfurt. In 1505, at the urging of his father, he began to study law; but within the year he decided to abandon law and enter the religious life by becoming an Augustinian monk. Later in life, Luther credited this sudden decision to having been caught in a thunderstorm and dashed to the ground by a bolt of lightning. In his fear, he renounced the world and entered the Augustinian monastery at Erfurt in July 1505. Luther became an outstanding theologian and Biblical scholar. He earned his doctorate in theology in 1512 and became professor of Biblical literature at Wittenberg University.

The seriousness with which Luther took his religious vocation led him into a severe personal crisis: how, he wondered, is it possible to reconcile the demands of God's law with human inability to live up to the law? He found his answer in the New Testament book of Romans: God had, in the obedience of Jesus, reconciled humanity to Himself. What was required of mankind, therefore, was not strict adherence to law or the fulfillment of religious obligations, but a response of faith that accepted what God had done. Such faith would lead to an obedience based on love, not fear.

This belief of Luther's led him into his first major confrontation with the Catholic church in 1517. Pope Leo X, in order to raise money for the building of St. Peter's Basilica in Rome, offered indulgences for sale to the people. These offered partial remission of the penalty for sins to those who made donations of money. Luther strongly objected to this practice.

On October 31, 1517, Luther nailed to the door of the church in Wittenberg a list of 95 theses, or propositions. They denied the right of the pope to forgive sins by the sale of indulgences, among other challenges. The theses were widely circulated in Germany and caused a great controversy.

The pope ordered Luther to appear before Cardinal Cajetan in Augsburg. The cardinal demanded that Luther retract all he had said. Luther refused to do this unless it could be proved to him from the Bible that he was wrong.

Early in 1521 the pope issued a Bull of Excommunication against Luther and ordered Emperor Charles V to execute it. Instead, the emperor called a "diet," or council, at Worms and summoned Luther for examination. The diet demanded that Luther recant, but he refused and was outlawed.

With the help of his friend the elector of Saxony, Luther hid in the castle of Wartburg, near Eisenach. There he remained in disguise. During his time at Wartburg he began to translate the New Testament into German.

Finally the emperor's preoccupation with the war he was waging with France made it safe for Luther to return to his work at Wittenberg. While Luther was in concealment some of his followers had carried the reform movement further than he had intended. On Luther's return he tried to correct these excesses but was not successful. In 1524 many of the German peasants used his teachings as a reason for revolting.

In 1525 Luther married a former nun, Katharina von Bora. This emphasized his rejection of monasticism and celibacy for the clergy. The remainder of Luther's life was spent in writing, preaching, and organizing the reformed church in Saxony. He replaced the Latin service of the mass with a service in the German language and wrote many hymns that are still in use, notably the famous 'Ein feste Burg ist unser Gott' ("A Mighty Fortress Is Our God"). Luther died on February 18, 1546, at Eisleben, his birthplace.

MALCOLM X

(b. 1925–d. 1965)

A black militant, Malcolm X championed the rights of African Americans and urged them to develop racial unity. He was known for his association first with the Nation of Islam, sometimes known as the Black Muslims, and later with the Organization of Afro-American Unity, which he founded after breaking with the Nation of Islam.

Malcolm Little was born in Omaha, Nebraska, on May 19, 1925, the seventh of eleven children. The family soon moved to Lansing, Michigan. There they were harassed by whites who resented the black nationalist views of the father, Earl Little, an organizer for Marcus Garvey's "back-to-Africa" movement.

When Malcolm was six his father was murdered. His mother later suffered a nervous breakdown, and the family was separated by welfare agencies. Later in his life Malcolm came to believe that white people had destroyed his family.

Placed in a series of schools and boardinghouses, Malcolm became a fine student and dreamed of becoming a lawyer. A teacher, however, told him that because he was black he should learn carpentry instead. Discouraged, he left school after the eighth grade to live with a relative in Boston, Massachusetts.

Malcolm X.

Malcolm shined shoes and worked at a soda fountain, in a restaurant, and on a railroad kitchen crew. In 1942 he moved to the black Harlem section of New York City. He lived as a hustler, cheating to make money. He was wary of the police. A pusher, he sold drugs and became an addict himself. Pursued by a rival hustler, he went back to Boston, where he organized a burglary ring. In 1946 he was sent to prison for burglary. While serving in prison Malcolm adopted the Islamic religion as practiced by a group that later became known as the Nation of Islam. They stressed ethical conduct with other African Americans but taught that white people were "devils." Released from prison in 1952, Malcolm joined his younger brother in Detroit, Michigan, where, in Muslim fashion, he replaced his slave last name with an X to symbolize his lost "true African family name."

Malcolm X soon became an active participant in the Nation of Islam. He assisted the national leader, Elijah Muhammad, by starting many new Muslim groups throughout the United States. His success as a recruiter was a result of his skill as a speaker, as he worked to instill racial pride in his black listeners and recounted the sufferings of blacks under white domination. In 1954 he returned to New York to become minister of the important Harlem temple, and in 1957 he founded the Muslim newspaper *Muhammad Speaks*.

By the early 1960s the Nation of Islam had become nationally known.

Malcolm X was their most effective national minister and their most recognized spokesman. He was increasingly ignored, however, by Black Muslims who accused him of seeking personal glory. In 1963 Malcolm X was officially silenced for his remark that the assassination of President John F. Kennedy was a case of "the chickens coming home to roost." Elijah Muhammad suspended him from the movement.

In 1964 Malcolm X broke completely with the Nation of Islam and began building his own Organization of Afro-American Unity (OAAU). He made the hajj to Mecca, Saudi Arabia, to learn about "true Islam." Impressed by the fellowship he observed among pilgrims of all colors, Malcolm X came to believe that whites, like blacks, were victims of a racist society. He thought that Islam could unite people of all races. After the hajj he adopted the name el-Hajj Malik el-Shabazz.

During later trips to African nations, where he was honored by their statesmen, Malcolm X began to advocate Pan-Africanism. He believed blacks all over the world should join to combat racism.

During the winter of 1964–65 Malcolm X received several death threats, and his home was bombed. On February 21, 1965, while speaking at an OAAU rally in Harlem, he was shot and killed. Three members of the Nation of Islam were convicted of the murder. His death saddened white and black people alike who admired his striving to build black pride and who shared his hopes that all races might someday be joined. Malcolm X was survived by his wife, Betty Shabazz, whom he had married in 1958. They had six daughters. His autobiography, published posthumously in 1965, was written by Alex Haley, author of Roots. The book was based on interviews Haley conducted with Malcolm X shortly before his assassination. In 1992 director Spike Lee released the movie Malcolm X, starring Denzel Washington in the title role. The film revived interest in the slain leader, especially among young African Americans.

NELSON MANDELA

(b. 1918–d. 2013)

In January 1990 Nelson Mandela was serving his 27th year as a political prisoner in South Africa. He was freed the next month, and in April 1994 he was elected president of the country. Mandela was a leader in the struggle against apartheid—South Africa's official system of segregation and discrimination against the country's non-white majority. He became a worldwide symbol of victory against that system when he was freed from his life sentence in prison. Mandela served as South Africa's president from 1994 to 1999.

Mandela was born into the royal family of the Tembu, a Xhosa-speaking people, on July 18, 1918, near Umtata, in the Transkei region of South Africa. He was originally named Rolihlahla Mandela; one of his school teachers gave him the English name Nelson. Partly to avoid an arranged marriage, Mandela renounced his right to become chief of the Tembu and left his village. He studied at the University College of Fort Hare but was suspended in 1940 along with Oliver Tambo for taking part in a student protest. He earned a bachelor's degree from the University of South Africa in 1941 and began studying law. In 1952 he and Tambo opened the first black-owned law firm in South Africa.

In 1944 Mandela joined a black-liberation organization called the African National Congress (ANC) and helped found its influential Youth League. Mandela quickly rose to a position of leadership in the ANC, becoming a member of its National Executive Committee in 1949. His first jail sentence, which was suspended, was for helping lead the ANC's 1952 Defiance Campaign, in which thousands of volunteers peacefully violated the apartheid laws. Along with many other ANC leaders, Mandela was arrested and tried for treason in 1956. After a long trial, he was acquitted in 1961. Mandela divorced his first wife and married Nomzamo Winnie Madikizela (Winnie Mandela) in 1958 (they divorced in 1996).

The ANC's anti-apartheid protests had at first been wholly nonviolent. In 1960, however, after the police shot more than 200 unarmed black protesters at Sharpeville and the government banned the ANC, Mandela began to advocate acts of sabotage. He helped found a military wing of the ANC, called Umkhonto we Sizwe (Spear of the Nation), and became a fugitive.

In 1962 Mandela was caught and sentenced to five years in prison. A year later, while he was still serving that sentence, he was tried for sabotage, treason, and violent conspiracy, and in 1964 he was sentenced to life in prison. Mandela was kept in Robben Island Prison, off Cape Town, until 1982, when he was transferred to the maximum-security Pollsmoor Prison. Winnie Mandela spearheaded a campaign to free him, which gained vast support among both South Africa's black population and the international community that condemned apartheid. Mandela was set free on February 11, 1990, by the administration of President F.W. de Klerk.

Once freed, Mandela continued with the work of ending apartheid. He became the ANC's deputy president in March 1990 and its president in July 1991. In that office, he negotiated landmark agreements with de Klerk to bring about the peaceful transformation of South Africa into a majority-rule democracy. Mandela and de Klerk shared the 1993 Nobel Peace Prize for their achievements.

Along with millions of other black South Africans, Mandela voted for the first time in the election that brought him to power in April 1994. During his presidency, Mandela focused on improving the living standards of the country's black population, while advocating peaceful reconciliation with the white population. In 1995 he established the Truth and Reconciliation Commission (TRC) to investigate human rights violations committed during the apartheid era. He signed into law a new democratic constitution in 1996. The following year, Mandela resigned his post with the ANC. He retired from active politics in 1999, after his term as the country's president ended. Mandela married Graça Machel, the widow of former president of Mozambique Samora Machel, in 1998.

Mandela's writings and speeches were collected in *No Easy Walk to Freedom* (1965), *I Am Prepared to Die*, 4th rev. ed. (1979), and *The Struggle Is My Life*, 3rd ed. (1990). His autobiography, *Long Walk to Freedom*, was published in 1994. Mandela died on December 5, 2013, in Johannesburg, South Africa.

THURGOOD MARSHALL

(b. 1908–d. 1993)

U.S. lawyer Thurgood Marshall became the first African American justice of the Supreme Court of the United States. He was a champion of civil rights, both as a lawyer and later as a judge.

Marshall was born in Baltimore, Maryland, on July 2, 1908. He attended Lincoln University and graduated first in his class from Howard University law school in 1933. He began private practice in Baltimore before joining the legal staff of the National Association for the Advancement of Colored People (NAACP) in 1936, where he specialized in civil rights cases. He became its chief counsel in 1938. Of the 32 cases that Marshall argued before the Supreme Court, he won 29. His most notable victory came with *Brown vs. Board of Education of Topeka* (1954), in which the Supreme Court struck down the "separate but equal" policy that had been used to justify racial segregation in public schools.

Marshall later served as a judge of a U.S. court of appeals from 1962 to 1965 and as U.S. solicitor general from 1965 to 1967, upon which President Lyndon B. Johnson appointed him an associate justice of the Supreme Court. As a liberal Supreme Court justice, Marshall was known for attacking discrimination, opposing the death penalty, and championing free speech and civil liberties. He retired from the bench in 1991. Marshall died in Bethesda, Maryland, on January 24, 1993.

HARVEY MILK

(b. 1930–d. 1978)

Harvey Bernard Milk was an American politician and gay-rights activist.

After graduating from the New York State College for Teachers in Albany (1951), Milk served in the U.S. Navy during the Korean War and was discharged in 1955 (Milk later said that he was dishonorably discharged due to his homosexuality, but military records do not support this claim). He held several jobs before becoming a financial analyst in New York. In 1972 he moved to San Francisco, where he opened a camera store and soon gained a following as a leader in the gay community. His popularity grew when he challenged the city's gay leadership, which he thought was too conservative in its attempts to gain greater political rights for homosexuals.

In 1973 Milk ran for a seat on the city's Board of Supervisors but was defeated. After another unsuccessful bid in 1976, he was elected in 1977, becoming one of the first openly gay elected officials in U.S. history. The following year Milk and the city's mayor, George Moscone, were shot and killed in City Hall by Dan White, a conservative former city supervisor. At White's murder trial, his attorneys successfully argued that his judgment had been impaired by a prolonged period of clinical depression, one symptom of which was the former health enthusiast's consumption of junk food. The attorneys' argument, mischaracterized as the claim that junk food had caused White's diminished capacity, was derided as the "Twinkie defense" by the satirist Paul Krassner while reporting on the trial for the San Francisco Bay Guardian. White's conviction on the lesser charge of voluntary manslaughter sparked an uproar in the city that was subsequently termed the "White Night Riot." Numerous books and films were made about Milk, including the 1984 documentary *The Times of Harvey Milk*, which earned an Academy Award; an opera, *Harvey Milk* (1995); and *Milk* (2008), a cinematic depiction of his political career that starred Sean Penn. In 2009 Milk was posthumously awarded the Presidential Medal of Freedom.

MICHAEL MOORE

(b. 1954–d.)

Michael Francis Moore is an American filmmaker, author, and political activist, who was best known for a series of documentaries—often controversial—that addressed major political and social issues in the United States.

Following his graduation from high school, Moore, as an 18-year-old member of the Flint school board, began his populist assault on what he viewed as the injustices of American capitalism. In 1976, after having attended but not graduating from the University of Michigan at Flint, Moore started a radical weekly newspaper, the *Flint Voice* (later *Michigan Voice*), which he edited for 10 years. He was later hired to edit the San Francisco-based left-wing magazine *Mother Jones* but was fired after a few months (he later accepted an out-of-court settlement for a wrongful-dismissal suit).

Michael Moore.

Returning to Flint, Moore filmed his first documentary, *Roger & Me* (1989), which chronicles the effects of unemployment in Flint due to the closing of two General Motors (GM) factories and the company's longer-term policy of downsizing. At the center of the film were Moore's "in-your-face" efforts to gain an audience with GM's chairman, Roger Smith. Mixing humour and poignancy with indignation, *Roger & Me* was a hit with critics and at the box office. Moore subsequently moved to New York City and established Dog Eat Dog Films. He also created an organization to finance social-action groups and other filmmakers.

After producing three television series and other limited-release films—including the comedy *Canadian Bacon* (1995), in which a U.S. president starts a cold war with Canada in order to boost his approval ratings—Moore achieved major success with *Bowling for Columbine* (2002). The film, which profiles gun violence in the United States, won the Academy Award for best documentary. In his next documentary, *Fahrenheit 9/11* (2004), Moore criticized U.S. President George W. Bush's handling of the September 11 attacks and the administration's decision to start the Iraq War. Although highly controversial, it won the Golden Palm at the Cannes film festival and earned more than $222 million worldwide to become the highest-grossing documentary. In 2007 Moore released *Sicko*, an examination of the health care industry in the United States. For his next documentary, *Capitalism: A Love Story* (2009), Moore took a critical look at the U.S. economy, including the subprime mortgage crisis of 2007–08 and the subsequent bailout of banks.

In addition to filmmaking, Moore wrote a series of best-selling books, including *Downsize This!* (1996); *Stupid White Men* (2002), which assails the legitimacy, methods, and motives of President Bush's administration; *Dude, Where's My Country?* (2003), a call for "regime change" in the United States; and *Mike's Election Guide* (2008), a guidebook to the 2008 U.S. presidential election. In 2011 he published *Here Comes Trouble*, a collection of autobiographical stories.

LUCRETIA MOTT

(b. 1793–d. 1880)

For most of her life Lucretia Mott campaigned against slavery. She also fought for equal rights for women. Lucretia Coffin was born to Quaker parents in Nantucket, Massachussetts, on January 3, 1793. At the age of 13 she entered a Quaker boarding school in Poughkeepsie, New York. There she met James Mott, a teacher in the school. They were married in 1811 and had six children.

For a time Mott conducted a small school in Philadelphia. She eventually became more active in the church and began speaking at Quaker meetings. In 1821 she became an official Quaker minister. When the Quakers split over the slavery question in 1827, she and her husband joined the Hicksites, an antislavery faction led by Elias Hicks.

In 1833 Mott helped found the American Anti-Slavery Society. She went to London in 1840. There she attended a world antislavery conference as the society's delegate. When the convention refused to seat women, she began a campaign for women's rights. She met Elizabeth Cady Stanton in London, and together they planned a women's rights convention. It was held in 1848 in Seneca Falls, New York. It launched the first woman suffrage movement in the United States.

When the Fugitive Slave Act was passed in 1850, Mott made her home in Philadelphia a stop on the Underground Railroad. During the American Civil War, however, she lived in retirement. She hated slavery, but because of her pacifist convictions she could not approve of the war. Mott died near Abington, Pennsylvania, on November 11, 1880.

JOHN MUIR

(b. 1838–d. 1914)

Because of American naturalist, explorer, and writer John Muir, the United States national park system was greatly expanded. In 1903 he made a camping trip in Yosemite with President Theodore Roosevelt, who absorbed Muir's enthusiasm for nature. During the remainder of Roosevelt's presidency, 148 million acres (60 million hectares) were set aside as national forests; 16 national monuments, including Muir Woods in California, were established; and the number of national parks doubled.

Muir was born on April 21, 1838, in Dunbar, Scotland. In 1849 the family immigrated to the United States and settled on a farm near Portage, Wisconsin. In 1860 Muir entered the University of Wisconsin in Madison, but he left without a degree in 1863 because he studied only the subjects that interested him—chemistry, geology, and botany.

After leaving Madison, Muir worked on mechanical inventions. In 1867, however, an accident at a wagon factory in Indianapolis nearly cost him an eye, causing him to abandon that career and devote himself to nature. Muir then walked all the way from Indianapolis to the Gulf of Mexico, keeping a journal as he went; after his death the journal was published as *A Thousand-Mile Walk to the Gulf*. In 1868 he made his way to California, where for six years he lived alone in the Yosemite Valley, exploring the glaciers and forests of the Sierra Nevada. From California he took many trips into Nevada, Utah, Oregon, Washington, and Alaska, inspired by his interest in glaciers and forests. In Alaska he discovered Glacier Bay and the great glacier named for him. After his marriage in 1880 Muir devoted ten years to his California fruit ranch. His gift for growing plants and for developing new varieties of fruits and flowers brought him success and the freedom to travel and write.

As early as 1876, Muir urged the federal government to adopt a forest conservation policy. He became a central figure in the debate over land use, advocating on behalf of land preservation primarily through articles published in popular periodicals. Muir was largely responsible for the establishment of California's Sequoia and Yosemite national parks in 1890.

On May 28, 1892, Muir founded the Sierra Club, an organization devoted to protecting the environment. He served as its first president, a position he held until his death. He died in Los Angeles on December 24, 1914.

A. J. MUSTE

(b. 1885–d. 1967)

Abraham Johannes Muste was a Dutch-born American clergyman best known for his role in the labor and left-wing movements of the 1920s and '30s and for his leadership of the American peace movement from 1941 until his death in 1967. He also had considerable influence on the American civil rights movement and was an outspoken critic of Christian neoorthodoxy in liberal Protestantism after World War II.

When he was six years old, Muste's family emigrated from the Netherlands to Grand Rapids, Michigan, where his father worked at a factory. In 1909, after being ordained in the Dutch Reformed Church, he married Anna Huizenga, with whom he would have three children. The couple moved to New York City, where Muste was introduced to liberal theology and pragmatism. He joined the Boston chapter of the National Civil Liberties Union (which later became the American Civil Liberties Union) and the pacifist Fellowship of Reconciliation. When the United States entered World War I, Muste, whose pacifist views put him at odds with his conservative congregation, was forced to resign his pastorate. From then on his spiritual home would be on the political left rather than in the church.

During the interwar years, Muste was a prominent figure in the progressive wing of the labor movement. He led striking textile workers in Lawrence, Massachusetts, in 1919 and served as general secretary of the Amalgamated Textile Workers of America. From 1921 to 1933, he served as the director of Brookwood Labor College, a training school for the Congress of Industrial Organizations. In 1929, after he was accused of being a communist by the American Federation of Labor, he founded the Conference for Progressive Labor Action (CPLA) to agitate for militant industrial unionism. In 1933 the CPLA became the American Workers' Party (AWP), which led a number of important strikes and organized the National Unemployment League. In 1935 the AWP merged with the Trotskyists to become the Workers' Party USA, with Muste as national secretary.

In 1936 Muste had a religious experience that persuaded him to break with Marxism-Leninism and rededicate himself to Christian pacifism. After briefly serving as minister of Labor Temple in New York City, he became national secretary of the Fellowship of Reconciliation, from which he published the book *Nonviolence in an Aggressive World* (1940) and trained a generation of activists in nonviolent direct action against racial segregation. When the civil rights movement emerged in the 1950s, he served as an adviser to Bayard Rustin and Martin Luther King, Jr., among others.

The issue that most preoccupied Muste during the postwar years was American militarism and the Cold War. In 1947 he published *Not by Might*, a book that called for draft resistance and nonpayment of taxes. In 1948 he became chairman of the Peacemakers, a radical pacifist group, and in 1957 he helped to found the Committee for Nonviolent Action, which opposed nuclear proliferation through dramatic civil disobedience campaigns. During these years, Muste also attempted to build a nonsectarian New Left as coeditor of the magazine *Liberation* and offered theological critiques of Reinhold Niebuhr and other Christian realists who supported the Cold War. Muste's commitment to direct action and his opposition to the Vietnam War endeared him to the New Left, who joined him in organizing the coalition that later became known as the National Mobilization Committee to End the War in Vietnam (MOBE). Muste was chairman of MOBE until his death.

RALPH NADER

(b. 1934–d.)

Credit for launching the late-20th-century consumer movement probably cannot be given to Ralph Nader, but he is responsible for much of the momentum it gained worldwide from the late 1960s. His book *Unsafe at Any Speed: The Designed-in Dangers of the American Automobile*, published in 1965, made him famous and led to the passing of auto-safety legislation.

Nader was born in Winsted, Connecticut, on February 27, 1934. He graduated from Princeton University in 1955 and received his law degree from Harvard in 1958. He settled into a law practice in Hartford, Connecticut, where he devoted most of his time to studying auto accident cases and writing about the issue of auto safety.

Convinced that he could make no headway against automobile manufacturers by working at the local level, Nader became a consultant for the United States Department of Labor. There he worked on a study about federal responsibility for auto safety. Publication of his book in 1965 made him an instant celebrity. The book became a best-seller and led directly to the passage of the National Traffic and Motor Vehicle Safety Act in 1966, which gave the government the power to enact safety standards for all automobiles sold in the United States. By 1969 the General Motors (GM) Corvair, the object of most of Nader's criticisms, had been withdrawn from production.

GM went to exceptional lengths to discredit Nader, including hiring a private detective to follow him. Nader sued for invasion of privacy. The case was settled after GM admitted wrongdoing before a Senate committee. With the funds he received from the lawsuit and aided by impassioned activists, who became known as Nader's Raiders, he helped establish a number of advocacy organizations, most notably his Washington, D.C.–based Public Citizen. Nader's Raiders became involved in such issues as nuclear safety, international trade, regulation of insecticides, meat processing, pension reform, land use, and banking. Among his other books are *The Menace of Atomic Energy* (1979) and *Who's Poisoning America?* (1981).

Although Nader and his associates did not invent the idea of consumer advocacy, they did radically transform its meaning, focusing on fact-finding research, analysis, and governmental lobbying for new laws on key consumer issues. Nader was also instrumental in the passage in 1988 of California's Proposition 103, which provided for a rollback of auto insurance rates.

Nader, who collected only 700,000 votes when he ran for U.S. president in 1996, was the Green party's nominee for the 2000 U.S. presidential election. His campaign focused on universal health care, environmental and consumer protections, campaign finance reform, and strengthened labor rights. Realizing that he had little hope of winning the election, Nader concentrated on obtaining 5 percent of the national vote, the minimum necessary to secure federal matching funds for the Green party for future presidential campaigns. To meet this goal, some Nader supporters initiated a vote-swapping program on the Internet. Nader Traders, as they were called, agreed to vote for Democratic candidate Al Gore in states where the race was close between Gore and Republican candidate George W. Bush and in exchange Gore's supporters would cast ballots for Nader in states where the contest was uncompetitive. Nader was opposed to the plan, and in the end it had little impact on the election as he managed to win only 3 percent of the national vote.

BARACK OBAMA

(b. 1961–d.)

In only four years Barack Obama made an improbable rise from the state legislature of Illinois to the highest office of the United States. The first African American to win the presidency, he made history with his resounding victory in the election of 2008. His eloquent message of hope and change attracted voters across the country, even in states that had gone decades without supporting a Democratic presidential candidate. He was elected to a second term in 2012.

In his first months in office, Obama worked to restore the international image of the United States, which many believed had been tarnished by the policies of the Bush Administration. He ordered the closing of the controversial military detention facility in Guantánamo Bay, Cuba, within a year (a deadline that was not met). He vowed to work toward the elimination of nuclear weapons and to improve strained relations with Russia. In June 2009 he traveled to the Middle East and gave a speech calling for a new relationship between the United States and the Muslim world. In recognition of such efforts, Obama was awarded the 2009 Nobel Peace Prize, with the Nobel committee citing his "extraordinary efforts to strengthen international diplomacy and cooperation between peoples."

Obama's top domestic priority was the ongoing economic recession. Aided by Democratic majorities in both the Senate and the House of Representatives, Obama pushed through Congress a massive stimulus package that pumped hundreds of billions of dollars into the struggling economy. By late 2009 the stimulus had reversed the dramatic decline in the gross domestic product. Perhaps the most encouraging sign of recovery was the dramatic turnaround of General Motors (GM). In June 2009 the auto manufacturer had declared bankruptcy, prompting a $60 billion government rescue and takeover of about three-fifths of its stock. By May 2010 GM, under a new business plan, had shown its first profit in three years. Despite these gains, however, unemployment remained high, and Republicans complained that the stimulus had been too costly.

A sweeping financial reform bill passed in July 2010 was another response to the recession. Aimed at preventing the conditions that led to the economic crisis, the bill empowered the government to take over and shut down large troubled financial firms and created a council of federal regulators to monitor the financial system, among other provisions. The passage of the bill was a major legislative victory for the president.

Another early priority of Obama's presidency was reforming the country's health care system. During the election campaign, Obama had called for reforms that would make health care insurance more affordable and extend coverage to tens of millions of Americans who lacked it. The issue provoked a prolonged and sometimes bitter debate, with Republicans complaining that Democratic proposals constituted a costly "government takeover" of health care. A new conservative populist movement, the Tea Party, loudly objected to the proposed health care reforms in a series of town hall meetings in summer 2009. More

Barack Obama.

generally, Tea Party members opposed what they saw as excessive taxes and government involvement in the private sector.

In late 2009 the Democratic-controlled House of Representatives and Senate each passed a version of the health care bill. As Congressional leaders prepared to negotiate a compromise between the two versions, the triumph of a Republican in a special election held to fill the Senate seat vacated by Ted Kennedy's death destroyed the Democrats' filibuster-proof majority. In March 2010, as the historic measure teetered on the brink of defeat, Obama and other Democratic leaders mounted a last-ditch campaign to pass it. The president became more forceful in promoting the bill, both to Congress and to the American people. Later that month Congress passed the bill with no Republican support. Officially called the Patient Protection and Affordable Care Act, it also became commonly known as Obamacare.

Obama's key foreign-policy challenges were the ongoing wars in Iraq and Afghanistan. Throughout the presidential campaign he had argued that the focus of U.S. military efforts should be in Afghanistan rather than Iraq. In keeping with this philosophy, Obama set an 18-month timetable for the withdrawal of U.S. combat troops from Iraq. The situation in Iraq continued to improve, and in August 2010, on schedule, the U.S. combat mission in Iraq ended. The withdrawal of some 50,000 U.S. troops who had remained in the country as a transitional force was completed in December 2011, ending the Iraq War. Meanwhile, as the Taliban experienced a resurgence in Afghanistan, Obama increased the number of U.S. troops there. On May 1, 2011, he announced that U.S. special forces had killed Osama bin Laden, leader of the terrorist group al-Qaeda, in a firefight in a compound in Abbottabad, Pakistan.

Elsewhere in the Middle East, popular uprisings collectively known as the Arab Spring brought abrupt ends to longtime authoritarian governments in Tunisia and Egypt and widespread protests and conflict in other countries. The Obama Administration voiced its support for the protesters' democratic goals while trying to avoid direct intervention in the affairs of other countries. In Libya, however, Obama felt U.S. intervention was necessary when longtime dictator Muammar al-Qaddafi unleashed a brutal military crackdown on protests against his rule. In March 2011 U.S. and European forces launched air strikes against targets in Libya in an effort to disable that country's air force and air defense systems. A week later the Obama Administration relinquished command in Libya to the North Atlantic Treaty Organization.

Obama officially kicked off his bid for reelection in May 2012. His Republican opponent was Mitt Romney, a former governor of Massachusetts. As in 2008, the economy was the central issue of the race. Though economic conditions continued to improve, the recovery was slow and uneven. Profits were up again for many corporations, and the financial system had regained stability; however, the housing market continued to struggle, and the unemployment rate, though down from the highs of 2009, remained high. Romney spent much of his campaign criticizing Obama's handling of the economy, but the Republican effort fell short. On November 6, 2012, Obama was reelected for a second term as president.

After the election, Obama entered into negotiations with Republican leaders regarding the federal budget. At issue were a series of economic measures set to expire at the start of 2013. Chief among them were the tax cuts introduced during Bush's presidency. Another critical issue was sequestration—automatic spending cuts to military and nonmilitary programs required by the Budget Control Act of 2011. A compromise bill signed in January 2013 preserved the Bush-era income tax cuts for most Americans but raised taxes on individuals earning $400,000 or more annually and couples earning $450,000 or more. The compromise delayed but did not prevent the cuts to military and social spending, which began in March.

Republicans tried to use the budget negotiations to aid their ongoing battle against Obamacare. With another deadline looming in October 2013, Republicans associated with the Tea Party movement led an attempt to include a one-year delay in funding for Obamacare in the new budget resolution. After Congress reached a stalemate over the resolution, the federal government partially shut down for the first time in 17 years, closing government offices and putting hundreds of thousands of employees temporarily out of work. The shutdown continued for 16 days before Congress passed a bill that funded the government through January 15, 2014. By the end of 2013 Congress passed a two-year budget agreement that replaced most of the automatic spending cuts required by sequestration with targeted cuts. The compromise also raised discretionary spending in military and nonmilitary programs.

With the temporary resolution of the budget battle, public attention shifted to the disastrous rollout of Obamacare in October 2013. The trouble centered on HealthCare.gov, the Web site set up as the place to apply for health insurance. The site was often slow or simply inoperable, preventing many users from enrolling in the program. As HealthCare.gov's performance improved, however, millions of Americans bought insurance plans through the site. At the beginning of April 2014, after the end of the first open enrollment period, the president announced that 7.1 million people had signed up for Obamacare, meeting the administration's goal.

Obama also angered Republicans with his use of executive orders—directives that do not require the approval of Congress. The president use his executive power to address issues that remained bogged down in Congress. In February 2014 Obama, unable to persuade Congress to raise the federal minimum wage, signed an executive order raising the hourly minimum wage of federal contract workers to $10.10. In June he took on global warming, directing the Environmental Protection Agency to introduce new restrictions on the carbon emissions of power plants. Although Republicans criticized Obama for misusing his executive powers, the president maintained that his actions were necessary to get anything done in the midst of Congressional gridlock.

For many Americans, Obama's election as the first African American president represented a historic step forward in the country's troubled history of race relations. In his second term, however, racial tensions once again came into the national spotlight. In August 2014 the fatal shooting of Michael Brown, an unarmed African American teenager, by a white police officer resulted in days of protests in Ferguson, Missouri. Although President Obama carefully sought not to take sides, a series of high-profile incidents kept the issue of police violence against African Americans in the headlines and spawned a protest movement known by the slogan "black lives matter." The country was even more stunned and saddened when, in June 2015, nine African Americans were shot and killed, allegedly by a young white man, in a hate crime in a historic black church in Charleston, South Carolina. Obama delivered a eulogy for one of the shooting's victims, addressing race relations and gun control.

In foreign affairs, the Middle East continued to be a major focus in Obama's second term. In Syria, the government's violent crackdown against pro-democracy protestors had escalated into civil war. Fighting between government forces and rebel groups pushed the civilian death toll higher and higher. Obama, seemingly seeking to avoid involvement in another Middle Eastern conflict, had been cautious in his response to the situation in Syria. As reports surfaced of the use of chemical weapons by Syrian government forces, however, the United States took a more active role, sending food and financial aid to the opposition. After suspected chemical weapons attacks killed hundreds of Syrians in August 2013, Obama announced that U.S. forces were prepared to intervene. The threat of military action faded as a diplomatic solution was sought. In September an agreement between Syria, Russia (Syria's ally), and the United States placed Syria's chemical weapons under international control.

In early summer 2014, nearly three years after the removal of the final U.S. troops from Iraq, Obama was again forced to respond to events there. For more than a year the country's U.S.-supported government had been fighting a militant Sunni group called the Islamic State in Iraq and the Levant (ISIL; also known as the Islamic State in Iraq and Syria [ISIS]). In June 2014 Obama sent some 300 U.S. Special Operations troops to train Iraqi security forces. In August and September the United States launched air strikes against ISIL in Iraq and Syria. At the same time, Obama helped to build a coalition of some 20 countries to join the military campaign against ISIL. U.S. and coalition air strikes continued into 2015.

In December 2014, Obama announced the formal end of the U.S.-led combat mission in Afghanistan. The 13-year conflict was the longest war ever fought by the United States.

GEORGE ORWELL

(b. 1903–d. 1950)

As a journalist and writer of autobiographical narratives, George Orwell was outstanding. But he will be remembered primarily for two works of fiction that have become 20th-century classics: *Animal Farm*, published in

1944, and *Nineteen Eighty-four* (1949).

George Orwell is a pen name. His real name was Eric Arthur Blair, and he was born in 1903 at Montihari in Bengal, India, where his father was a minor British official. His family had social status but little money, a fact that influenced Orwell's later attitude toward the English class system and the empire's treatment of its subject peoples. In about 1911 the family returned to England. Blair was sent to school in Sussex, where he was distinguished both by his poverty and his intelligence. He later wrote of his miserable school years in *Such, Such Were the Joys* (1953). He attended Eton in the years 1917 to 1921 but decided against going on to a university. Instead he went to Burma (now Myanmar) as a member of the British imperial police.

His own poverty, plus his growing aversion to Britain's imperial policies, led him to resign from the government in 1928. He then spent several years among the poor and outcast of Europe and among the unemployed miners in the north of England. These experiences were recounted in *Down and Out in Paris and London* (1933) and *The Road to Wigan Pier* (1937). Orwell then went to Spain to report on the Spanish Civil War. His experiences in Spain were described in *Homage to Catalonia* (1938), one of his best books.

During World War II Orwell wrote for the British Broadcasting Company and worked as a literary editor for the *London Tribune*. The success of *Animal Farm* in 1944 allowed him to devote himself to writing. He bought a house on the island of Jura, where he wrote *Nineteen Eighty-four*. By the time it was published, Orwell was already ill from the tuberculosis from which he died on January 21, 1950, in London.

ROSA L. PARKS

(b. 1913–d. 2005)

By refusing to give up her bus seat to a white man in the segregated South, Rosa Parks sparked the United States civil rights movement. Her action led to the 1955–56 Montgomery, Alabama, bus boycott, and she became a symbol of the power of nonviolent protest.

Rosa Louise McCauley was born on February 4, 1913, in Tuskegee,

Alabama. She briefly attended Alabama State Teachers College (now Alabama State University) and in 1932 married Raymond Parks, a barber. She worked as a seamstress and became active in the National Association for the Advancement of Colored People (NAACP), serving as secretary of the Montgomery chapter from 1943 to 1956.

On her way home from work one day in 1955, Parks was told by a bus driver to surrender her seat to a white man. When she refused, she was arrested and fined, an action that motivated local black leaders to take action. Emerging civil rights leader Martin Luther King, Jr., led a boycott of the bus company that lasted more than a year. In 1956 the U.S. Supreme Court upheld a lower court's decision declaring Montgomery's segregated bus seating unconstitutional.

Rosa L. Parks.

Parks moved to Detroit, Michigan, in 1957. She worked in the office of Michigan congressman John Conyers, Jr., from 1965 until she retired in 1988. She remained active in the NAACP and other civil rights groups. The Southern Christian Leadership Conference established the Rosa Parks Freedom Award in her honor, and in 1979 the NAACP awarded her its Spingarn Medal. In 1987 she cofounded an institute to help educate young people and teach them leadership skills. An autobiography, *Rosa Parks: My Story*, appeared in 1992. She was the recipient of two of the U.S. government's most prestigious civilian honors—the Presidential Medal of Freedom (1996) and the Congressional Gold Medal of Honor (1999)—for her contributions to the civil rights movement. Parks died on October 24, 2005, in Detroit.

FRANCES PERKINS

(b. 1882–d. 1965)

Fannie Coralie Perkins was a U.S. secretary of labor during the presidency of Franklin D. Roosevelt. Besides being the first woman to be appointed to a cabinet post, she also served one of the longest terms of any Roosevelt appointee (1933–45).

Perkins graduated from Mount Holyoke College in 1902 and for some years taught school and served as a social worker. She worked briefly with Jane Addams at Hull House in Chicago and then resumed her studies, first at the Wharton School of Finance and Commerce of the University of Pennsylvania and then at Columbia University, where she took an M.A. in social economics in 1910. From that year until 1912 she was executive secretary of the Consumers' League of New York. In that position she lobbied successfully for improved wages and working conditions, especially for women and children. From 1912 to 1917 she was executive secretary of the New York Committee on Safety and from 1917 to 1919 executive director of the New York Council of Organization for War Service. She was appointed in 1919 to New York's State Industrial Commission by Governor Alfred E. Smith, and in 1923 she was named to the State Industrial Board, of which she became chairman in 1926. Smith's successor, Franklin D. Roosevelt, appointed Perkins state industrial commissioner in 1929. She was, both before and after the onset of the Great Depression of the 1930s, a strong advocate of unemployment insurance and close government supervision of fiscal policy.

When Roosevelt entered the presidency in 1933 he named Perkins secretary of labor, making her the first woman to serve in a cabinet position. After the initial controversy of her appointment died away she settled into a 12-year term of effective administration of her department. She pushed for a minimum wage and maximum workweek, a limit on employment of children under 16, creation of the Civilian Conservation Corps, and unemployment compensation—all of which were enacted. She helped draft the Social Security Act and supervised the Fair Labor Standards Act (1938). When the focus of labor activity shifted in the late 1930s from government to unions, Perkins played a less visible role. Her most important work was then the building up of the Department of Labor, particularly the strengthening of the Bureau of Labor Statistics.

Two months after Roosevelt's death, Perkins resigned from the Cabinet, but she remained in government as a U.S. civil service commissioner until 1953. From then until her death, she lectured on the problems of labor and industry. In 1934 she published *People at Work*, and *The Roosevelt I Knew*, a record of her association with the late president, appeared in 1946.

WENDELL PHILLIPS

(b. 1811–d. 1884)

For nearly 50 years Wendell Phillips was one of the foremost abolitionists, reformers, and orators in the United States. Although he often faced ridicule and the threat of mob violence, his belief in abolition and basic human rights was greater than any desire for popularity and any fear of danger.

Phillips was born on November 29, 1811, in Boston, Massachusetts. His father, a prominent judge, was the city's first mayor. An excellent student, Phillips attended the Boston Latin School, Harvard College, and Harvard Law School. He first gained recognition in 1837 with a stirring speech he delivered in Boston's Faneuil Hall, condemning the murder in Illinois of the antislavery editor Elijah P. Lovejoy. He advocated the disunion of free states from slave states and welcomed the American Civil War. During the war Phillips criticized President Abraham Lincoln for delaying emancipation. Phillips also advocated temperance, better working conditions, heavier taxation of the rich, and women's rights, and he condemned the history of ill-treatment of Indians in the United States. In 1870 he ran unsuccessfully for governor of Massachusetts as the candidate of the Labor and Prohibition parties. He died in Boston on February 2, 1884.

HOMER PLESSY

(b. 1863–d. 1925)

Homer Plessy was an American shoemaker who was best known as the plaintiff in the landmark U.S. Supreme Court case *Plessy vs. Ferguson* (1896), which sanctioned the controversial "separate but equal" doctrine for assessing the constitutionality of racial segregation laws.

Three years after Plessy's father died, his widowed mother married a post office clerk from a family of shoemakers. Plessy chose to follow his stepfather's family and learn the shoemaking trade. He was also influenced by his stepfather's participation in the Unification Movement, a civil rights organization formed in the 1870s. The group worked across racial lines, seeking political equality for all and an end to discrimination.

Plessy's first venture into social activism came in 1887, when he became involved in education reform as vice president of the Justice, Protective, Educational, and Social Club. The group had unsuccessfully challenged the segregation of Orleans Parish public schools, despite a provision in the Louisiana State Constitution that prohibited the establishment of separate schools on the basis of race. Moreover, because so many of the city's wealthier white families sent their children to one of nearly 200 private schools, the public schools were beset with financial difficulties, leaving many African American children to drop out and wander the streets. The Social Club committed its resources to establishing a library and trying to ensure good teachers for the African American schools.

Like many of the *gens de couleur* (the class consisting of free Creole people of colour in Louisiana), Plessy could easily have passed for white, and he described himself as "seven-eighths Caucasian and one-eighth African blood," which nonetheless made him "colored" under the terms of the Separate Car Act of 1890. But he and other light-complected Creoles chose not to turn their backs on their African ancestry and tried to protect the rights that they believed were guaranteed to them by the Fourteenth Amendment to the U.S. Constitution (which, among other things, prohibited the states from denying to anyone "the equal protection of the laws").

On June 7, 1892, Plessy walked into the Press Street Depot in New Orleans, bought a first-class ticket to Covington, and boarded the East Louisiana Railroad's Number 8 train, fully expecting to be forced off the train or arrested—or both. As the train pulled away from the station, the conductor asked Plessy if he was a "colored" man; Plessy said he was, and the conductor told him to move to the appropriate car, which Plessy refused to do. Plessy told the trainman that he was an American citizen, that he paid for a first-class ticket, and that he intended to ride in the first-class car. The conductor stopped the train, and Detective Christopher Cain boarded the car, arrested Plessy, and forcibly dragged him off the train with the help of a few other passengers. After a night in jail, Plessy appeared in criminal court before Judge John Howard Ferguson to answer charges of violating the Separate Car Act.

The Citizens' Committee to Test the Constitutionality of the Separate Car Act, of which Plessy was a member, posted a $500 bond for his release. Plessy was not arraigned until October 1892, four months after his arrest, and his attorneys entered a plea claiming that the act was unconstitutional because it imposed a "badge of servitude" in violation of the Thirteenth Amendment (which prohibited slavery) and because it denied to Plessy the equal protection of the laws provided for in the Fourteenth Amendment. They also claimed that the matter of race, both as to fact and to law, was too complicated to permit the legislature to assign that determination to a railway conductor.

Plessy failed in court, and his subsequent appeal to the state supreme court (in *Ex parte Plessy*, 1893) was similarly unsuccessful. An appeal to the U.S. Supreme Court followed, but time was hardly on Plessy's side. Between the filing of the appeal in 1893 and oral argument before the U.S. Supreme Court in Washington, D.C., in April 1896, both the general climate and the attitude of the court had hardened. Throughout the country, but especially in the South, conditions for blacks were quickly deteriorating.

The Supreme Court ruling that followed on May 18, 1896, and that bore the names of Plessy and Ferguson (*Plessy vs. Ferguson*) upheld the Separate Car Act, holding that the law violated neither the Thirteenth Amendment (because it did not reimpose slavery) nor the Fourteenth Amendment (because the accommodations provided to each race were equal). The decision solidified the establishment of the Jim Crow era, thus inaugurating a period of legalized apartheid in the United States.

Shortly after the Supreme Court decided the case, Plessy reported to Ferguson's court to answer the charge of violating the Separate Car Act. He changed his plea to guilty and paid the $25 fine. For the rest of his life, Plessy lived quietly in New Orleans, working as a laborer, warehouseman, and clerk. In 1910 he became a collector for a black-owned insurance company and continued to be active in the African American community's benevolent and social organizations, such as the Société des Francs-Amis and the Cosmopolitan Mutual Aid Association.

A. PHILIP RANDOLPH

(b. 1889–d. 1979)

A. Philip Randolph was a trade unionist and civil rights leader who was a dedicated and persistent leader in the struggle for justice and parity for the black American community.

The son of a Methodist minister, Randolph moved to the Harlem district of New York City in 1911. He attended City College at night and, with Chandler Owen, founded (1912) an employment agency, attempting, through it, to organize black workers. In 1917, following the entry of the United States in World War I, the two men founded a magazine, the *Messenger* (after 1929, *Black Worker*), that called for more positions in the war industry and the armed forces for blacks. After the war, Randolph lectured at New York's Rand School of Social

Science and ran unsuccessfully for offices on the Socialist Party ticket.

In 1925, as founding president of the Brotherhood of Sleeping Car Porters, Randolph began organizing that group of black workers and, at a time when half the affiliates of the American Federation of Labor (AFL) barred blacks from membership, took his union into the AFL. Despite opposition, he built the first successful black trade union; the brotherhood won its first major contract with the Pullman Company in 1937. The following year, Randolph removed his union from the AFL in protest against its failure to fight discrimination in its ranks and took the brotherhood into the newly formed Congress of Industrial Organizations (CIO). He then returned to the question of black employment in the federal government and in industries with federal contracts. He warned President Franklin D. Roosevelt that he would lead thousands of blacks in a protest march on Washington, D.C.; Roosevelt, on June 25, 1941, issued Executive Order 8802, barring discrimination in defense industries and federal bureaus and creating the Fair Employment Practices Committee. After World War II, Randolph founded the League for Nonviolent Civil Disobedience Against Military Segregation, resulting in the issue by President Harry S. Truman on July 26, 1948, of Executive Order 9981, banning segregation in the armed forces.

When the AFL merged with the CIO in 1955, Randolph was made a vice president and member of the executive council of the combined organization. He was the first president (1960–66) of the Negro American Labor Council, formed by Randolph and others to fight discrimination within the AFL-CIO.

In an echo of his activities of 1941, Randolph was a director of the March on Washington for Jobs and Freedom, which brought more than 200,000 persons to the capital on August 28, 1963, to demonstrate support for civil rights policies for blacks. Two years later, he formed the A. Philip Randolph Institute for community leaders to study the causes of poverty. Suffering chronic illness, he resigned his presidency of the Brotherhood of Sleeping Car Porters in 1968 and retired from public life.

PAUL ROBESON

(b. 1898–d. 1976)

Multitalented U.S. actor, singer, and social activist Paul Robeson enjoyed success that was unparalleled among African Americans in the United States in the 1930s and 1940s. However, even as he toured extensively, befriended luminaries, and promoted his message of unity among cultures, he managed to maintain close bonds with the African American community and the working class. At the height of his artistic career Robeson turned his attention to human rights, becoming an eloquent and often controversial speaker against racial discrimination in the United States, colonialism in Africa, and economic injustice throughout the world. His refusal to compromise his progressive political convictions in the face of mounting pressure during the 1950s, however, damaged and eventually shortened his career.

Paul Leroy Robeson was born in Princeton, New Jersey, on April 9, 1898, to William Drew and Maria Louisa (Bustill) Robeson. His father was a former slave who worked his way through Lincoln University in Pennsylvania to become a minister, and his mother, who died when Paul was six, was a schoolteacher from a distinguished family of abolitionists. After graduating from Sommerville High School with honors at age 17, he accepted an academic scholarship to become only the third African American student to attend Rutgers College (now Rutgers University). He excelled in academics, winning his class oratorical prize four years in a row and election to Phi Beta Kappa, the national college academic honor society. He also excelled in athletics, earning 17 athletic letters in baseball, basketball, football, and track. He was selected as an All American in football in 1917 and 1918, becoming both the first player from Rutgers and the first African American to receive the honor. He was the valedictorian of the 1919 graduating class at Rutgers. He next attended Columbia University, where he earned a law degree while supporting himself by playing professional football on the weekends. In 1923 he took a job at a New York law firm.

While in law school Robeson had married fellow student Eslanda

(Essie) Cardozo Goode, with whom he had one son, Paul Jr. She persuaded him to accept his first amateur stage role in a 1921 YMCA production in the Harlem section of New York. She also encouraged him to turn to acting as a career when racial hostility mounted against him at his law firm. He left the firm after a few months and joined the Provincetown Players, a theater company associated with playwright Eugene O'Neill. Robeson first appeared on the professional stage in *Taboo* in 1922 and made his London debut in the same play, retitled *Voodoo*, later that year. O'Neill soon gave him leading roles in New York productions of his plays *All God's Chillun Got Wings* (1924) and *The Emperor Jones* (1925), which brought Robeson critical acclaim. He branched out into feature films in 1924 with *Body and Soul*. Despite having no formal training in singing, Robeson gave his first recital in New York's Greenwich Village in 1925. He established his reputation as an outstanding interpreter of African American spirituals during tours of the United States and Europe. His role as Joe in the London production of the musical *Show Boat* (1928) showcased his superb bass-baritone voice, particularly in his show-stopping rendition of "Ol' Man River." His international fame grew with his acclaimed performance in the title role of William Shakespeare's *Othello* in London (1930).

During the 1930s Robeson's performing career became intertwined with his increasing social and political awareness. He continued to appear in stage productions, such as *The Hairy Ape* (1931) and *Stevedore* (1935), and reprised his stage roles in film versions of *The Emperor Jones* (1933) and *Show Boat* (1936), among other films. At the same time, however, Robeson began to voice his opposition not only to the stereotypical roles usually offered to African American actors, but also to inequality throughout the world and particularly in American society.

Robeson studied more than 20 languages and toured Europe, giving concerts to the working poor and developing ties with leftist political organizations and labor unions. In 1934 he traveled to the Soviet Union on a trip that would change his life. Overwhelmed by his warm welcome, Robeson found himself strongly attracted to the communist system because it seemed to be free of racial prejudice and imbued with the spirit of equality. He became an enthusiastic advocate of the Soviet Union and socialism and supported anti-fascist movements, speaking out against

Nazism and entertaining Loyalist troops in Madrid during the Spanish Civil War. He also contributed to the World War II effort in the United States by performing patriotic songs on the radio and in concerts and participating in United Service Organization tours, which were organized to entertain troops. In 1943 and 1944 he appeared in the New York production of *Othello*, which was the longest-running Shakespearean play in Broadway history up to that time. During this period he received numerous honors for his efforts, including the Spingarn Medal from the National Association for the Advancement of Colored People (NAACP) in 1945.

The onset of the Cold War following World War II, however, led to a decline in Robeson's popularity and professional fortunes. Called before the House Committee on Un-American Activities in 1946 because of his leftist sympathies, Robeson defied his questioners and was branded a communist. He came under surveillance by the Federal Bureau of Investigation and was denounced even by the NAACP as he continued to speak out against the United States government and what he characterized as its racist treatment of African Americans. Right-wing rioters led by members of the Ku Klux Klan and the American Legion forced the cancellation of Robeson's Peekskill, New York, concert for minority trade unionists and pacifists in 1949. Following the riot, the campaign of repression against Robeson intensified: He was barred from appearing in concert halls, and his records were removed from store shelves. After he refused to pledge that he was not a communist, the United States Department of State suspended his passport in 1950. He performed in churches and for trade unions in defiance of the government's censorship while the African American community and progressive organizations abroad campaigned on his behalf. He accepted the Stalin Peace Prize from the Soviet Union in 1952.

Robeson sued the state department and finally won the restoration of his passport in 1958, the year that saw the publication of his autobiography, *Here I Stand*. He left the United States to live and perform in Europe and the Soviet Union, where he was given a hero's welcome. He returned to the United States in poor health in 1963 and soon retired from public life. After his wife died in 1965, Robeson went to Philadelphia to live in seclusion with his sister. More than two decades removed from his days of outspoken activism, he died there quietly on January 23, 1976, at the age of 77.

JACKIE ROBINSON

(b. 1919–d. 1972)

"A life is not important except in the impact it has on other lives," reads the tombstone of Jackie Robinson, the first African American athlete to play in baseball's major leagues in the 20th century. By breaking the color barrier in 1947, Robinson made great strides not only for black athletes but also for all concerned with racial justice.

Jack Roosevelt Robinson was born on January 31, 1919, in Cairo, Georgia, but grew up in Pasadena, California. After demonstrating exceptional athletic ability during high school and junior college, he excelled at baseball, football, basketball, and track at the University of California at Los Angeles (UCLA) and became the first student at the school to earn four letters in one year. He left UCLA in 1941 and briefly played professional football before being drafted into the United States Army. During his service, he refused to sit at the back of a bus and was threatened with a court-martial, but the charges were dropped and he was given an honorable discharge in 1945.

While playing baseball for the Kansas City Monarchs in the Negro National League, Robinson caught the eye of a scout for the Brooklyn (now Los Angeles) Dodgers and was brought to the attention of team president Branch Rickey. Major league baseball was closed to black players at the time. Rickey thought that this was wrong, and he wanted to find someone who could successfully integrate the sport. After meeting Robinson and being impressed with his courage as well as his skill, Rickey signed him on October 23, 1945, to play for the Dodgers' AAA team in Montreal. During the 1946 season, Robinson batted .349 with the farm club and led the team to victory in the Little World Series.

Robinson made his major league debut in April 1947. The chief problem he had to overcome was controlling his fiery temper in the face of continual racial slurs from the crowds and other ballplayers, including some of his own teammates. Robinson did not break his promise to Rickey to remain silent, though pitchers sometimes deliberately threw at him, hotels at away games often would not accommodate him, and he and his family received death threats. He instead let his actions do the talking by batting .297 and leading the National League in stolen bases. He was chosen rookie of the year at season's end.

Robinson's .342 average made him the league's batting champion and most valuable player in 1949. During his career, which he spent primarily as a second baseman, Robinson helped the Dodgers capture six National League pennants and one World Series title. He retired in 1956 with a .311 lifetime batting average and 197 total stolen bases. The Dodgers later retired his number 42 jersey. When he was elected to the Baseball Hall of Fame in 1962 he was the first black player to be so honored.

After he left baseball Robinson pursued business interests while continuing to work on behalf of civil rights. Diabetes and heart problems plagued his later life, and he died on October 24, 1972, in Stamford, Connecticut. His wife established the Jackie Robinson Foundation the following year to provide minority scholarships. In 1997, major league baseball held a season-long celebration marking the 50th anniversary of his historic debut.

ELEANOR ROOSEVELT

(b. 1884–d. 1962)

Great reformer and humanitarian Eleanor Roosevelt strove to improve the lives of people all over the world. As the wife of Franklin Delano Roosevelt, 32nd president of the United States, she had the distinction of being First Lady longer than any other presidential wife—slightly more than 12 years (1933–45)—and her defense of the rights of minorities, youth, women, and the poor during her tenure helped to shed light on groups that previously had been alienated from the political process. After her husband's death, as a delegate to the United Nations, she helped write the Universal Declaration of Human Rights (1948).

Anna Eleanor Roosevelt was born in New York City on October 11,

1884. Her uncle, Theodore Roosevelt, later became 26th president of the United States. Eleanor grew up in a wealthy family that attached great value to community service. Both her parents and a brother died before she was 10, and Eleanor and her surviving brother were raised by their strict grandmother. The death of Eleanor's father, to whom she had been especially close, was very difficult for her.

Relatives hoped to polish 15-year-old Eleanor—a girl considered sweet but plain and awkward—by enrolling her at Allenswood, a girls' boarding school outside London. There she came under the influence of the French headmistress Marie Souvestre, whose intellectual curiosity and taste for travel and excellence awakened similar interests in Eleanor, who later described her three years there as the happiest time of her life. Reluctantly, Eleanor returned to New York in the summer of 1902 to prepare for her debut into society that winter. Following family tradition, she devoted time to community service, including teaching in a settlement house on Manhattan's Lower East Side.

Soon after Eleanor returned to New York, Franklin Roosevelt, her distant cousin, began to court her. He especially was attracted to her intellect and kind nature. Despite the objections of his mother, with whom Eleanor continued to have problems throughout her married life, the couple wed on March 17, 1905, in New York City, with Uncle Theodore (then president) giving away the bride. Between 1906 and 1916 Eleanor gave birth to five healthy children—Anna; James; Elliott; Franklin, Jr.; and John—and another son who died in infancy.

After Franklin won a seat in the New York Senate in 1911, the family moved to Albany, where Eleanor was initiated into the job of political wife. When Franklin was appointed assistant secretary of the navy in 1913, the family moved to Washington, D.C., and Eleanor spent the next few years performing expected social duties. With the entry of the United States into World War I in April 1917, Eleanor was able to resume her volunteer work. She visited wounded soldiers and worked for the Navy-Marine Corps Relief Society and in a Red Cross canteen.

In 1918 Eleanor discovered that Franklin had been having a love affair with her social secretary, Lucy Mercer. Mindful of his political career and fearing the loss of his mother's financial support, Franklin refused Eleanor's offer of a divorce and agreed to stop seeing Mercer.

The Roosevelts' marriage settled into a routine in which the two kept independent agendas while remaining respectful of and affectionate toward each other.

Franklin ran unsuccessfully for vice president on the Democratic ticket in 1920. At this time Eleanor's interest in politics increased, partly as a result of her decision to help in her husband's political career after he was stricken with poliomyelitis in 1921 and partly as a result of her desire to work for important causes. She joined the Women's Trade Union League and became active in the New York state Democratic party. As a member of the Legislative Affairs Committee of the League of Women Voters, she began studying the Congressional Record and learned to evaluate voting records and debates.

When Franklin became governor of New York in 1929, Eleanor found an opportunity to combine the responsibilities of a political hostess with her own burgeoning career and personal independence. She continued to teach at Todhunter, a girls' school in Manhattan that she and two friends had purchased, making several trips a week back and forth between Albany and New York City.

Entering the White House during the Great Depression, Mrs. Roosevelt helped to plan work camps for girls, to establish the National Youth Administration in 1935, and to launch projects to employ writers, artists, musicians, and actors. She insisted that women's wages be equal to men's. Throughout the 1930s she supported Arthurdale, an experimental homestead community for destitute mining families in West Virginia.

The unprecedented breadth of Eleanor's activities and her advocacy of liberal causes (leading some people to charge that she supported communism) made her nearly as controversial a figure as her husband. Although she earned a great deal of praise, some people accused her of being an interfering busybody, of wasting government funds, and of neglecting her family. Despite such criticism, she influenced public opinion and official policy.

Eleanor instituted regular White House press conferences for women correspondents, and wire services that had not formerly employed women were forced to do so in order to have a representative present. In deference to the president's disability, she helped serve as his "eyes and ears" throughout the nation, embarking on extensive tours and reporting to him on conditions, programs, and public opinion. These unusual excursions drew criticism and ridicule from her opponents, but many people responded warmly to her compassionate interest in their welfare. Beginning in 1936 she wrote a daily syndicated newspaper column, "My Day," and she also gave frequent radio talks. A widely sought-after speaker at political meetings and at various institutions, she showed particular interest in child welfare, housing reform, and equal rights for women and racial minorities.

In 1939, when the Daughters of the American Revolution (DAR) refused to let Marian Anderson, an African American opera singer, perform in Constitution Hall, Eleanor resigned her membership in the DAR and arranged to hold the concert at the nearby Lincoln Memorial; the event turned into a massive outdoor celebration attended by 75,000 people. On another occasion, when local officials in Alabama insisted that seating at a public meeting be segregated by race, Eleanor carried a folding chair to all sessions and carefully placed it in the center aisle. She also was concerned about the improvement of health and education on Indian reservations and fought for the preservation of Native American culture.

After her husband's death on April 12, 1945, Eleanor made plans to retire, but she did not keep them. President Harry S. Truman appointed her a delegate to the United Nations (UN), where she served as chairman of the Commission on Human Rights (1946–51) and played a major role in the drafting and adoption of the Universal Declaration of Human Rights. In the 1950s she toured India, Pakistan, the Middle East, and the Soviet Union, investigating social conditions and discussing the problems of world peace.

In the United States, Eleanor worked for the election of Democratic presidential candidates and supported social welfare legislation. In 1961 President John F. Kennedy appointed her chairman of his Commission on the Status of Women, and she continued with that work until shortly before her death from a rare form of tuberculosis on November 7, 1962, in New York City. She was buried at Hyde Park, her husband's family home on the Hudson River and the site of the Franklin D. Roosevelt Library.

FRANKLIN DELANO ROOSEVELT

(b. 1882–d. 1945)

Everyone had strong feelings about Franklin D. Roosevelt during his 12 years as president. Many people hated him. They thought he was destroying the country and the American way of life. Most people loved him. They believed he was a great president, truly interested in people.

Roosevelt became president in 1933. The United States was then in the grip of a worldwide business depression. Millions of people had no work and no money. Roosevelt used his powers to create jobs and to help those who needed help. To do this he had to change the government's part in national life. For good or ill, many of Roosevelt's ideas of government are still part of the law of the land.

Roosevelt was a great leader. During World War II he was the real commander in chief of the American armed forces. He took charge of the industrial might of the country. He played a major part in setting up the United Nations. In peace and in war he always had the people behind him. Some of his methods may be questioned, but his aims were good.

When Franklin D. Roosevelt assumed the presidency of the United States in 1933, the nation's economy was in a state of turmoil. Following the stock market crash of 1929 that signaled the onset of the Great Depression, the Dow Jones Industrial Average went on to lose an additional 80 percent of its value through the early 1930s. Industrial production slowed to about half its pre-depression level, agricultural and other commodity prices tumbled to half of their previous value, and unemployment soared to 25 percent. Roosevelt responded to the nation's state of panic by immediately putting into action an aggressive recovery agenda known as the New Deal.

In March 1933 Roosevelt outlined a set of measures designed to curb deflation and foreclosures and to put millions of people to work through government programs. Most historians consider the New Deal as having two parts. The first included emergency policies and programs aimed at stabilizing the national economy. The second, begun in the mid-1930s, was a set of broader social welfare measures designed to combat poverty and provide an economic safety net.

One of the first New Deal measures to be enacted was the National Industrial Recovery Act, which created the National Recovery Administration (NRA). The law enabled businesses to work together to fix prices and quotas while protecting labor by setting minimum wages and allowing collective bargaining. Its effect on the economy was arguable, however, and both businesses and labor chafed at its regulations. The Supreme Court declared the NRA unconstitutional in 1935. One of the more effective programs in the early years of the New Deal was the Agricultural Adjustment Act (AAA), which subsidized farmers for producing less and thereby raised commodity prices. Two other early programs, the Civilian Conservation Corps and the Public Works Administration, employed many people while helping to improve the nation's infrastructure. The Tennessee Valley Authority harnessed the power of the Tennessee River for the first time and helped to lift the region out of poverty.

While the early measures went some distance toward stabilizing prices and raising production levels and employment, the United States was still mired in the depression in the mid-1930s. With the broad support of the American public, Roosevelt launched the second phase of the New Deal, which would build the foundation for the modern welfare state. Most importantly, perhaps, was the passage of the Social Security Act in 1935, which provided a pension system for the aged and the disabled. The Works Progress Administration (WPA) employed eight million Americans between 1935 and 1942 in building roads, schools, airports, and other public works. The second phase of the New Deal also saw programs designed to employ artists and students, to bring electricity to rural areas, and to improve public infrastructure in general.

BAYARD RUSTIN

(b. 1910–d. 1987)

American civil rights activist Bayard Rustin took an active role in the struggle for racial equality. He disagreed with racial segregation and believed in pacifist agitation. Rustin was the chief organizer of the 1963 March on Washington, a massive demonstration to rally support for civil rights legislation that was pending in Congress.

Rustin was born on March 17, 1910, in West Chester, Pennsylvania. After finishing high school, he held odd jobs and traveled widely. During this time he also received five years of university schooling at the City College of New York (in New York City) and at other institutions, but he never completed a degree. From 1941 to 1953 Rustin worked for the Fellowship of Reconciliation, a nondenominational religious organization. Simultaneously in 1941, he organized the New York branch of another reformist group, the Congress on Racial Equality.

In the 1950s Rustin became a close adviser to the civil rights leader Martin Luther King, Jr., and he was the chief organizer of King's Southern Christian Leadership Conference. In August 1963 Rustin helped organize the March on Washington, which brought together an interracial group of more than 200,000 people to demand equal justice for all citizens under the law. In 1964 he directed a one-day student boycott of New York City's public schools in protest against racial imbalances in that system. Rustin subsequently served as president of the A. Philip Randolph Institute, a civil rights organization in New York City, from 1966 to 1979. Rustin died on August 24, 1987, in New York. In 2013 he was posthumously awarded the Presidential Medal of Freedom.

OSCAR ARIAS SÁNCHEZ

(b. 1941–d.)

President of Costa Rica from 1986 to 1990 and from 2006, Oscar Arias Sánchez worked during his first term to bring economic stability to his country and to end the guerrilla wars that had engulfed several Central American countries. He was awarded the 1987 Nobel Peace Prize in recognition of his efforts to bring peace to the region.

Arias was born on September 13, 1941, in Heredia, Costa Rica. His family was one of the wealthiest coffee-growing families in the country. He studied economics at the University of Costa Rica and earned a Ph.D.

Oscar Arias Sánchez.

from the University of Essex in England. In the 1960s he began working for the moderate socialist National Liberation Party (Partido de Liberación Nacional; PLN), and in 1972 he was appointed minister of planning in the government of President José Figueres, a post he held until 1977. He was elected leader of the PLN in 1979 and won the Costa Rican presidency in 1986 with the platform "roofs, jobs, and peace."

As president in the late 1980s, Arias took measures to cope with Costa Rica's economic problems, but his main interest was in trying to restore peace and political stability to the strife-torn countries of Central America. Although harshly critical of the Sandinista government in neighboring Nicaragua, he forbade that regime's guerrilla opponents (the "Contras") from operating militarily on Costa Rican soil. In February 1987 he proposed a regional peace plan for the Central American countries that called for cease-fires in all guerrilla wars in the region, a stop to outside military aid and media censorship, a general amnesty for political prisoners, and eventual free elections and reductions in civil- and human-rights abuses.

Arias and the leaders of Guatemala, El Salvador, Honduras, and Nicaragua signed this plan in August 1987. Owing in part to opposition from the United States, the plan was never fully implemented. When Arias's presidential term ended in 1990, he returned to his former post as PLN leader. He used his Nobel prize money to establish the Arias

Foundation for Peace and Human Progress, which promoted peace and equality throughout the world. Arias was reelected president in 2006.

MARGARET SANGER

(b. 1883–d. 1966)

The founder of the U.S. birth control movement was Margaret Sanger, a nurse who worked among the poor on the Lower East Side of New York City. There she witnessed firsthand the results of uncontrolled fertility, self-induced abortions, and high rates of infant and maternal mortality.

Sanger was born Margaret Higgins in Corning, New York, on September 14, 1883. She took her nurse's training at the White Plains Hospital and the Manhattan Eye and Ear Clinic. She married William Sanger in 1900. Although she later divorced him she kept the last name by which she had become well known, even after she remarried in 1922.

Sanger believed in a woman's right to plan the size of her family. In 1912 she gave up nursing to devote herself full time to the cause of birth control. In 1914 she founded the National Birth Control League and in that same year was indicted for sending out copies of the periodical *The Woman Rebel*, which advocated birth control. At that time the federal Comstock Law of 1873 classified such literature as obscene. Her case was dismissed in 1916. Later that year she opened the first birth-control clinic in the United States in Brooklyn, New York. She was arrested and served 20 days in jail in 1917 for creating a public nuisance. Continued government harassment brought public opinion to her side, and in 1936 the 1873 law was modified.

In 1921 Sanger founded the American Birth Control League and served as its president until 1928. That and later organizations became in 1942 the Planned Parenthood Federation of America. Sanger organized the first World Population Conference in Geneva, Switzerland, in 1927 and was also the first president of the International Planned Parenthood Federation, organized in 1953. She helped promote family planning in India and Japan. She wrote several books, including *My Fight for Birth Control* (1931). Sanger died in Tucson, Arizona, on September 6, 1966.

KAILASH SATYARTHI

(b. 1954–d.)

Kailash Satyarthi, original name Kailash Sharma, is an Indian social reformer who campaigned against child labor in India and elsewhere and advocated the universal right to education. In 2014 he was the corecipient of the Nobel Peace Prize, along with teenage Pakistani education advocate Malala Yousafzai, "for their struggle against the suppression of children and young people and for the right of all children to education."

Sharma was born to a Brahman police officer and a homemaker. As a child he formed a football (soccer) club to raise money to help pay the school fees of underprivileged students and campaigned for the development of a textbook bank for them as well. He attended Samrat Ashok Technological Institute in Vidisha, earning a degree in electrical engineering in 1974. Sharma then pursued graduate work and taught at the institute for two years. In 1977 he relocated to New Delhi, where he worked for a publisher of literature for Arya Samaj, a Hindu reform movement. Sharma later exchanged his Brahman (or high-caste) surname for "Satyarthi," which was derived from *Satyarth Prakash* (*Light of Truth*), a volume written (1875) by Dayananda Sarasvati, the founder of Arya Samaj. Dayananda had urged reforms such as the abolition of the caste system and child marriages in addition to advocating a return to a literal interpretation of the Hindu Vedas.

Motivated by those principles, Satyarthi established a magazine, *Sangharsh Jaari Rahega* ("The Struggle Will Continue"), which documented the lives of vulnerable people. He grew increasingly concerned by the prevalence of child labour in India, which was regulated only by a sparse patchwork of legislation. Pervasive poverty frequently led to the repayment of parental debt through the bonded servitude of their children. Satyarthi began working under the tutelage of Swami Agnivesh, an Arya Samaj

Kailash Satyarthi.

adherent and activist who advocated on behalf of women and children. He later broke away from the more religiously motivated activism of his mentor and in 1980 founded the nonprofit Bachpan Bachao Andolan (BBA; "Save the Childhood Movement"). Agnivesh, with whom Satyarthi retained an alternatingly close and antagonistic relationship, founded the more legislatively focused Bandhua Mukti Morcha (BMM; "Bonded Labour Liberation Front") in 1981.

The BBA took a radically confrontational approach, with members descending on guarded brick and carpet factories (often accompanied by police) and liberating children who had been forced into servitude by their parents in exchange for loans or by lenders hoping to recoup losses incurred by their parents. Satyarthi and his comrades were beaten on multiple occasions, and several members of the organization were assassinated in retribution. The BBA claimed to have freed thousands of children and by the 1990s had established several ashrams where the youths could reacclimate and begin their educations. Bal Mitra Gram (BMG), a program for "child friendly" villages in which child labour was banned and all children were enrolled in school, was launched in 2011.

Satyarthi urged the BBA toward international cooperation.His efforts led to the formation of the South Asian Coalition on Child Servitude (SACCS), which partnered NGOs and unions in nearby Bangladesh, Nepal, Pakistan, and Sri Lanka. In 1994 Satyarthi launched RugMark (now GoodWeave), an initiative to certify that carpets had not been manufactured by children. The organization was credited with major reductions in the use of child labor in the rug-making industry, though in India it drew criticism for accepting German funds owing to that country's competing carpet industry. Satyarthi also helped to catalyze the 1998 Global March Against Child Labor, a series of demonstrations and marches across some 100 countries in which more than seven million people participated. The movement resulted in the passage (1999) of the Convention Concerning the Prohibition and Immediate Action for the Elimination of the Worst Forms of Child Labour by the International Labour Organization (ILO) of the UN and coalesced into a permanent international collective. In 1999 Satyarthi was among the cofounders of the Global Campaign for Education, which championed education as a universal human right, and in 2001 he became a founding member of the UNESCO High-Level Group on Education for All.

Satyarthi's receipt of the Nobel Peace Prize with young Pakistani education reformer Malala Yousafzai in 2014 was heralded as a long-overdue acknowledgement of the human rights struggles of children. However, some Indian and Pakistani publications lambasted the Nobel committee's choice as a ponderously symbolic call to political and religious rapprochement between the two countries.

DRED SCOTT

(b. 1799–d. 1858)

In the 1840s an enslaved African American named Dred Scott sued for his freedom on the grounds that his residence on free soil in the United States had liberated him from the bonds of slavery. The U.S. Supreme Court's denial of Scott's plea in a landmark 1857 decision immediately became a violently divisive issue in national politics and served to push the country closer toward the outbreak of the American Civil War.

Scott was born about 1799 in Southampton County, Virginia. In the early 1830s he was sold by the Peter Blow family to Dr. John Emerson of Missouri. In 1834 Emerson began a series of moves as part of his service in the U.S. military. He took Scott from Missouri (a slave state) to Illinois (a free state) and finally into the Wisconsin Territory (a free territory under the provisions of the Missouri Compromise). During this period, Scott met and married Harriet Robinson, who became part of the Emerson household. In the early 1840s the Emersons (Dr. Emerson had married in 1838) and the Scotts returned to Missouri. Dr. Emerson died in 1843.

Dred Scott reportedly attempted to purchase his freedom from Emerson's widow, who refused the sale. In 1846, with the help of antislavery lawyers, Harriet and Dred Scott filed individual lawsuits for their freedom in Missouri. It was later agreed that only Dred's case would move forward; the decision in that case would apply to Harriet's case as well.

The Dred Scott case eventually reached the U.S. Supreme Court, which announced its controversial decision on March 6, 1857. Soon thereafter, however, members of the Blow family purchased both Dred and Harriet and freed them later in 1857. Dred died of tuberculosis the following year. Little is known of Harriet's life after that time.

PETE SEEGER

(b. 1919–d. 2014)

American singer Pete Seeger was one of the foremost figures of American folk music, spending decades popularizing his own brand of pop-folk both as a member of various groups and as a solo performer. His most famous songs—"If I Had a Hammer" and "Where Have All the Flowers Gone?"—became well-known pop-folk classics, and "Turn! Turn! Turn!" was a number-one hit for the Byrds.

Peter Seeger was born on May 3, 1919, in New York, New York. Both his father, a musicologist, and his mother, a violin teacher, were on the faculty of the Juilliard School. By the time he was a teenager, Seeger was adept at playing the ukulele, banjo, and guitar. His interest in folk music began when he visited a folk festival in the southern United States. After attending private schools in Manhattan, New York, Seeger enrolled at Harvard University in Cambridge, Massachusetts, where he studied sociology for two years.

In the late 1930s Seeger worked at the Archive of Folk Song in the Library of Congress and appeared on radio programs. He formed the Almanac Singers with Woody Guthrie, Lee Hays, and Millard Lampell in 1940 and released his debut album, *Talking Union and Other Union Songs* (1941), just as the United States was entering World War II. After serving in the U.S. Army, Seeger became the national director of People's Songs, Inc., where he used the term "hootenanny" to describe the group's pro-labor, antifascist songs. In the late 1940s, Seeger formed the Weavers, a quartet known for popularizing folk songs such as "On Top of Old Smokey" and "Goodnight Irene."

A performer with a strong social consciousness, Seeger was blacklisted for his alleged communist sympathies during the 1950s and was unable to get work on network television for 17 years. Throughout this period, he continued to sing and record, though his public appearances were limited. By the early 1960s, Seeger had found a new audience among young Americans who increasingly embraced his commitment to political and social change, especially his opposition to American involvement in the Vietnam War. Seeger's albums during that period, such as *We Shall Overcome* (1963) and *Songs of Struggle and Protest* 1930—1950 (1964), reflected his antiwar stance. The Byrds' recording of his song "Turn! Turn! Turn!," which became a number-one hit in 1965, was a fusion of folk and pop with lyrics adapted from a biblical passage in Ecclesiastes.

An accomplished storyteller, music historian, author, and instructor, Seeger educated and influenced many other performers. He played a pivotal role in popularizing the five-string banjo and introduced a variety of instruments into folk music. In the 1990s he continued to perform in concerts that typically included active audience participation.

Seeger was inducted into the Rock and Roll Hall of Fame in 1996, and the following year he received his first Grammy Award, for the album *Pete* (1996). In 2009 he won a second Grammy Award, for his album *At*

89 (2008), a collection that found the artist approaching his 90th birthday with undiminished spirit and hope. In 2010 he released *Tomorrow's Children*, an album dedicated to environmental awareness that Seeger recorded with the Rivertown Kids, a group of students who attended middle school near Seeger's home. The album won a Grammy Award for best musical album for children in 2011. Seeger's "musical autobiography," *Where Have All the Flowers Gone*, was published in 1993. He died on January 27, 2014, in New York City.

UPTON SINCLAIR

(b. 1878–d. 1968)

Deeply committed to social justice, Upton Sinclair believed in the power of literature to improve the human condition. He wrote more than 90 novels but is best remembered for *The Jungle* (1906), in which he describes the wretched sanitary and working conditions in the Chicago meat-packing industry.

Upton Beall Sinclair was born on September 20, 1878, in Baltimore, Maryland. He received a bachelor's degree from the City College of New York and did some graduate work at Columbia University. Sinclair published several unsuccessful novels before writing *The Jungle* for serialization in the socialist newspaper *Appeal to Reason*. Publication of the novel placed Sinclair in the ranks of the early 20th-century muckraking writers who used their pens to expose corruption and social injustice. Although it was intended to arouse sympathy for the conditions of the workers, the novel instead led to the passage of the first food inspection laws in the United States.

Sinclair published numerous other protest novels, including *King Coal* (1917) and *The Profits of Religion* (1918). He also wrote 11 historical novels known as the Lanny Budd series. One of these novels, *Dragon's Teeth*, won the 1943 Pulitzer Prize. Throughout his life Sinclair was a vocal supporter of socialism. He died in Bound Brook, New Jersey, on November 25, 1968.

ELLEN JOHNSON SIRLEAF

(b. 1938–d.)

On January 16, 2006, Ellen Johnson Sirleaf was sworn in as president of Liberia. In her inaugural speech she vowed to end civil strife and corruption, establish unity, and rebuild the country's devastated infrastructure. Johnson Sirleaf's victory in her country's 2005 presidential election was the culmination of a long and often hazardous political career and made the "Iron Lady" Africa's first elected woman head of state.

She was born in Monrovia, Liberia, on October 29, 1938, of mixed Gola and German heritage. (Her father was the first indigenous Liberian to sit in the national legislature.) She was educated at the College of West Africa in Monrovia and at age 17 married James Sirleaf (they were later divorced). In 1961 Johnson Sirleaf went to the United States to study economics and business administration. After obtaining a master's degree in public administration from Harvard University in 1971, she entered government service in Liberia.

Johnson Sirleaf served as assistant minister of finance (1972–73) under Pres. William Tolbert and as finance minister (1980–85) in Samuel K. Doe's military dictatorship. She became known for her personal financial integrity and clashed with both heads of state. During Doe's regime she was imprisoned twice and narrowly avoided execution. In the 1985 national election, she campaigned for a seat in the Senate while openly criticizing the military government, which led to her arrest and a 10-year prison sentence. She was released after a short time and was allowed to leave the country. During 12 years of exile in Kenya and the United States, she became an influential economist for the World Bank, Citibank Corp., and other international financial institutions. From 1992 to 1997 she was the director of the Regional Bureau for Africa of the United Nations Development Programme.

Johnson Sirleaf ran for president in the 1997 election, representing the Unity Party. She emphasized her financial experience, her noninvolvement in the civil war, and the personal qualities of compassion, sacrifice, and wisdom that she had developed as a mother of four. She

Ellen Johnson Sirleaf.

finished second to Charles Taylor and was forced back into exile when his government charged her with treason. By 1999 Liberia had again collapsed into civil war. Taylor was persuaded to go into exile in Nigeria in 2003, and Johnson Sirleaf returned to Liberia to chair the Commission on Good Governance, which oversaw preparations for democratic elections. In the runoff presidential election on November 8, 2005, she won 59.5 percent of the vote against retired association football (soccer) legend George Weah, who turned down a post in her administration but later issued a public statement of support.

With more than 15,000 UN peacekeepers in Liberia and unemployment running at 80 percent, the new president faced serious challenges. In her first 100 days in office, Johnson Sirleaf visited Nigeria and the United States to seek debt amelioration and aid from the international community, established a Truth and Reconciliation Commission to probe corruption and heal ethnic tensions, fired the entire staff of the Ministry of Finance, and issued a program for the expansion of girls' education. By late 2010 Liberia's entire debt had been erased, and Johnson Sirleaf had secured millions of dollars of foreign investment in the country.

Johnson Sirleaf was one of three recipients, along with Leymah Gbowee and Tawakkul Karman, of the 2011 Nobel Peace Prize for their efforts to further women's rights. Later in 2011 Johnson Sirleaf was reelected as Liberia's president.

ELIZABETH CADY STANTON

(b. 1815–d. 1902)

A pioneer in the modern quest for women's rights, Elizabeth Stanton helped to organize a political movement that demanded voting rights for women. She was a prominent leader in the campaign for what became the 19th Amendment to the U.S. Constitution.

Elizabeth Cady was born in Johnstown, New York, on November 12, 1815. She received a better education than most of her female peers. It was while studying law with her father, who later became a New York Supreme Court judge, that she became aware of the legal discrimination against women and took up the cause of women's rights. Cady also actively advocated the abolition of slavery and she opposed the use of liquor.

Cady married Henry Brewster Stanton in 1840 and the same year accompanied him to London for a world antislavery convention, where she met Lucretia Mott. Female delegates to the convention were refused recognition, and the two women became allies in the fight for women's rights.

Elizabeth Stanton circulated a petition that led to a statute recognizing the property rights of married women in New York. In 1848 she and Mott convened the first women's rights convention, held in Seneca Falls, New York. Stanton read a Declaration of Sentiments she had written that was modeled on the Declaration of Independence. The convention adopted numerous resolutions, including a demand for women's right to vote. Mott opposed this resolution and the convention was ridiculed in the press.

In 1869 Stanton founded the National Woman Suffrage Association and served as its president for the next 21 years. With Susan B. Anthony, Stanton edited and wrote much of *Revolution*, a weekly newspaper devoted to women's rights. With Matilda Joslyn Gage they also compiled the first three volumes of the six-volume *History of Woman Suffrage*. Stanton wrote and lectured extensively. In 1920 the 19th Amendment to the Constitution made Stanton's dream of woman suffrage a reality. Stanton died in New York City on October 26, 1902.

LINCOLN STEFFENS

(b. 1866–d. 1936)

Lincoln Steffens was an American journalist, lecturer, and political philosopher, a leading figure among the writers whom U.S. President Theodore Roosevelt called muckrakers.

After attending the University of California, Steffens studied psychology with Wilhelm Wundt in Leipzig and with Jean-Martin Charcot in Paris, which confirmed his basic positivist orientation. During nine years of New York City newspaper work ending in 1901, Steffens discovered abundant evidence of the corruption of politicians by businessmen seeking special privileges. In 1901 after he became managing editor of *McClure's* magazine, he began to publish the influential articles later collected as *The Shame of the Cities* (1906), a work closer to a documented sociological case study than to a sensational journalistic exposé.

Many nationwide lecture tours won Steffens recognition. He raised rather than answered questions, jolting his audience into awareness of the ethical paradox of private interest in public affairs by comic irony rather than by moral indignation. He revealed the shortcomings of the popular dogmas that connected economic success with moral worth, and national progress with individual self-interest.

The Mexican Revolution (1910–20) and the Russian Revolution of 1917 turned Steffens's attention from reform to revolution. After a trip to Petrograd (now St. Petersburg) in 1919, he wrote a friend, "I have seen the future; and it works." His unorthodoxy lost him his American audience during the 1920s; he continued to study revolutionary politics in Europe and became something of a legendary character for younger expatriates.

After the great success of his *Autobiography* (1931), he supported many communist activities but refused identification with any party or doctrine.

GLORIA STEINEM

(b. 1934–d.)

U.S. feminist, political activist, and editor Gloria Steinem was an advocate of the women's liberation movement during the late 20th century. She was the founder of *Ms.* magazine, through which she hoped to explore current issues from a feminist perspective.

Steinem was born on March 25, 1934, in Toledo, Ohio. When she was young she traveled with her parents in a house trailer. The couple divorced in 1946, and Gloria settled with her mother in Toledo. For the first time she was able to attend school on a regular basis. She was also responsible for taking care of her chronically depressed mother. During

Steinem's senior year of high school, she moved to Washington, D.C., to live with her older sister.

Steinem graduated from Smith College in 1956 and went to India on a scholarship. There she participated in nonviolent protests against government policy. Returning to the United States, she began working as a writer and journalist in New York City in 1960. Her 1963 article "I Was a Playboy Bunny," which related her experience as a waitress at Hugh Hefner's Playboy Club, brought her immediate notoriety. A few years later Steinem's work turned more political, and she began writing a column, "The City Politic," for *New York* magazine. After attending a meeting of a radical feminist group, the Redstockings, in 1968, her involvement in feminism strengthened. As a result, Steinem founded the National Women's Political Caucus, an organization dedicated to furthering women in politics, in July 1971 with Betty Friedan, Bella Abzug, and Shirley Chisholm. That same year she began developing *Ms.* magazine, which first appeared as an insert in the December issue of *New York*.

During the late 1970s and the '80s, Steinem became the spokesperson for the women's liberation movement. She helped found the Coalition of Labor Union Women, Voters for Choice, and Women Against Pornography. Her books include *Outrageous Acts and Everyday Rebellions* (1983), *Revolution from Within* (1992), and *Moving Beyond Words* (1994). Steinem was awarded the Presidential Medal of Freedom in 2013.

I. F. STONE

(b. 1907–d. 1989)

I. F. Stone, original name Isidor Feinstein, was a spirited and unconventional American journalist whose newsletter, *I.F. Stone's Weekly* (later *I.F. Stone's Bi-Weekly*), captivated readers with the author's unique blend of wit, erudition, humanitarianism, and pointed political commentary.

Feinstein worked on newspapers while still in high school. After studying at the University of Pennsylvania (1924—d. 27), he worked for the *Philadelphia Inquirer*. Feinstein moved to New York City and worked for both the *New York Post* (1933–39) and the *Philadelphia Record*. He changed his name to I. F. Stone in 1937. In 1938 Stone became an associate editor of the liberal weekly the *Nation*, eventually becoming its editor (1940–46). During this period he also worked as a reporter for *PM*, an experimental liberal daily. When *PM* folded in 1948, Stone worked for the *New York Star*, then went back to the *Post*, and then to the *New York Daily Compass*. When this paper folded in 1952, Stone decided to start his own weekly.

From the outset *I.F. Stone's Weekly* (1953–67; *I.F. Stone's Bi-Weekly*, 1967–71) had an influence far greater than the size of its readership. Among early subscribers were Albert Einstein, Bertrand Russell, and Eleanor Roosevelt. The newsletter, staffed only by Stone and his wife, was researched, written, and edited by Stone. It set high journalistic standards and could be found in the homes of some of the most prominent politicians, academicians, and journalists in the nation.

Stone became known for his espousal of unpopular causes long before they became popular with the liberal establishment. He was an early supporter of civil rights and an early opponent of President Harry S. Truman's Cold War policies and of McCarthyism. He was also an early opponent of the United States' involvement in the Vietnam War.

Stone also wrote numerous books, including *The Court Disposes* (1937), about the U.S. Supreme Court; *Business as Usual: The First Year of Defense* (1941), an indictment of the U.S. military's unpreparedness for World War II; and *Underground to Palestine* (1946), detailing his involvement with the struggle of Jewish refugees to reach a homeland. Collections of Stone's columns were published in *The Haunted Fifties* (1963), *In a Time of Torment* (1967), and *Polemics and Prophecies, 1967—1970* (1971).

AUNG SAN SUU KYI

(b. 1945–d.)

The leader of the opposition to the ruling military government in Myanmar (formerly Burma), Aung San Suu Kyi brought international attention to the struggle for human rights and the restoration of democracy in her country. An advocate of nonviolent protest, she was under house arrest in Yangon when she was awarded the 1991 Nobel Peace Prize.

Aung San Suu Kyi was born on June 19, 1945, in Rangoon (now Yangon). Her father, Aung San, was regarded as the founder of modern Burma after he negotiated the country's independence from Britain. He was assassinated in 1947. Her mother, Khin Kyi, a prominent diplomat, was named ambassador to India in 1960. After studying in India, Aung San Suu Kyi earned a bachelor's degree at the University of Oxford, where she met her future husband, British scholar Michael Aris. She subsequently worked for the United Nations in New York City and in 1985–86 was a visiting scholar in Southeast Asian studies at Kyoto University in Japan. She returned to Burma in April 1988 to care for her ailing mother, who died later that year.

By the end of 1988 Suu Kyi was heavily involved in the protest movements sweeping the country against the brutal rule of military strongman Ne Win. She initiated a nonviolent struggle for democracy and human rights, helping to form the National League for Democracy (NLD), a political party. In July 1989 the military government of newly named Myanmar placed her under house arrest. The military offered to free her if she agreed to leave Myanmar, but she refused to do so until the country was returned to civilian government. In the 1990 parliamentary elections, the NLD won more than 80 percent of the seats that were contested. The military government ignored the election results, however, and did not allow the new parliament to meet. *Freedom from Fear: And Other Writings*, a collection of her articles and speeches edited by Aris, was published in 1991 following the Nobel Prize announcement. Suu Kyi was eventually freed from house arrest in July 1995.

Despite her release, Suu Kyi was officially barred from leading the NLD, and her movements remained restricted. In 1998 she announced the formation of a representative committee that she declared was the country's legitimate ruling parliament. The military regime once again placed her under house arrest from September 2000 to May 2002.

Following clashes between the NLD and pro-government demonstrators in 2003, the government returned Suu Kyi to house arrest. The international community continued to call for her release. In May 2009, shortly before her sentence was to be completed, an intruder (a U.S.

Aung San Suu Kyi.

citizen) entered her compound and spent two nights there. Suu Kyi was arrested and convicted of breaching the terms of her house arrest.

It was believed that this conviction was to prevent her from participating in the 2010 multiparty parliamentary elections—the first since 1990. Indeed, in 2010 new election laws barred individuals convicted of a crime from participating. They also prohibited anyone who was married to a foreign national (as she was) from running for office. In support of Suu Kyi, the NLD refused to reregister under these new laws (as was required) and was disbanded. In the November 2010 elections, the government parties won an overwhelming majority of legislative seats amid widespread allegations of voter fraud. Six days after the elections, Suu Kyi was released from house arrest. She vowed to continue her opposition to military rule.

Government restrictions on Suu Kyi's activities were further relaxed during 2011. She was allowed to meet with Myanmar's new civilian president as well as the prime minister of Thailand and the U.S. Secretary of State. Meanwhile, rules on political participation were eased, and the NLD was officially reinstated. Suu Kyi was permitted to run for parliament in elections in April 2012. She easily won a seat representing Yangon. Later in 2012 she traveled outside Myanmar for the first time since 1988. On a tour of Europe, Suu Kyi gave the acceptance speech for her 1991 Nobel Prize in Oslo, Norway, and she addressed the British Parliament in London, England.

Suu Kyi and the NLD campaigned vigorously for what turned out to be the country's first openly contested parliamentary election. The polling, held in early November 2015, produced a major victory for the NLD, which was able to secure large-enough majorities of seats in both legislative chambers to allow the party to form the next national government.

BLESSED MOTHER TERESA

(b. 1910–d. 1997)

One of the most highly respected women in the world, Mother Teresa was internationally known for her charitable work among the victims of poverty and neglect—particularly in the slums of Calcutta (now Kolkata), India. In 1979 she was awarded the Nobel Peace Prize in recognition of her humanitarian efforts. She also received the Jewel of India, India's highest civilian medal, as well as honorary degrees from academic institutions worldwide.

Mother Teresa's original name was Agnes Gonxha Bojaxhiu. She was born in Skopje, Macedonia, of Albanian ancestry. She was baptized there on August 27, 1910. At the age of 18 she decided to become a nun, and she ventured to Dublin, Ireland, to join the Sisters of Loretto, a community of Irish nuns with a mission in the Archdiocese of Calcutta. After a year she left Ireland to join the Loretto convent in Darjeeling, India. Her work included a teaching post at St. Mary's High School in Calcutta, where she witnessed the destitution that marked the city's slums. In 1946, Mother Teresa later recalled, she received a "call within a call," experiencing what she considered divine inspiration to begin a new chapter in her life, one devoted to helping the sick and impoverished. In that year she founded a new religious order, the Missionaries of Charity. This new order was officially recognized by the Roman Catholic Church in 1950. The order organized schools and opened centers to treat the blind, the aged, lepers, the disabled, and the dying. In 1952 Mother Teresa founded the Nirmal Hriday ("Place for the Pure of Heart") in Calcutta—a home to which terminally ill people could go to die with dignity. Despite her own religious beliefs, Mother Teresa demanded that the volunteers and workers at the Nirmal Hriday respect the religious beliefs of those who came for sanctuary in their last days. Under her guidance a leper colony called Shanti Nagar ("Town of Peace") was built near Asansol in West Bengal.

In the years after its inception, the Missionaries of Charity established centers throughout the world. In 1968 Pope Paul VI called Mother Teresa to Rome to found a home there. In 1971 he awarded her the first Pope John XXIII Peace Prize. Under Mother Teresa's direction, the Missionaries of Charity established orphanages, nutrition centers, health care centers, and schools, bringing relief to diverse people, from impoverished blacks in South Africa to Christians and Muslims in war-torn Lebanon in the early 1980s to the poor in New York City's Harlem section.

After Mother Teresa suffered a heart attack in 1989, she was fitted

Mother Teresa.

with a pacemaker. Because of her health problems, she resigned as superior general of the order in April 1990. She was voted out of retirement by the members, however, and returned to her post in September. In early 1997 Mother Teresa began to suffer from increasingly severe health problems, including heart and kidney disorders. Only a few months after stepping down permanently from leadership of the Missionaries of Charity, she died of a heart attack in Calcutta on September 5, 1997, at the age of 87. At the time of her death, missions of Mother Teresa's order existed in more than 90 countries and had grown to include some 4,000 nuns and hundreds of thousands of lay workers and volunteers. Sister Nirmala, a longtime member of the order, succeeded her as head of the organization.

Within two years of Mother Teresa's death, the process to declare her a saint was begun, with special authorization from Pope John Paul II. She was beatified on October 19, 2003, reaching the ranks of the blessed in the shortest time in the history of the Roman Catholic Church.

MARGARET THATCHER

(b. 1925–d. 2013)

The first woman to be elected prime minister of the United Kingdom was Margaret Thatcher, who was also the first woman to hold such a post in the history of Europe. The first prime minister since the 1820s to win three consecutive elections, Thatcher held office longer than any other 20th century British leader.

Margaret Hilda Roberts was born on October 13, 1925, at Grantham, Lincolnshire, England. She ran errands for the Conservative Party in the 1935 election and maintained this association as a member of the Oxford University Conservative Association. A science graduate of Oxford, she worked as a research chemist.

Her first attempts to win a seat in Parliament were in 1950 and 1951. She lost both elections. In 1951 she married businessman Denis Thatcher. To equip herself for politics she began studying law, with an emphasis on taxation and patent policy. In 1959 Thatcher ran again for Parliament from a safe Conservative north London district and won. She served as secretary to the Ministry of Pensions and Insurance from 1961 to 1964 and as secretary of state for education and science in Edward Heath's Cabinet from 1970 to 1974. After the Conservative Party's loss of two general elections in 1974, she followed Heath as head of the party. When the Conservative Party won the 1979 elections, Thatcher became prime minister.

She belonged to the most conservative wing of her party, advocating cuts in taxation, an end to government controls, and reductions in public expenditures. Her early policies caused widespread unemployment and a number of business bankruptcies. A popular victory in the Falkland Islands conflict of 1982, however, led to a landslide victory in the 1983 elections. Her stature as a world leader increased when she visited the Soviet Union in March 1987, less than three months before she won another remarkable victory.

Thatcher's declared objective was to "destroy socialism." Her "unfinished revolution" to reshape British political, economic, and social life—mainly through privatization—was labeled Thatcherism. Because of her strong leadership, she was called the Iron Lady. She supported the NATO alliance and the European Communities, though her opposition to "Europe 1992" integration adversely affected her popularity and helped lead to her resignation in November 1990.

Despite her official withdrawal from office, Thatcher continued to cast a shadow over world politics. She was especially outspoken in her opposition to Britain's participation in several institutions of the European Union, and she outlined her position in her book *Statecraft: Strategies for a Changing World* (2002). In 1991 she established the Margaret Thatcher Foundation, which promotes democracy and free markets, particularly in the formerly communist countries of Eastern and Central Europe. She was made a peeress for life in the House of Lords in 1992, and in 1995 Queen Elizabeth II conferred upon her the Order of the Garter, the highest British civil and military honor. In March 2002, after suffering a series of minor strokes, Thatcher announced her retirement from public life. She died on April 8, 2013, in London, England.

NORMAN THOMAS

(b. 1884–d. 1968)

As clergyman, social reformer, and frequent candidate for political office, Norman Thomas was often called the "conscience of America." For 40 years he shaped the views of the socialist party in the United States and kept the party free of communist influence. He ran for the presidency of the United States six times, beginning in 1928. Although he never won, he succeeded in keeping his progressive ideas before the public.

Thomas was born in Marion, Ohio, on November 20, 1884. He graduated from Union Theological Seminary in New York City in 1911 and became a Presbyterian clergyman. At his East Harlem Church and in the American Parish settlement house, the problems of poverty led him to support the social gospel that was then popular. By 1918 he was a socialist. He resigned as minister of the East Harlem Church that year to devote himself to politics. For a time he was an editor of the influential weekly, the *Nation*. In 1920 he was one of the people who started the American Civil Liberties Union. He ran for governor of New York in 1924 and for mayor of New York City in 1925 and 1929, losing each time.

Among his writings are *The Test of Freedom*, published in 1954, and *Socialism Re-examined* (1963). Thomas died in Huntington, New York, on December 19, 1968. Throughout his life he remained a staunch defender of individual rights.

SOJOURNER TRUTH

(b. 1797–d. 1883)

Children, I talk to God and God talks to me!" This was the usual opening of abolitionist speaker and civil rights pioneer Sojourner Truth. Her real name was Isabella Van Wagener, and she was born a slave in Ulster County, New York, in about 1797.

The circumstances surrounding her liberation are uncertain, but her surname was taken from Isaac Van Wagener, who was reportedly the last of several masters and the man who freed her in 1827. She moved to New York City, where she worked as a domestic servant. There she became closely associated with a Christian evangelist named Elijah Pierson. In 1843 she left New York, took the name Sojourner Truth, and began a life of preaching that carried her throughout the Northern states. Her growing reputation and personal magnetism drew large crowds wherever she appeared. She supported herself by selling copies of *The Narrative of Sojourner Truth*, which she had dictated to a friend.

She was a powerful foe of slavery, and in the 1850s she added the women's rights movement to her causes. During the Civil War she served as a counselor to freed slaves in Washington, D.C. Her later years were spent helping freed slaves and lecturing in the North. She died at her home in Battle Creek, Michigan, on November 26, 1883.

HARRIET TUBMAN

(b. 1820–d. 1913)

A runaway slave herself, Harriet Tubman helped so many blacks escape to freedom that she became known as the "Moses of her people." During the Civil War she served the Union Army as a nurse, cook, scout, and spy.

Harriet Tubman was born Araminta Ross about 1820 on a plantation near Bucktown, Maryland. She was one of 11 children of a slave couple. At seven she was hired out to do housework and to care for white children on nearby farms. Later she became a field hand. While still a teenager, she was struck on the head by an overseer. As a result of the blow, she fell asleep suddenly several times a day for the rest of her life. Hard work toughened her, and before she was 19 she was as strong as the men with whom she worked.

In 1844 Ross married a free black, John Tubman. She left him in 1849, when her fear of being sold farther south spurred her to escape. She traveled at night, aided by the Underground Railroad, a secret network of people who helped fugitive slaves reach the Northern states and Canada.

In Philadelphia, Pennsylvania, and later at Cape May, New Jersey, Tubman worked as a maid in hotels and clubs. By December 1850 she had saved enough money to make the first of 19 daring journeys back into the South to lead other slaves out of bondage. In 1851 she returned for her husband but found he had remarried.

Tubman worked closely with the Underground Railroad. Often she left fugitives in the care of other "conductors" after leading them part of the way herself. She maintained strict discipline during the perilous journeys to the North. If a runaway lagged behind or lost faith and wished to turn back, she forced him on at gunpoint. Before the Civil War she freed her parents and most of her brothers and sisters as well as hundreds of other slaves.

Slaveowners were constantly on the lookout for Tubman and offered large rewards for her capture, but they never succeeded in seizing her or any of the slaves she helped escape during her work for the Underground Railroad. Much later in life she proudly recalled: "I never ran my train off the track, and I never lost a passenger."

Tubman supported her parents and worked to raise money for her missions into the South. She spoke at abolitionist meetings and at women's rights assemblies, often concealing her name for protection from slave hunters. Her forceful leadership led the white abolitionist John Brown to refer to her admiringly as "General" Tubman. She helped Brown plan his October 1859 raid on the federal arsenal at Harpers Ferry, West Virginia, and promised that many of the slaves she had freed would join him. Only illness prevented her from fighting at Brown's side during the raid itself.

During the Civil War Tubman served the Union Army. She nursed and cooked for white soldiers, for example, as well as for sick and starving blacks who sought protection behind Union lines. She acted as both a scout and a spy, often bravely leading Union raiding parties into Confederate territory. For this, she won the respect of many grateful Union officers. But her efforts went unrewarded. She spent many decades trying to collect 1,800 dollars in back pay from the federal government, which refused to recognize her wartime services. When in 1899 she was finally granted a pension, it was given to her not for her own deeds but because she was the widow of Nelson Davis, a Civil War veteran whom she had married in 1869.

Tubman had settled in Auburn, New York, in 1857. After the Civil War she fed, sheltered, and nursed any blacks who came to her home for aid. Although she was in poor health, she worked to support two schools for freedmen in the South and continued to provide a home for her parents. She often had to borrow money for food from friends who gratefully remembered her heroic exploits in the fight against slavery. After many years of effort, she was able to sponsor a home for needy blacks in Auburn, which was opened in 1908.

Scenes in the *Life of Harriet Tubman*, her first biography, published in 1869, was written by Sarah Hopkins Bradford to raise money for her support. In subsequent editions the title was changed to *Harriet Tubman: the Moses of Her People*. Harriet Tubman died in Auburn on March 10, 1913, and was buried with military honors. A year later the city unveiled a tablet in her memory.

DESMOND TUTU

(b. 1931–d.)

South African Anglican bishop and outspoken social activist Desmond Tutu received the Nobel Peace Prize in 1984 for his efforts to bring a nonviolent end to apartheid, South Africa's policy of racial segregation.

Desmond Mpilo Tutu was born on October 7, 1931, in Klerksdorp, Transvaal Province, South Africa. His father was a teacher, and after graduating from the University of South Africa in 1954, Tutu himself taught at a high school for three years. Resigning his post in 1957, he began to study theology and was ordained an Anglican parish priest in 1961. He later moved to London, where he earned an M.A. from Kings College and from 1972 to 1975 was an assistant director for the World Council of Churches. He served as dean of St. Mary's Cathedral in Johannesburg from 1975 to 1976—the first black to hold that position.

In 1976 Tutu was named bishop of Lesotho. Two years later he accepted an appointment as the general secretary of the South African Council of Churches and became a leading spokesperson for the rights of black South Africans. Gaining national and international attention, he emphasized peaceful means of protesting apartheid and encouraged the application of economic pressure by countries dealing with South Africa. *The Divine Intention*, a collection of his lectures, was published in 1982, followed by *Hope and Suffering*, a collection of his sermons, in 1983. In presenting him the Nobel Peace Prize, the Nobel Committee described Tutu as "a unifying leader."

In 1985 Tutu became Johannesburg's first black Anglican bishop, and a year later he was elected the first black archbishop of Cape Town, thus becoming head of South Africa's 1,600,000-member Anglican church; he stepped down as head of the church in 1996, becoming archbishop emeritus. In 1995 South African President Nelson Mandela appointed Tutu head of the Truth and Reconciliation Commission, which investigated allegations of human rights abuses during the apartheid era. Since 1987 Tutu has been chancellor of the University of the Western Cape in Bellville, South Africa.

Tutu published *God Has a Dream: A Vision of Hope for Our Time*, a collection of personal reflections, in 2004. In 2009 he was awarded the U.S. Presidential Medal of Freedom.

Desmond Tutu.

WILLIAM TYNDALE

(b. 1492–d. 1536)

During the Protestant Reformation, English scholar William Tyndale translated part of the Bible from Greek and Hebrew into English. Unlike Roman Catholics, Protestants believe that the Bible is the sole source of religious authority. For this reason, Protestant reformers believed that it is important for people to be able to read the Bible for themselves in their own language. The Roman Catholic Church insisted, however, that it alone had the authority to interpret the meaning of the Bible for the people. Roman Catholic authorities suppressed Tyndale's translation and ultimately had him executed. His work nevertheless became the model for a series of English biblical translations, which culminated in the celebrated King James Version, or Authorized Version (1611).

Tyndale was born about 1490–94, near Gloucestershire, England. He was educated at the University of Oxford and became an instructor at the University of Cambridge. At Cambridge in 1521 he fell in with a group of humanist scholars who were meeting at the White Horse Inn. Tyndale became convinced that the Bible alone should determine the practices and doctrines of the church. He decided to translate the Bible into English to make it accessible to all English believers.

Church authorities in England prevented Tyndale from translating the Bible there. With financial support from wealthy London merchants, he went to Germany in 1524. There he completed an English translation of the New Testament in July 1525. He had it printed in Germany, first at Cologne and, when Roman Catholic authorities there suppressed it, at Worms. In 1526 the first copies of his translation reached England, where it was soon banned.

Tyndale then began work on an Old Testament translation. He published English-language versions of the five books of the Pentateuch in Marburg, Germany, in 1530. Before he was able to complete the rest of his translation, however, he was captured in Antwerp (now in Belgium). Tyndale was executed on October 6, 1536, at Vilvoorde (now in Belgium).

At the time of his death, several thousand copies of his New Testament had been printed. Today, two complete volumes and a fragment are all that remain.

Tyndale was not the first person to translate the Bible into English. John Wycliffe and his followers had produced the first complete English-language version of the Bible in 1382. However, Tyndale's translation was highly influential. It was the first part of the Bible to be printed in English (as opposed to copied out by hand). Tyndale's greatest achievement lay in striking a balance between the needs of scholarship, simplicity of expression, and literary gracefulness—all in a uniform style of language. Tyndale's style of biblical translation served as the model for all subsequent English versions of the Bible for nearly 400 years.

VOLTAIRE

(b. 1694–d. 1778)

In his 84 years Voltaire was historian and essayist, playwright and storyteller, poet and philosopher, wit and pamphleteer, wealthy businessman and practical economic reformer. Yet he is remembered best as an advocate of human rights. True to the spirit of the Enlightenment, he denounced organized religion and established himself as a proponent of rationality.

Voltaire was born François-Marie Arouet on November 21, 1694, in Paris. At 16 he became a writer. He wrote witty verse mocking the royal authorities. For this he was imprisoned in the Bastille for 11 months. About this time he began calling himself Voltaire.

Another dispute in 1726 led to exile in England for two years. On his return to Paris he staged several unsuccessful dramas and the enormously popular *Zaïre*. He wrote a life of Swedish king Charles XII, and in 1734 he published *Philosophical Letters*, a landmark in the history of thought. The letters, denouncing religion and government, caused a scandal that forced him to flee Paris. He took up residence in the palace of Madame du Châtelet, with whom he lived and traveled

Voltaire.

until her death in 1749.

In 1750 Voltaire went to Berlin at the invitation of Prussia's Frederick the Great. Three years later, after a quarrel with the king, he left and settled in Geneva, Switzerland. After five years his strong opinions forced another move, and he bought an estate at Ferney, France, on the Swiss border. By this time he was a celebrity, renowned throughout Europe. Visitors of note came from everywhere to see him and to discuss his work with him. Voltaire returned to Paris on February 10, 1778, to direct his play *Irene*. His health suddenly failed, and he died on May 30.

Candide, the strongly anti-Romantic comic novel, is the work by Voltaire most read today. His other writings include *Zadig* (1747), *The Century of Louis XIV* (1751), *Micromégas* (1752), *The Russian Empire under Peter the Great* (1759–63), *The Philosophical Dictionary* (1764), and *Essay on Morals* (1756).

LECH WAŁĘSA

(b. 1943–d.)

Solidarity, Poland's first independent trade union under a communist regime, was founded by Lech Wałęsa in 1980. He gained recognition around the world as the leader of millions of Poland's workers. In an attempt to crush the union, the government imposed martial law on December 13, 1981, an act that only enhanced Wałęsa's reputation. He was awarded the Nobel Peace Prize in 1983.

Wałęsa was born in Popowo, Poland, on September 29, 1943. His father was a carpenter, and young Wałęsa received only elementary schooling followed by vocational training. In 1967 he went to work as an electrician at the Lenin Shipyard in Gdańsk. In 1970 there were worker riots against higher food prices. Many of the demonstrators were gunned down by government troops.

On August 14, 1980, during more antigovernment protests, Wałęsa urged the workers to strike. When strikers in other factories asked him to continue the strike in solidarity with them, he agreed. An inter-factory strike committee was formed and a general strike proclaimed. On August 31 the government agreed to permit the formation of independent unions. The strike committee was transformed into Solidarity. After the government imposed martial law in 1981, Solidarity was outlawed and most of its leaders arrested. Wałęsa was detained for nearly a year.

It was the re-legalization of Solidarity as a trade union in April 1989 and the agreement to hold partially free parliamentary elections that appeared to open the door for the radical reforms that influenced other countries of the Soviet bloc in their effort to challenge the communist system. Solidarity candidates scored a stunning victory in June elections, and in August a prominent member became premier—the first instance of a non-communist being chosen head of a communist nation in Eastern Europe.

In November Wałęsa visited the United States, where he addressed a joint session of Congress. A split in Solidarity was prompted by Wałęsa's criticism of the government. In December 1990 he was elected president of Poland, succeeding Gen. Wojciech Jaruzelski. After serving one term, he was defeated by ex-communist Aleksander Kwasniewski in the November 1995 presidential election.

WILLIAM WALLACE

(b. 1270?–d. 1305)

The Scottish national hero William Wallace as a young man killed an Englishman who insulted him. For this he was outlawed. He then collected a band of followers and began a struggle against the English rule of King Edward I.

Gradually the number of his followers grew. Wallace defeated and almost destroyed the English army at Stirling on September 11, 1297, drove the enemy entirely out of Scotland, and devastated the whole northern part of England. As a reward Wallace was knighted and proclaimed guardian of Scotland. Edward soon led a new and larger English army against him, and on July 22, 1298, Wallace's forces were overpowered in the battle of Falkirk. Wallace was later captured and taken to London. There he was executed as a traitor on August 23, 1305.

Wallace had failed to free his country from the yoke of England, but he had inspired others to carry on the struggle. A few years later Scotland's independence was temporarily secured under Robert Bruce.

EARL WARREN

(b. 1891–d. 1974)

As chief justice of the Supreme Court of the United States from 1953 to 1969, Earl Warren presided during a period of sweeping changes in U.S. constitutional law, especially in the areas of race relations, criminal procedure, and legislative apportionment. Warren is also remembered for heading a committee that investigated the 1963 assassination of President John F. Kennedy.

Warren was born on March 19, 1891, in Los Angeles, California. He was educated at the University of California, Berkeley, earning a bachelor's degree in 1912 and a law degree in 1914. He practiced in a local law office until the United States entered World War I, when he joined the Army and served as a bayonet instructor.

From 1925 to 1939 Warren served as district attorney for Alameda County, California, where he became nationally known for his no-nonsense attitude and his insistence that law officials act fairly. While serving as attorney general of California (1939–43), Warren—in the name of national security—supervised the controversial relocation of more than 100,000 Japanese Americans during World War II. He was elected governor of the state for three terms (1943–53), supporting issues such as prison reform, educational and health-care system improvements, and equal pay for equal work.

Warren's only defeat at the polls came in the 1948 presidential election, when he was the running mate of Republican Thomas Dewey. Warren, putting aside his own presidential aspirations, helped Dwight D. Eisenhower win the Republican nomination in 1952 by swinging the California delegation in his favor. As president, Eisenhower nominated Warren interim chief justice of the U.S. Supreme Court in 1953, and the Senate confirmed him in 1954.

In his first term on the bench, Warren spoke for a unanimous court in the leading school-desegregation case, *Brown vs. Board of Education of Topeka* (1954), declaring unconstitutional the separation of public-school children according to race. Rejecting the "separate but equal" doctrine that had prevailed since 1896, Warren stated that "separate educational facilities are inherently unequal." Although the composition of the Court changed throughout his years of leadership, Warren—through his skill at finding common ground and his ability to foster communication between members—was able to keep all decisions about racial segregation unanimous, sending powerful messages to the public.

As he had throughout his career, Warren continued to support the autonomy of law enforcement officials while also believing that suspects have a right to fair treatment. *Mapp vs. Ohio* (1961) prevented prosecutors from using evidence seized in illegal searches, and the landmark *Miranda vs. State of Arizona* (1966) ruled that police, before questioning a criminal suspect, must inform him of his rights to remain silent and to have counsel present (appointed for him if he is unable to afford representation) and that a confession obtained in defiance of these requirements is inadmissible in court. *Terry vs. Ohio* (1968) helped law enforcers by expanding their ability to stop and frisk people suspected of having weapons.

Although hesitant to take on the assignment, Warren agreed in late November 1963 to President Lyndon B. Johnson's request to head a committee looking into both the assassination of Kennedy and the murder of the presumed assassin, Lee Harvey Oswald. The report of the Warren Commission—concluding that Oswald acted alone—was submitted in September 1964 and was published later that year. Historians continue to study the document, and many have expressed doubts about its accuracy and consistency.

Warren retired from the Supreme Court in spring 1969 and spent his remaining years traveling, delivering speeches, and writing his memoirs (published in 1977). He died on July 9, 1974, in Washington, D.C.

GEORGE WASHINGTON

(b. 1732–d. 1799)

Many United States presidents were honored for their great achievements, and George Washington's achievements distinguished him as the Father of His Country. Washington was commander in chief of the Continental Army during the American Revolution, chairman of the convention that wrote the United States Constitution, and the first president of the United States. He led the people who transformed the United States from a British colony into a self-governing nation. His ideals of liberty and democracy set a standard for future presidents and for the entire country.

George's father died in 1743, and his property was divided among his nearest heirs. Ferry Farm was left to George's mother, Mary Ball Washington. George's half brother, Lawrence, inherited Epsewasson, and his other half brother, Augustine, inherited Wakefield. Lawrence married Anne Fairfax, a neighbor, and added her adjoining land to the property at Epsewasson. He renamed the estate Mount Vernon, in honor of Adm. Edward Vernon, the British naval officer under whom he served in the West Indies.

After his father's death, George went to live with Augustine at Wakefield and attended Henry Williams's school, one of the best schools in Virginia. By age 15 George was skilled in mathematics and mapmaking and developed an interest in practical surveying.

In 1748 George went to live with his other half brother, Lawrence, at Mount Vernon. There he met Lord Thomas Fairfax, a cousin of Anne Fairfax. Lord Fairfax owned more than five million acres (two million hectares) in Virginia, and he hired George to help survey his land beyond the Blue Ridge Mountains. Surveying was difficult and dangerous work, but George adapted well and excelled at his new profession. On July 20, 1749, through Lord Fairfax's influence, George Washington was appointed surveyor of Culpeper County, his first public office. Through his experiences as a surveyor, Washington became more knowledgeable and resourceful about the land and gained an enthusiasm for colonizing the West.

During the years he lived with Lawrence and his family at Mount Vernon, Washington heard many stories of his brother's experiences in the British Navy. These tales inspired Washington to pursue a military career. When Lawrence died in July 1752, Washington inherited Mount Vernon, thus becoming a landowner. In November 1752 Lieutenant Governor Robert Dinwiddie of Virginia appointed Washington adjutant, or assistant, officer for the southern district of Virginia. The following year, Dinwiddie made Washington a major of an army militia and sent him with a message to the French commander of Fort Le Boeuf (now Waterford, Pennsylvania). The message demanded that the French abandon their forts on the British territory between Lake Ontario and the Ohio River. Washington delivered the message and returned to Virginia in January 1754 with a full report on the French army's plan to take possession of the Ohio River valley. After studying Washington's report, Dinwiddie convinced the British government that the French posed a serious threat to the British colonies. Washington's perilous journey had taken 10 weeks, and twice he nearly lost his life. Once, a Native American shot at him from close range; a few days later, Washington was thrown from a raft into an ice-filled stream.

George Washington.

In April 1754 Washington was made lieutenant colonel of the militia. He was ordered to lead nearly 200 troops to take possession of Fort Duquesne, which was located in the Ohio River valley where the Allegheny and Monongahela rivers meet. The French had a strong hold on Fort Duquesne, and Washington's small militia was unable to overtake the fort. He located an area nearby at Great Meadows (now Confluence, Pennsylvania) and built Fort Necessity for his army. On May 28, 1754, Washington's troops and their Native American allies ambushed and killed or captured all of a French scouting party near Fort Necessity. The French commander, Coulon de Jumonville, was killed in the attack, and this encounter contributed to the start of the French and Indian War.

Washington's skillful maneuvers in the ambush against the French scouting party was recognized by his superior officers, and he was immediately promoted to colonel. He was given command of a small army of Virginia and North Carolina troops and Native American allies. In July 1754 Washington's troops attacked the French forces at Fort Duquesne, but the French and the Native Americans loyal to the French outnumbered them and forced Washington to surrender. The French allowed Washington's army to return to Virginia after he released the French prisoners of war. Despite his defeat, Washington was commended for his valiant efforts against the French by the Virginia House of Burgesses, the representative assembly in colonial Virginia.

In February 1755 Washington was sent to serve as aide to British Major General Edward Braddock in another offensive against Fort Duquesne. Braddock acknowledged and respected Washington's merit and leadership abilities. He allowed Washington to advise and express his opinions on military strategies. On July 9, 1755, French forces ambushed and defeated Braddock's forces, and Braddock was killed in the battle. Washington displayed initiative and poise as he assembled the remaining troops and led them back to Virginia.

In August 1755 Lieutenant Governor Dinwiddie appointed Washington commander of all Virginia militia forces. Virginia expanded its forces to 1,000 soldiers, and Washington directed the patrols and defense of the entire 400-mile (640-kilometer) western frontier. In 1758 Washington accompanied British General John Forbes and finally defeated the French at Fort Duquesne, which was burned to the ground by the retreating French troops. Forbes established Fort Pitt (now Pittsburgh, Pennsylvania) on the site, and Washington resigned from the army with the honorary rank of brigadier general. While serving in the final campaign against Fort Duquesne, Washington was elected to the Virginia House of Burgesses.

On January 6, 1759, Washington married a young widow, Martha Dandridge Custis. Martha had two children from her previous marriage—a son named John and a daughter, Martha, who was called Patsy. The Custis estate covered nearly 15,000 acres (6,000 hectares) of land near Williamsburg, Virginia. From the time of his marriage, Washington supervised both Mount Vernon and the Custis estate, thus becoming one of the wealthiest and most industrious landowners in Virginia. In addition to the prosperous farming, planting, and industry on his estates, Washington continued to serve in the Virginia House of Burgesses. During its sessions, Washington attended dances and banquets hosted by other members of Virginia's aristocracy, and in return, he hosted picnics and dinner parties at Mount Vernon.

After the French and Indian War ended in 1763, Great Britain was in debt as a result of war expenditures. A stronger British military was needed to protect the increased British possessions in the colonies acquired during the war. Parliament, the legislative body of Great Britain's government, implemented several acts aimed at generating revenue from the colonies to alleviate these costs. The Stamp Act of 1765 imposed a tax on newspapers, legal documents, and other business papers. The colonists considered this act an intrusion on their rights, and Great Britain repealed it in 1766. However, Great Britain continued to regulate the colonies in matters of taxation and legislation with the Townshend Acts of 1767, which placed taxes on imported British commodities. In April 1769 Washington presented a plan to the House of Burgesses for boycotting British-made goods.

Hostilities between the colonists and the British government escalated after the Boston Massacre on March 5, 1770, when British soldiers fired on a group of angry citizens in Boston who were threatening the soldiers. Colonists protested vehemently over British taxation without colonial representation in Parliament. On December 16, 1773, a group of colonists threw 342 chests of tea into Boston Harbor to protest a tea tax.

This rebellion, known as the Boston Tea Party, prompted Great Britain to retaliate by passing the Intolerable Acts in 1774. These acts were a series of punitive laws directed against the colonies; among other things, they called for the closing of Boston Harbor and the installation of a military government in Massachusetts. The acts also forced the colonists to provide housing for British troops in colonial dwellings.

Washington's political career expanded as dissension grew between the colonists and Great Britain. He believed that the British had attacked the rights of the colonists with heavy taxes and oppressive laws, and he was ready to defend these rights. In May 1774 Washington and other Virginia legislators signed the resolutions calling for a Continental Congress. He was elected to the Virginia delegation that attended the First Continental Congress in Philadelphia on September 5, 1774. He also attended the Second Continental Congress in 1775.

Many Continental Congress members demanded independence from Great Britain. In April 1775 skirmishes between British troops and the colonists at Lexington and Concord further intensified colonial hostilities toward Great Britain. Washington was not yet in favor of independence, but he was prepared to support armed resistance against British authority throughout the colonies.

Recognizing Washington's military experience and leadership, the Continental Congress made him commander in chief of all colonial military forces in June 1775. He asked for no pay beyond his actual expenses because he considered the assignment his duty to protect the rights and values of the citizens whom he served.

Reports of how courageously the colonial militia fought against British soldiers at Bunker Hill in June 1775 gave Washington confidence about the impending war. However, he faced a multitude of hardships as he assembled the Continental Army. His recruits were untrained and poorly paid, terms of army enlistment were short, and his officers frequently quarreled among themselves. Washington persevered to build his army into trained soldiers equipped with adequate supplies.

Washington commanded the respect of his troops through his confidence, poise, and determination as a general. In March 1776 his army staged a siege and eventually expelled British troops from Boston. Washington also instilled a sense of national pride in his troops. He maintained discipline within his army by punishing dishonest soldiers and deserters. At the same time, he attended to the welfare of his men by petitioning to the Continental Congress for better rations and pay.

On July 4, 1776, the Continental Congress adopted the Declaration of Independence for the 13 colonies. Congress wrote the Articles of Confederation, the first constitution in the United States, to implement a national government.

In December 1776 Washington's forces crossed the Delaware River from Pennsylvania to New Jersey and won battles at Trenton and Princeton. The Continental Army gained an advantage in the war with General Horatio Gates's victory in New York at the Battle of Saratoga in October 1777. However, Washington's army suffered losses against the British forces in Pennsylvania at the battles of Brandywine and Germantown in the fall of 1777. In December 1777 Washington withdrew to Valley Forge, Pennsylvania, where he set up winter quarters and reorganized his army despite the bitter cold.

By 1778 France recognized the United States as an independent nation and sent military support to help Washington's forces fight the British. In July 1778 a French naval fleet blockaded the British troops in New York City, leaving the British isolated from reinforcements. After 1779 the theater of war shifted to the South with major battles in Charleston, South Carolina, and Richmond, Virginia.

On October 19, 1781, Washington's army, combined with the French naval fleet and ground troops, staged a siege at Yorktown, Virginia. The commander of the British Army, General Charles Cornwallis, was forced to surrender. The Treaty of Paris was signed on September 3, 1783, officially ending the American Revolution. Washington remained with the Continental Congress until December 1783, when he resigned his commission and returned to his home at Mount Vernon.

Washington's stepdaughter, Patsy, died in 1773, and his stepson, John, died in 1781. George and Martha Washington adopted John's two children, George and Eleanor Custis. Washington acquired more than 50,000 acres (20,234 hectares) in the western territories, and his farms continued to thrive. He recognized the Potomac River as a great waterway for settlers and trade goods, and he predicted that western territories such as Kentucky, Tennessee, and Ohio would become states.

Washington was chosen to preside over the Constitutional Convention of 1787 in Philadelphia. Under the Articles of Confederation, the United States government was incapable of governing the instabilities that existed within the states. By July 1788 a new constitution had been drafted and 11 of the 13 states had ratified the United States Constitution. By 1790 the remaining two states, North Carolina and Rhode Island, had also ratified the Constitution, and Congress became the governing body of the United States government.

On February 4, 1789, the electors granted all 69 electoral votes to George Washington, thereby unanimously electing him as president of the United States. John Adams was elected vice president. Washington was inaugurated into office on April 30, 1789. His presidency was to be a time of adjustment to a new type of government for the people of the United States.

The newly formed United States government consisted of a legislative branch, the Congress; a judicial branch, the Supreme Court; and an executive branch, which was headed by Washington and included his Cabinet. The first Cabinet members included Thomas Jefferson as secretary of state, Henry Knox as secretary of war, Edmund Randolph as attorney general, and Alexander Hamilton as secretary of the treasury. In 1790 Washington approved a permanent location for the United States capital on the Potomac River. The capital was moved from New York City to Philadelphia until the new capital was established.

During Washington's administration, the authority of the federal government was greatly strengthened. Washington and Alexander Hamilton chartered the Bank of the United States in 1791, and the federal government assumed responsibility for both national and state debts. Taxes were placed on imported goods and certain private property within the states, and money was deposited into the national treasury for paying debts. Also in 1791 the states ratified the Bill of Rights, the first 10 amendments to the Constitution, which granted United States citizens their basic rights.

Washington was reelected to a second term as president in 1792, with John Adams again serving as his vice president. Three new states were admitted to the United States during Washington's administration—Vermont in 1791, Kentucky in 1792, and Tennessee in 1796.

When war broke out between France and Great Britain in 1793, Washington decided that the United States should remain neutral in foreign affairs. Even though the United States owed France a debt for assistance in the American Revolution and had promised to help France in any future conflicts, Washington felt that the United States was not prepared to enter another war so soon. Accordingly, he issued the Proclamation of Neutrality in April 1793, which stated that the United States must maintain a sense of national identity, independent from any other country's influence. Several future presidents, including James Monroe, followed Washington's neutrality policy.

National political parties emerged as a result of Washington's foreign policies. Washington and Alexander Hamilton were opposed to the segregation of the government that political parties created. Hamilton, however, led the Federalist Party with John Adams to support their policies. James Madison and Thomas Jefferson founded the Republican Party (later called the Democratic-Republican Party). The Federalists advocated a strong central government and wanted to maintain close ties with Great Britain. The Republicans were opposed to the authority of a strong national government that decreased the power of state and local governments. Republicans also wanted to preserve their old alliance with France. Washington favored the Federalist ideals of government but worked to sustain a balance between the two parties.

The United States government met its first serious domestic challenge with the Whiskey Rebellion in July 1794. Washington set a tax on whiskey to help pay the national debt. Farmers in western Pennsylvania who relied on the income from selling whiskey were outraged by the tax. These farmers resisted the tax by assaulting federal revenue officers. After negotiations between the federal government and the farmers failed, Washington dispatched local state militias and federal troops to quell the rebellion. The national government prevailed over a rebellious adversary and won the support of state governments in enforcing federal law within the states.

Washington's administration faced boundary disputes with the

Native Americans on the western frontier, Great Britain in the northeast and northwest, and Spain in the south. Settlers in the Ohio River valley fought Native Americans over claims on the western frontier boundaries. Washington dispatched an army under the command of Gen. Anthony Wayne to defend the settlements from the Native Americans. Wayne built a chain of forts from Ohio to Indiana to protect the settlements. He finally defeated the Native Americans at the Battle of Fallen Timbers on August 20, 1794.

Washington authorized John Jay, chief justice of the Supreme Court, to negotiate boundary disputes with Great Britain. In the Jay Treaty, signed on November 19, 1794, Great Britain and the United States negotiated the boundaries between the United States and British North America. Great Britain also granted the United States trading privileges with England and the British East Indies.

Thomas Pinckney, an American diplomat, was sent to Spain for negotiations concerning U.S. interests in Spanish-owned territories. Pinckney's Treaty, signed on October 27, 1795, established the southern boundary of the United States at 31° N. latitude, opened the Mississippi River to U.S. trade through Spanish territories, and granted Americans a tax-free port in New Orleans.

From 1794 to 1798 the Barbary pirates of North Africa attacked U.S. merchant ships in the Atlantic. The Continental Navy, created in 1775 and disbanded in 1784, was restored in 1794 to protect U.S. vessels. Washington signed the Navy's first commission to John Barry, who was made captain of the frigate United States. In April 1798 Congress created the Department of the Navy.

When Washington's second term ended in 1796, he refused to run for a third term. Washington's Farewell Address was first published in the *American Daily Advertiser*, a Philadelphia newspaper, on September 19, 1796. It was written largely by Alexander Hamilton but was remolded by Washington and expressed Washington's ideas. The address gave the people of the United States Washington's reasons for not accepting a third term in office. He considered it unwise for one person to hold such a powerful position for so long. All successive U.S. presidents served no more than two terms except Franklin D. Roosevelt, who was elected to four terms. In 1951 the 22nd Amendment to the U.S. Constitution was ratified and stated: "No person shall be elected to the office of the President more than twice."

Washington's Farewell Address offered his advice to the country on several issues. He denounced the new political party system as divisive and dangerous to the nation's unity. In foreign affairs, he cautioned his successors to "steer clear of permanent alliances with any portion of the foreign world" and not to "entangle our peace and prosperity in the toils of European ambition, rivalship, interest, humor, or caprice." His warnings laid the foundation for America's isolationist foreign policy—a national policy of neutrality, or avoiding political or economic entanglements with other countries—which lasted through most of U.S. history before World War II. His warnings also set the stage for the Monroe Doctrine.

Washington was succeeded by John Adams, who was sworn in as president on March 4, 1797. Thomas Jefferson was his vice president.

CORNEL WEST

(b. 1953–d.)

Cornel West is an African American philosopher, educator, writer, and activist, born on June 2, 1953, in Tulsa, Oklahoma. He was praised for his keen insights into the difficulty of growing up black in America. West stood out as a social critic with strong religious ties who discussed the importance of class and economic issues in the black community, both as a professor and as a sought-after lecturer at rallies and churches.

West's father was an Air Force administrator, and his mother was a teacher and elementary school principal. The family moved often in his youth, and West was a rebellious youngster. When West discovered that his hero, Teddy Roosevelt, had studied at Harvard University, West decided that was the place he wanted to study as well. He graduated magna cum laude in 1973 from Harvard with a bachelor's degree in Near Eastern languages and literature. He received a master's degree from

Princeton University in 1975 and a Ph.D. in 1980. West taught religion at Princeton and led the university's Afro-American Studies department beginning in 1988. He also taught at Yale University, Barnard, Williams, Haverford, and the University of Paris.

His book *Race Matters* (1993) comprised eight essays about black American crises. He blamed these crises on poverty as well as on the overwhelmingly negative attitude of African Americans. Of West's many books, *Race Matters* was the first one aimed at a general audience. In some of the essays, West also raised the issues of sexism and homophobia as attitudes important for the African American community to combat.

Some of his earlier books were *Prophecy Deliverance! An Afro-American Revolutionary Christianity* (1982), a work of philosophy combining the ideas of black writers, Christianity, and such traditional philosophers as René Descartes; 'Prophetic Fragments' (1988), an essay covering many philosophical issues; *The American Evasion of Philosophy* (1989); *The Ethical Dimensions of Marxist Thought* (1991); *Breaking Bread: Insurgent Black Intellectual Life* (1991), which recorded a series of conversations with the renowned social critic bell hooks; and *Prophetic Reflection: Notes on Race and Power in America* (1993), which contained many of West's speeches.

Cornel West.

West was noted for his fiery speaking style, and he brought his appreciation of philosophy together with a fervor for contemporary issues to his students and listeners. His essays were published in a wide variety of magazines, including *Spin*, the *Yale Law Journal*, the *Nation*, and *Christianity and Crisis*.

ELIE WIESEL

(b. 1928–d.)

A prolific writer, teacher, and philosopher, Elie Wiesel was awarded the Nobel Peace Prize in 1986 for his efforts against violence, hatred, and oppression. He was a survivor of the Nazi Holocaust, and his writings and lectures provided a sober, passionate testament to the destruction of European Jewry during World War II.

Eliezer Wiesel was born on September 30, 1928, in Sighet, Romania. When he was 16 his family was deported to the Auschwitz death camp along with all the Jews of Sighet. His parents and sister were killed, but Wiesel was forced into slave labor at Buchenwald, another German death camp. After the war Wiesel settled in France, where he studied at the Sorbonne and worked as a journalist. In 1956 he moved to the United States, becoming a citizen in 1963. From 1976 he taught at Boston University.

In his first book, *Night*, Wiesel recounts the horrors of his experiences at the hands of the Nazis. Other works—including *The Town Beyond the Wall*, *A Beggar in Jerusalem*, and *The Fifth Son*—reflect the influence of Hasidic tradition, the Talmud, and French existentialism. Wiesel received the Congressional Gold Medal and the Presidential Medal of Freedom and was named a commander in the French Legion of Honor.

Elie Wiesel.

MALALA YOUSAFZAI

(b. 1997–d.)

While a teenager, Pakistani activist Malala Yousafzai spoke out publicly against the Taliban's prohibition on the education of girls. She gained global attention when she survived an assassination attempt at age 15.

Malala Yousafzai was born on July 12, 1997, in Mingora, Swat Valley, Pakistan. The daughter of an outspoken social activist and educator, Yousafzai was an excellent student. Her father—who established and administered the school she attended, Khushal Girls High School and College in the city of Mingora—encouraged her to follow in his path. In 2007 the Swat Valley, once a vacation destination, was invaded by the Taliban. Led by Maulana Fazlullah, the Pakistani Taliban began imposing strict Islamic law, destroying or shutting down girls' schools, banning women from any active role in society, and carrying out suicide bombings. Yousafzai and her family fled the region for their safety, but they returned when tensions and violence eased.

On September 1, 2008, when Yousafzai was 11 years old, her father took her to a local press club in Peshawar, Pakistan, to protest the school closings, and she gave her first speech—"How Dare the Taliban Take Away My Basic Right to Education?" Her speech was publicized throughout Pakistan. Toward the end of 2008, the Taliban announced that all girls' schools in Swat would be shut down on January 15, 2009. The British Broadcasting Corporation (BBC) approached Yousafzai's father in search of someone who might blog for them about what it was like to live under Taliban rule. Under the name Gul Makai, Yousafzai began writing regular entries for BBC Urdu about her daily life. She wrote from January through the beginning of March of that year 35 entries that were also translated into English. Meanwhile, the Taliban shut down all girls' schools in Swat and blew up more than 100 of them.

In February 2009 Yousafzai made her first television appearance, when she was interviewed by Pakistani journalist and talk show host Hamid Mir on the Pakistan current-events show *Capital Talk*. In late February the Taliban, responding to an increasing backlash throughout Pakistan, agreed to a cease-fire, lifted the restriction against girls, and allowed them to attend school on the condition that they wear burkas (a garment that covers the body from head to toe and veils the face). However, violence resurged only a few months later, in May, and the Yousafzai family was forced to seek refuge outside of Swat until the Pakistani army was able to push the Taliban out. In early 2009 the *New York Times* reporter Adam Ellick worked with Yousafzai to make a documentary, *Class Dismissed*, a 13-minute piece about the school shutdown. Ellick made a second film with her, titled *A Schoolgirl's Odyssey*. The *New York Times* posted both films on their Web site in 2009. That summer she met with U.S. special envoy to Afghanistan and Pakistan Richard Holbrooke and asked him to help with her effort to protect the education of girls in Pakistan.

Malala Yousafzai.

With Yousafzai's continuing television appearances and coverage in the local and international media, it had become apparent by December 2009 that she was the BBC's young blogger. Once her identity was known, she began to receive widespread recognition for her activism. In October 2011 she was nominated by human rights activist Desmond Tutu for the International Children's Peace Prize. In December of that year she was awarded Pakistan's first National Youth Peace Prize (later renamed the National Malala Peace Prize).

On October 9, 2012, Yousafzai was shot in the head by a Taliban gunman while she was en route home from school. Fazlullah and the Pakistani Taliban took responsibility for the attempt on her life. She survived the attack and was flown from Peshawar to Birmingham, England, for surgery. The incident elicited protests, and her cause was taken up around the world, including by the United Nations (UN) special envoy for global education, Gordon Brown, who introduced a petition that called for all children around the world to be back in school by 2015. That petition led to the ratification of Pakistan's first Right to Education bill. In December 2012 Pakistani President Asif Ali Zardari announced the launch of a $10 million education fund in Yousafzai's honor. About the same time, the Malala Fund was established by the Vital Voices Global Partnership to support education for all girls around the world. In 2013 Yousafzai became the youngest nominee for the Nobel Peace Prize.

Yousafzai recovered, staying with her family in Birmingham, where she returned to her studies and to activism. On July 12, 2013, her 16th birthday, for the first time since being shot she made a public appearance and addressed an audience of 500 at the UN in New York City. Among her many awards, in 2013 Yousafzai won the United Nations Human Rights Prize, awarded every five years. She was named one of Time magazine's most-influential people in 2013 and appeared on one of the seven covers that were printed for that issue. With Christina Lamb (foreign correspondent for The Sunday Times), Yousafzai coauthored a memoir, *I Am Malala: The Girl Who Stood Up for Education and Was Shot by the Taliban* (2013). In 2014 Yousafzai became the youngest person to win the Liberty Medal, awarded by the National Constitution Center in Philadelphia, Pennsylvania, to public figures striving for people's freedom throughout the world.

MUHAMMAD YUNUS

(b. 1940–d.)

Bangladeshi economist Muhammad Yunus was the founder of the Grameen Bank, an institution that provides small loans to poor people to help them establish financial self-sufficiency. In 2006 Yunus and Grameen received the Nobel Peace Prize.

Muhammad Yunus was born on June 28, 1940, in Chittagong, East Bengal (now Bangladesh). He taught economics at Chittagong University from 1961 to 1965 and then studied and taught at Vanderbilt University until 1972, earning a Ph.D. in economics in 1969. After his time at Vanderbilt, Yunus returned to Chittagong University as head of the economics department. He began studying the economic aspects of poverty in 1974 as famine swept through Bangladesh. Yunus's findings convinced him that in order for the underprivileged to succeed, they needed access to money that would help them build small businesses. In 1976 Muhammad Yunus began a program of "micro" loans, a credit system in which borrowers, whose loans may be little more than $25, join lending groups. The group members provide support, as well as peer pressure, to ensure that the borrowers repay their loans. The Bangladesh government made the Grameen Bank Project an independent bank in 1983. The Grameen model has spurred other forms of microlending around the world.

In February 2007 Muhammad Yunus formed a political party, Nagorik Shakti (Citizen Power), and declared his intention to contest the upcoming election. His actions came while the country was in a state of upheaval and severe conflicts had erupted between the two main political parties, the Awami League and the Bangladesh National Party. Although Yunus's movement sought to restore good governance and eliminate corruption, he dropped his efforts to establish the party in May due to a lack of support.

In addition to winning the Nobel Peace Prize in 2006, Muhammad Yunus was the recipient of many honors. These honors include Bangladesh's prestigious Independence Day Award (1987), the World

Muhammad Yunus.

Food Prize (1994), and the U.S. Presidential Medal of Freedom (2009). He was the first person to receive the King Hussein Humanitarian Award (2000).

GLOSSARY

ADVOCATE A person who argues for or supports a cause or policy.

AVANT-GARDE A group of people who develop new and often very surprising ideas in art and literature.

BOHEMIAN A person (such as a writer or an artist) living an unconventional life, usually in a colony with others.

CAMPAIGN A series of activities designed to produce a particular result.

CONDEMN To give (someone) a usually severe punishment.

CONSENSUS An idea or opinion that is shared by all the people in a group.

CONSERVATIVE Believing in the value of established and traditional practices in politics and society.

CREDIBILITY The quality of being believed or accepted as true, real, or honest.

DEMONSTRATION An event in which people gather together in order to show that they support or oppose something or someone.

DEPLORABLE Very bad in a way that causes shock, fear, or disgust.

DISAVOW To deny that you know about or are involved in (something).

DISBAND To end an organization or group (such as a club).

EXILE A person who has been forced to live in a foreign country.

HARASSMENT To create an unpleasant or hostile situation, especially by uninvited and unwelcome verbal or physical conduct.

INTOLERANCE A reluctance to grant rights to other people.

MANDATE An official order to do something.

MULTIFACETED Having many different parts.

OUTSPOKEN Talking in a free and honest way about your opinions.

PIONEER A person who helps create or develop new ideas or methods.

PROTEST An event at which people gather together to show strong disapproval about something.

REFUGEE Someone who has been forced to leave a country because of war or for religious or political reasons.

RESISTANCE An effort made to stop or to fight against someone or something.

SUBCULTURE A group that has beliefs and behaviors that are different from the main groups within a culture or society.

TOLERANCE A willingness to accept feelings, habits, or beliefs that are different from your own.

UNORTHODOX Different from what is usually done or accepted.

UPHEAVAL A major change or period of change that causes a lot of conflict, confusion, or anger.

VENERABLE Valued and respected because of old age or long use.

INDEX

A

B

C

D

E

F

G

H

I

J

K

R

S

T

U

V

W

Y